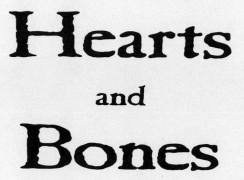

Hearts
and
Bones

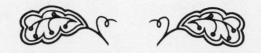

Hearts

and

Bones

Margaret Lawrence

AVON BOOKS ▲ NEW YORK

HEARTS AND BONES is an original publication of Avon Books. This work has never before appeared in book form. This work is a novel. Any similarity to actual persons or events is purely coincidental.

AVON BOOKS
A division of
The Hearst Corporation
1350 Avenue of the Americas
New York, New York 10019

Library of Congress Cataloging in Publication Data:

Lawrence, Margaret K.
    Hearts and bones / Margaret Lawrence.
        p.   cm.
I. Title.
PS3562.A9133H4   1996   96-2394
813'.54—dc20   CIP

First Avon Books Hardcover Printing: September 1996

Avon Books are available at special quantity discounts for bulk purchases for sales promotions, premiums, fund raising or educational use. Special books, or book excerpts, can also be created to fit specific needs.

For details write or telephone the office of the Director of Special Markets, Avon Books, Dept. FP, 1350 Avenue of the Americas, New York, New York 10019, 1-800-238-0658.

To Ann,
who always knew Hannah was there

"We never knows wot's hidden in each other's hearts; and if we had glass winders there, we'd need keep the shutters up, some on us, I do assure you!"

—Mrs. Sairy Gamp, midwife in
Martin Chuzzlewit, by Charles Dickens

PROLOGUE:
HOW HE KILLED HER

Whatever they thought when they found her was bound to be wrong.

Those who were simple would assume she was as simple as themselves, and those who were not would mistake her sex, her poverty, her ignorance, even her profound and tortured vision of the clear face of evil for stupidity and inferiority and madness, not knowing her history as he did himself.

Her death would be dismissed, the whole concentration focused on the murderer. On him.

It seemed for a moment that he must be thinking of some other man, and when he realized that the word *murderer* now applied to him, he laughed softly at the thought of it. She, too, would have laughed.

Nobody else in the village had heard her laugh, he was sure. Nobody knew her. There would be no one to say how she grew melodramatic and tore herself sometimes, cut her hair or her soft body, burned herself with candles or coals from the fire. How she spoke only in enigmas and scraps of doggerel, the verses of old songs, but never plain and to the purpose. How part of her lived with the dead and could not be rescued, nor even reached except with the urgent thrust of his sex, the only thing for which she had wanted him. How she imagined she had seen all her dead at various times, here in Maine, in Rufford, where they had never set foot in life. She believed she had met her bayoneted

1

brothers on the cobbled street, laughing and singing as they left Josh Lamb's tavern; had come home to find her mutilated sister spinning flax by her fireside or stitching at a quilt in the lap frame; had seen her bullet-riddled father calmly reading a book as he crossed the thick river ice of the Manitac on horseback by the Grange ford beyond Henry Markham's mill.

No one, certainly, to tell how she kept her own children too close out of fear, even inside her house—the boy tied by a leather leash attached to her apron, the little girl always at her breast or on her hip.

He himself had no children to carry his name. It was an ache in him.

There would be no one to say how *she* had ached.

How she was ruled by the dark places of her body, and how they had ruled him, too.

How she wept.

How she howled in her dreams.

How she hated God.

How she never surrendered.

Until she lay dead, he did not know how he had loved her, how much of him she had ruined. She had set him apart to destroy her, he knew that now. It was the only gift she had given him freely.

His knee was still on her chest, pinning her to the quilt she lay on. He had not expected so much resistance, because she was not strong and he had killed often enough in the War with muskets, knives, pistols, swords—every modern weapon of this dead-end of the eighteenth century.

His mind flickered and seemed for a second to be extinguished. He could not remember the year, nor the month of the year, though it was winter. He had always lived at a distance from himself, always kept his mask in place before friends, even family. Now the distance had invaded him, lifted and carried him until he had no more part in the everyday world of days and years, of sunrises and sunsets and slow-burnt hours.

He closed his eyes, his body still bent motionless above her dead breasts, his breath making a wisp of her hair drift softly away from her forehead, then fall back again. The sight of it broke him, a sharp sudden pain between his ribs.

Seventeen eighty-six. February. The pain brought his memory back.

No, he had killed with his hands only once before. It was strange, though not unpleasant. They no longer seemed to be attached to him, and he looked down at them calmly, wondering what they might choose to do next. He felt the last gulp of breath from the girl's nostrils, and under his knee her rib cage seemed to buckle with implosion, like small buildings he had seen struck by cannon-fire.

He hardly noticed her eyes staring at him, nor the slight smile that he still believed he could see at the corners of her mouth, as though she had what she wanted at last. He had had to stuff some of her own hair into it to stop her smiling. But it took no effect.

He released the pressure of his knee and straddled her body. He was still naked, as she was, and it was very cold in the room, the deep, bone-cold of a Maine winter. He wanted to go into the kitchen and build up the hearth fire, to heat water to wash, and then to dress and go back home.

It was almost morning, and in another hour or so he would be expected at morning prayer in his wife's parlor.

We thank Thee for our Peaceful Sleep, that Wakeful Thoughts from Sin doth Keep.

His wife had worked it in a sampler that hung above their bed. He tried to picture the room to himself, to imagine himself there.

But he could not go home. He could not take his hands away from the dead girl's throat. His fingers had taken root there and had a separate brain, a separate will from the rest of his body, the part of him that was now shivering violently with the cold.

Murderer, he thought. *Ah, surely not. Not I.*

At last he saw one hand move, then the other. He crawled away from her and rolled himself off the quilt-covered feather tick onto the straw matting of the floor, where her discarded shift still lay in a heap.

He had left his own clothes by the kitchen fire, where they would be warm when he wanted them. He got up from the icy floor and poured the wax from the guttering candle into its saucer. The light flared up again, and he walked to the door, his breath steaming and condensing in a thin frost on his brush of stubbly beard.

For a moment he thought of looking back at her to see if he had left his hands behind him, left them there with her.

But he resisted the impulse. If you looked back at them, the dead would control you forever. He had had enough of being controlled.

As he pushed the flannel draft-curtains aside and reached for the iron handle of the heavy plank door, he caught sight of his own hands where they belonged, and he felt relief. They were still there, and obeyed him again.

He heated water, washed, dressed himself, and raked his fingers through his stubborn hair, then retied it with the black ribbon at the nape of his neck. In the wicker cage, her songbird lay dead as he had left it, its feet sticking up absurdly, like stiff dry weeds on a peculiar stem.

Still, it seemed to him that the bird was watching him. He moved away from it, into the shadows. There, his back to the bird, he finished dressing, pulled on his high riding boots and fastened his breeches at the knees.

There was some half-frozen cheese and bread in the dresser on the far wall, and he ate that and drank some rum, putting the plate and mug carefully into the wooden tub in which she did the washing-up, then pouring the rest of the water from the kettle over it.

His work was almost done. He had still to fetch his gelding from the small stable behind the house, and he must hurry now, for it would be light in another half-hour. It had taken longer than he had supposed.

We thank Thee for our Daily Work, and Pray we shall not Fail nor Shirk.

He looked for a place to put the letter, where it would be sure to be found as he had promised her. Picking up the heavy pewter salt cellar in the middle of the table, he slipped the paper under it. For a moment he hesitated, studying the handwriting, the uneven strokes of brownish homemade ink scratched with the badly-sharpened quill.

Then he went down the hall and opened the door to her bedchamber once more.

Her body still lay there, the broken arm at a crazed angle, the legs splayed open as his sex had left her, the soft down of her inner thighs still smeared with his seed. She had struggled wildly at the last minute, clawing at him and biting as though she had not led him herself to the bed, dropped her shift to the floor as always, undressed and roused him as always.

At the last minute, she had fought. For what? Purity, chastity, fidelity to her husband—they were long gone. Life? She said she did not want it. It was her whole purpose to throw it away.

And yet, she fought him. And he had fought back and won.

He had done many things, terrible things, but he had never before raped a woman. He was not afraid of the fact nor of the word. But he felt it had changed something fundamental inside him, even more than her death had done. Broken something. The last thing he had left to break.

After it, he would be able to do anything. Destroy anyone. Perhaps that was what she had wanted, even more than she had wanted death.

He stood beside the bed, his cloak around his shoulders, his battered brown tricorn already perched on his head. The candle was in his hand, and he let the light play over her features. For a moment, he could not remember her Christian name, for he had called her by it seldom.

Mrs. Emory, he had called her. Or *My dear*. Or sometimes, *Nan*.

He rubbed a hand across his eyes, thinking. Then it reached him from somewhere. *Anthea*.

He lifted her hand to his face and let her limp fingers drift across his cheek.

"Poor cold Mouse," he said. He set the candle down and blew it out.

In the Name of the Father and the Son and the Holy Spirit, Amen.

ONE

THE FIRST JOURNAL OF HANNAH TREVOR, MIDWIFE

14 February, the year 1786

I begin on Saint Valentine's Day, these pages which are mine own.

The morning not so cold. Heavy fog over the river at least a mile above Gull's Hook. I cannot see across to the Grange Landing, which makes me sorry and peevish, for it rests me to see Major Josselyn walking there upon his own ground. God send he does not think of me.

Partly to relieve my soul, churned seven pounds butter, and baked. Nine loaves and six fine pies, and two plum cakes besides. Against my judgement, sold three of the pies and two loaves on promise to Judge Siwall's cook, Marjorie Kemp, for they are this week without grain, flour or meal and can buy none in Rufford or Wybrow so late in the season. I am owed fifteen pence, which I will no way forgive. Gaudy Improvidence Relies Upon Her Neighbors and Pays Them With Scorn!

Daughter spins the black wool Mrs. Kider paid for my attendance at her last delivery, which I shall knit for socks. Mother and babe well. This day I go with Aunt to wait with Mrs. Rugg, beyond the Training

Ground, who is very unwell and any moment expects her twelfth. Shall forgive her my fee.

Late toward noon, Tom Stockham called with our post from the Boston boat come in at Wybrow Head. Letter from the Rev. Rockwood. He says it is now proved my husband James Trevor is dead in Quebec, of a fever. So the scale of Divine Reason keeps its balance true. It is eight years since I saw my husband's face.

Mr. Stockham tarried to dinner, a fine fish pie my Uncle Henry favors, and a dish of stewed apples.

> My Aunt's Receipt for Fish Pie: Soak overnight ten or a dozen filets of salted cod. Next morning, wash away the salt and boil in pieces, with salt, pepper, and butter, a half pound, till the stock thicken. In good season, add the broken flesh of lobster, three or four pound, or other sea-fruit. Take slices of raw salt pork, and layer meat and fish together with the gravy in a good large pot till all is used, with a lid of biscuit dough upon the whole. Bake in an oven made hot enough for bread, an hour and half or two hours only.

It is fourteen years since my children died in Massachusetts, of whom the eldest was but five years and four months. God rest Susanna, Martha and Benjamin Trevor, and forgive the many failures of their mother, Hannah.

May God forgive James Trevor also, for I do not.

It is eleven years since I came to Rufford, Maine, to Two Mills Farm on the River Manitac, and but five years since the War's end.

It is twenty years since my foolish marriage, my own long War, which ends this day. I thank God I am free, and no man's wife forever.

Aunt and I this forenoon put into the frame my own Daughter Jennet's quilt, cut to my pattern of Hearts and Bones. I gave for this purpose my marriage gown of cranberry-colored merino.

The pattern is pieced to my sole devising, and it pleases me.

TWO

HANNAH TREVOR AND WHO SHE WAS

Lucy Hannah Trevor turned thirty-eight years old on that foggy St. Valentine's Day of the year 1786. She had the ripeness of a woman who has borne four children and the unconscious sensuality of one who thinks she has long since cured herself of needing men for more than idle conversation.

She had a slender face with sober, restless brown eyes behind square-cut wire spectacles that helped to disguise such emotions as she allowed herself to admit. Her hair was ash brown, not yet greying, and it was so stubbornly curly that she grew impatient sometime in her twenties and cut it short, like a boy's. So it had remained.

Nor did she conceal it with the usual demure white cap society expected of her. When a thing seemed useless nonsense, she took pains to ignore it.

Besides, so abundant were her curls that unless she nailed the thing on, a cap was more often on the ground than on her head.

"God knows, I do despair of you," Hannah's Aunt Julia often cried in exasperation. Her voice was a kind of raucous honk from years of making herself heard over the wailing of the many new-

9

born infants she had helped into the world, and though Julia herself came from a family of stonemasons, she had been, like her niece, educated somewhat above her station, for she could both read and write. She delivered her edicts in the peremptory tone of a duchess addressing a bootblack, and was for the most part obeyed.

After all, had she not had the good sense to marry a man of energy and consideration? Henry Markham now had not only Two Mills Farm and the lumber mill on the riverbank below it, but the new gristmill as well. They were not rich, as the Josselyns were, or as the Siwalls pretended to be. But they were prosperous, and they endured. They had been on the Manitac longer than almost anyone thereabouts.

The noon meal over, Julia saw her husband and Tom Stockham off down the path to the village high road, which ran parallel to the frozen river. Half a dozen houses between here and the Si- walls', and no doubt their cook, old Marjorie Kemp, had stopped at every one of them to sit in the kitchen and turn up her nose at the loaves she'd wheedled out of Hannah, and tell tales about the girl.

Julia sniffed and closed her gooseberry eyes in disgust. Marjorie had heard Mr. Stockham come in with the mail and tarried on purpose, hoping to nose out the contents of Hannah's letter from Boston. Hoping to get herself asked to dinner for fish pie and plum cake, too, no doubt!

"The day I sit down to my decent table with the likes of Marjorie Kemp," grumbled Julia, "I'll—I'll—sell my bones for butter!"

Still, Hannah did sometimes seem to set the gossip mills turn- ing on purpose. A word in season might do some good, after all. Julia lifted her chin another determined inch, pulled the laces of her bodice a trifle tighter out of self-discipline, and sailed into the steamy kitchen where Hannah, just finished with the washing- up, was cleaning the leftover baking ashes from the square oven built into the brick face of the great oak-mantled hearth. The old woman shook her head and the ruffled lace danced on cap and ample bosom.

"If you could see yourself, Hannah Trevor! Ashes from ear to ear like a scullery maid! No cap on that stubborn head, nor even a decent kerchief in the neck of your gown. I declare, there's ashes in your very bosom! What will Mrs. Kemp go back and tell the Siwalls about you?"

Hannah drew out the last shovelful of ash and straightened her back, pushing up her spectacles to peer down at her scandalous bosom. Her aunt was right, of course, she had got a smut of ashes there. Rather seductive, really. She bit her lip to suppress a smile and wiped it away with her cuff.

"Mrs. Kemp may tell that dried-up asparagus stalk of a wife of Siwall's anything she pleases," she replied. "I wouldn't give tuppence for the lot of them. Why, I could name you two swollen bellies on the North Bank we'll be helping through labor before the ice breaks, thanks to that fool son of theirs."

Though there were others, Hannah and her aunt were the best-known of Rufford's nurse-midwives, and the most successful—partly because they knew how to keep their mouths shut and their noses out of other people's dirty linen.

"Maidservants' gossip!" cried Julia. "I pay no heed to it! Nor should you, of all people."

Her eye drifted unconsciously to the corner of the room where Jennet, Hannah's eight-year-old daughter, sat cross-legged on a blanket chest, shelling dried corn for hominy. A mercy Jennet was born deaf and couldn't hear herself whispered bastard round every doorpost.

"Besides," Julia forged on, "Hamilton Siwall is a magistrate and Moderator of the Rufford congregation. He's a decent enough man."

"He certainly prays louder than most. And he's rich enough to buy Jem out of scrapes and pay his gaming debts, thanks to selling the land of foreclosed farmers at three times what he paid for it."

Hannah dumped the wood-ash into the lye barrel beside the fireplace and poured in water. In another month or so, when it

was spring, they would need all the lye they could get for
soapmaking.

"All that is beside the point," said her aunt "He's a man of
position, and Mistress Kemp is his cook. People listen to her.
And *you* are a woman without a husband."

Julia paused, studying Hannah's features. Behind her ash-dusted
spectacles, the brown eyes were cool and still as the surface of
the frozen river. But underneath, there was a deep current of what
Julia could only call rage. She had always known it was there, all
these years since James Trevor left Hannah here alone, in a small,
cold, half-ruined cottage down by the docks.

They had had her to live with them at once, of course, she
and Henry, here at Two Mills Farm. It was during the War, and
James was a Loyalist; alone, his wife would hardly have survived.
They would have broken her as they smashed the windows of
his house, or taken her as they took his case clock and his bed
curtains and his harp-backed chairs.

Julia knew very little of what had happened between James and
Hannah Trevor. But she did know it had not ended when James
escaped to Canada. Perhaps it would never end.

"Will you stop hating him now, Hannah, my dear?" the old
woman asked her softly. "Now it is proved he is dead?"

The placid surface of the brown eyes did not alter, but Hannah
Trevor brought her fist down so hard on the lid of the lye barrel
that the staves shook and quivered, and even little Jennet, who
was said to hear nothing, looked up, wide-eyed, from her corn
shelling and watched her mother's face.

Hannah stepped softly to Jennet's corner and brushed a hand
gently over the lock of red-brown hair that insisted on falling
over the small fair forehead. Before she replied, she drew closer
to Jennet, needing to bring the energy of the warm body against
her own. For once, Jennet let herself be held without wriggling
to be free.

"James Trevor has been no part of me since my other children
were lost," said Hannah at last. "Now I must leave him to God,
I suppose. But I shall not forgive him. Not I."

No, thought Julia Markham. *Nor forgive God, neither.*

Hannah let the child go and scrubbed at a smudge of ash she had left on Jennet's cheek. Then she turned to Julia. "That baby of Rugg's must be impatient of our arrival, Aunt. Shall I saddle Flash, or will you walk today, as I do?"

"I shall ride, of course. And sidesaddle, too, as you ought to do yourself, instead of wading through the snow in those old clothes like a hoyden!" Julia stood up and took her niece's face between her two hands. "You fly in the face of convention once too often, and it will turn and bite you! Must you always be giving old biddies like Mistress Kemp an excuse to cluck at you? Come, at least wear a cap to Mrs. Rugg's."

Hannah extracted herself from the old lady's embrace and marched off to get her cloak and boots. "No, Aunt-dear," she called over her shoulder. "You must pardon me. A cap doesn't suit me. Let them cluck as they please."

It was her way, and the gift James Trevor's betrayal had given her. Hannah had spent the last fourteen years becoming herself, or at least learning to live as boldly as she chose.

She worked bareheaded and bare-armed in her garden of herbs and simples in summer, and helped with the harvests of corn, turnips, pumpkins, beans, and flax, and with the calving, butchering, cidering and shearing to pay for her living at the farm, and for Jennet's. As a result, Hannah's skin was not the whey-faced white of London or Boston fashion, but a rich honey-color that faded in the dark Maine winters to a translucent ivory.

It made her seem fragile and a little remote in winter, as though she were made of bone, and grew brittle. Perhaps she did, for memory lives in the bones and asks a heavy price in the dark, slow winters of the north.

As to dress, Hannah possessed only two gowns aside from the merino wool that had been her wedding dress: a dark green winter gabardine with an embroidered sash, and a pale grey tucked linen for the summer. These she seldom wore except for weddings or burials, and their cut was a good fifteen years out of fashion now.

For the most part, she dressed in dull-colored skirts that did not quite reach to the ankles and therefore avoided the worst of the ever-present mud, above them separate scoop-necked bodices of homespun wool, linen, or occasionally of purchased calico, with a clean kerchief at the neck against the cold—when it was not inconvenient.

What else should be said of Hannah?

That she was an excellent dancer, though she seldom danced.

That she could not, as her uncle said, carry a tune "with a yoke and bucket," though she was fond of music.

That though she could read and write and was thus more educated than many women of her time, she had labored her way through only three books, and owned but one of them. Those books were: *The History of Rasselas, Prince of Abyssinia*, by Dr. Samuel Johnson; *The Tragedie of King Lear* by *Mr. William Shakspear, with Improvements by The Famous Actor, Mr. Colley Cibber*; and *Poor Richard's Almanack*, by Mr. Benjamin Franklin. She had sent to Boston for her own copy of *King Lear*.

What else?

That Hannah believed in what she called God, though she neither waited for nor prayed for His personal assistance. He had wound up the world like a clock and set it ticking. Whether it kept running or stopped was entirely immaterial to Him.

That she derived these beliefs from experience and had no patience with sermons of any kind, especially when delivered by pompous old fellows in wigs.

That she did not confuse her determination to be the equal of any man with the need to look like one, swear like one, prance like one, or brawl like one. She accepted her sexual self, and she accepted good, honest men and valued them, as she did good, honorable women. It was only fools of either sex she refused to suffer gladly.

That she made patchwork quilts only partially for use and beauty. Mostly, Hannah worked from an almost obsessive need

to discover a reasonable pattern in apparent waste and chaos—
the same need that led her into the mysteries of childbirth and
of violent and sudden death.

That until she discovered the body of Anthea Emory, they had
met only once. It was across a quilting frame.

And last, although she would have told you that she valued
self-knowledge above all things, it should be said that Hannah
Trevor, drawing perilously near to the age of forty, knew far less
about herself than she believed.

THREE

THE MAN AT THE WINDOW

Daniel Jossclyn—who had been waiting at his library window all afternoon for a glimpse of her—caught sight of Hannah through the thinning fog as a flash of bright scarlet against the snow-covered hill and the dense darkness of the pine forest beyond. She wore, as she always did in winter, a heavy hooded cloak of felted red wool, its right side drawn up and pinned to her left shoulder to keep her from tripping as she came downhill along the steep, rutted path. The snow was still very deep, and she had kilted up her grey-brown woolsey skirt and her quilted petticoats as high as the flared tops of her uncle's old riding boots, which she wore only partly to scandalize the likes of Marjorie Kemp.

Even on the ice and the patches of heavily-crusted February snow, she walked fast, taking long, purposeful strides, and when she fell—which she had done twice since Daniel began to watch her—she picked herself up without chagrin and marched on as if she were crossing a meadow in June.

Behind her, riding the old mare called Flash, Aunt Julia Markham shook her head and threw up both mittened hands in mock despair as her niece tripped yet again, for a fall was dangerous to a woman in more ways than one. Under the skirts and petticoats, women wore only thigh-high, gartered stockings and a loose shift that reached to just above the knee.

Under the shift, they wore nothing at all.

In most women, this fact induced a mincing gate, a need to ride sidesaddle, and a most cautious navigation of stairs, ladders, and steep hillsides, all accompanied by a constant and vivid sexual awareness. In most men, it induced a sense of imminent and adventurous—if not arousal, then certainly possibility.

And Dan Josselyn was no exception to the rule.

He sat very still at the library window, for stillness was his way, especially when he was angry. He was proof against Hamilton Siwall's blustering most of the time, but today his business partner's nattering threatened to rob him of a rare glimpse of Hannah, and that he could not forgive.

"*You* were born to soldiering, my friend," Siwall was saying, "but, damn me, *I* was born to *trade!* I know how to catch the tide of events and turn a profit from it. Thousands of men mustered out of the Continental army and looking for land to settle on, and here we sit with ten thousand acres of timberlands! I tell you, we must cut that precious section of yours! Raft the logs down to Markham's mill and sell 'em, ship 'em off! Then sell the bloody land for farm lots! Realize a double profit!"

He paused, remembering the presence across the room of Daniel's invalid wife, Charlotte, who sat on the damask sofa, propped up with pillows, a fine Shetland shawl across her knees and an issue of a French fashion paper spread out before her. "Beg pardon, Ma'am," Siwall said awkwardly. "Not the language of a gentleman. I forget myself when exercised."

She smiled politely, but his hunched figure did not relax.

Ham Siwall was a stocky man in his early fifties, with thinning hair worn lightly powdered and drawn back across his bald spot into a queue at the nape of his neck. It was tied today with a crimson ribbon almost as red as his face.

Daniel turned to confront him and couldn't help smiling. Siwall had not been bred a gentleman, and he had none of the veneer that made such confrontations a subtle and civilized game. He would have to school himself to conceal his passions better if he meant to be a politician. It was his one advantage as a partner, this inability to keep his feelings to himself. You could always tell when he was lying. But in a representative to the General Court in Boston, his transparent manners would seem to leave something to be desired.

Daniel studied his partner's excited countenance before he replied. "Siwall, I've told you before. Those acres are virgin timber, full of mink and marten and grey fox and ermine. The furs are worth far more than any price I might get for the land, even if I considered it wise to open it to farming. Which I do not. You agree, John?"

He turned to a big, shaggy man in a leather jerkin who stood with his back to the fire, turning and turning a battered three-cornered hat in his rough hands. He was John English, Daniel's steward and estate manager.

"Well, sir," he said slowly, one eye on Siwall's angry face and bull neck. "Them acres is high ground. Rocky. Good for trees and what lives amongst trees. But I do misdoubt a man could raise enough in corn and cabbage to keep a skinny wife up there, let alone children, even once he'd cleared and plowed. And that'd take best part of a year."

"What a man does with land once he's bought it is no concern of mine! That's business, damn you! Business, not sentimental claptrap!" shouted Siwall.

John English set his jaw and stared at his boots. "Well, then, that's as may be, sir. Maybe you *can* sell a pig in a poke if you wish, and maybe you *can* deliver a stone for a loaf of bread with a clear conscience and sleep sound as a drum at night. But a poor man can't eat stones, nor feed 'em to his children, and if he's ignorant enough to buy them, that don't forgive the seller his sins when the lot of 'em starves, now, does it?" He shook his shaggy head. "No, sir. I'll face my Maker with a clear mind and empty pockets, if I must. But that land's not fit for farming. Best left to trapping, I say. Since you ask."

"Then you are an ass, sir!" Siwall took a step toward Daniel. "Trapping takes time, Josselyn, and there are buyers for land now, waiting to come north from Boston in the spring! We must realize a profit while we can!"

Daniel Josselyn closed his eyes, thinking of Hannah. Then he opened them again. At his center lay a deep, empty hole, very dark, very silent, and from this unconscious well sometimes came actions he did not know he intended. They could be unflinchingly cruel, and they did not always consider consequences.

He opened the single drawer of his desk, drew out a small leather scrip, and shook down its contents at Hamilton Siwall's feet. A modest shower of gold and silver dollars and a few shillings and pence tumbled onto the heavy wool carpet.

"Those three thousand acres of high ground are mine, sir," he said quietly. "We divided the land equally when we began, and so our contract with the Bristol Company disposes. You did not want the high ground, and you did as you pleased with your acres on the lower slopes. You stripped them bare of trees and sold them off to small farmers. When the currency went bad after the War, you foreclosed on the first lot and sold their farms again at higher prices to other men. Now the money's spent to please your wife's pretensions and pay off your son's whores and his debts at cards. Your rightful share of the land is gone, and now you fancy the chance to use mine as if it were your own. I will not cut my upland timber. I will offer no more lots for sale in my logging trace." He paused, smiling softly. "However. I know you need money to finance your political ambitions. Take what I offer, in friendship and amity. It is all you will get from me and mine."

Daniel turned back to face the window again, his eyes fixed on the scarlet-clad figure that now made its way along the village high road.

Behind him, Hamilton Siwall swayed slightly, as though he might fall face forward onto the hearth rug.

"Am I not still a partner in this company? Have I no voice in its proceedings?" he hissed.

Daniel did not turn to face him again. "You have a voice, certainly. But you will not succeed in silencing mine. Keep to your contract, and I will keep to mine. I wish you good day, sir. Take your money and go."

Siwall bent and gathered a fistful of the coins. For a moment he stared at them. Then, with a force that sent live embers flying halfway across the room, he cast them into the fire. His hand, emptied of the silver, lifted and poised, as though it would strike Daniel a blow across the ear.

Before it could smash down on its target, John English caught Siwall's wrist, and as he did so, Charlotte's soft voice spoke, drifting like the motes of fine dust in the drafts of the high-ceilinged room.

"Do greet your good lady for me, Mr. Siwall, if you please. Will you ask her to come and take tea with me on Thursday afternoon? As you know, I am without much company, and good society alone makes these interminable American winters of yours bearable to me. I hope she will oblige me."

Siwall shook free of John's grip and turned, giving Charlotte a stiff bow. "I shall tell her, Madam. What Honoria does is her own business. But I pray she has better sense than to expose herself to the scorn that flourishes in this house. Good day to you."

Daniel heard Siwall's footsteps clatter across the polished walnut of the front hall, and the voice of Mrs. Twig, the housekeeper, as she bid him an obsequious good day.

"You shamed him too bitter, sir," said John English softly.

"I know," Daniel admitted. "He provoked me. I'll ride over to Burnt Hill and beg his pardon before dark."

English laid a big hand on his master's shoulder, a thing Daniel could not remember him doing before. "I doubt it will help, sir," he said. "He's not the forgiving kind. 'Twas a mercy he had no weapon to hand, for there's hate in him, and that's for certain.

No matter who it's meant for. Hate breeds harm, and hurts whatever it finds at hand. Ah, he's a dark man, that one."

"Ham Siwall?" Daniel looked up at his manager. It was the last thing he would have thought of Siwall, who seemed to wear his heart upon his sleeve.

But John English had said as much as he intended to, and did not explain. He slammed his old hat on his head and delivered one last troubling warning. "Provoke you he might, Major Josselyn, sir. Only—"

"Only what, John?"

"You know I'd say nothing against any man lightly."

"Of course not."

"Well, then. If Squire Siwall was my partner, I shouldn't never turn my back on him again."

THE BOX HE LIVED IN

When John English had gone, Daniel did not get up from the desk and join his wife on the divan. He remained at the window, hoping for a last glimpse of Hannah Trevor, now almost out of sight along the road.

The only sounds were the ticking of the case clock and the occasional turning of a page of Charlotte's fashion paper, and Daniel, straining to see beyond the remnants of the fog, became gradually aware that his broad hand moved of its own will and lifted itself to the square of frosty window glass that contained Hannah's disappearing image, saw his long, hardened, fingertip touch the moving fleck of blood-red that was her distant self. He allowed himself no conscious inventory of what he remembered of her body—though his memory was painfully distinct and included even the single slightly distended vein that showed dark blue through the skin of her thigh.

He made no sound except breathing. His index finger merely pressed itself onto the cold glass, trying to hold her still there, and then for an instant he saw instead his own watery reflection superimposed on hers in the windowpane.

Daniel closed his eyes and looked away. Since the War, he had avoided mirrors, polished surfaces, glass—anything in which he might be forced to see his own face. He preferred never to look at himself, if he had any choice.

Though it was not such a bad sight, on the whole.

A wide face, it was, with hooded eyes the color of good brandy. A straight nose thickened by an old break. Reddish hair no longer than his collar, worn untied and drifting soft around forehead and temples. An unfashionable stubble of red-brown beard and mustache.

When he was angry, as he had been with Siwall, the eyes burst into flame like brandy, too, with a glint of deep blue-black at the core that was not fire but ice, and never entirely melted. When he smiled, a web of crinkles appeared around the eyes and a deep dimple, barely disguised by the moustache, showed itself suddenly at the corner of his mouth.

But just now he no longer loved nor hated. Now he was a shadow that belonged nowhere and attached itself to nothing. If you touched him, you might have put your fingers straight through his body, like a cage of bones.

His finger lifted itself to his own face to be certain he was real.

"Will you take me back upstairs to bed now, Daniel?"

The voice belonged to Charlotte. He had hoped to please his wife by carrying her downstairs for an hour or two, but she had been so long confined mainly to her bed in the warm south chamber upstairs that when, at his urging, she ventured to sit with him in one of the large, elegant, high-ceilinged rooms downstairs, she grew angry and afraid, and the fear made her petulant.

All her comfort was now contained within her bedchamber, and he had spared no expense to make it whatever she chose— a high tester bed with crewel-embroidered hangings of her own design, a cherrywood rocker, a damask chaise longue from Paris, a washstand with blue-and-white Chinese ewer and basins, a basket for her eternal crewel yarns, a standing embroidery frame and another she could use even in her bed, and Mr. Richardson's latest sentimental novel, to be read aloud by Abby, the maid she had brought from London when she arrived after the War to join him here.

To amuse herself in her invalid situation, Charlotte had played at designing the library for him: walls papered Chinese red above head-high cherry-wood paneling and cases for his many books; a wide fireplace with a marble mantel; a fine divan and two lolling chairs covered with gold silk damask; a spinet and a harp in the far corner; and high, small-paned windows that looked out in summer across the blooming gardens to the river and old Henry Markham's slowly-turning mills.

Charlotte almost never sat there with him, in that elegant library. Even if she were not confined to her room, she found the place oppressive, she said. The truth was, she resented the room because it was his.

For under one of the windows stood Daniel's plain pine book-keeper's desk with its single locking drawer. It seemed as out-of-place in the library as he did himself, but it was a relic from his first days in the Manitac country of the Maine coast, and he prized it. Ugly, Charlotte called it, and promptly bought him a kidney-shaped monstrosity from a Boston joiner's catalogue.

But Daniel would not have it. He knew it was not so much the plain desk his wife minded as the fact that it fitted perfectly under the window, and that from that window he could sometimes see Hannah. The new desk would not have had enough space there, and would have been set away in the middle of the room, where he would be alone and without hope.

Where the box of his life would close on him and smash him, once and for all.

He pleaded the lack of light and had the gaudy thing carted up to one of the spare chambers. He must have his window and the fact of Hannah, moving, working, coming and going on her visits of midwifery or nursing. The sight of her goaded him back to living.

Since the day of the new desk's banishment, Charlotte had never joined him in the library except at his urging. It was the seal to his secret defection, and she did not forgive him.

Now he blamed himself silently. She was persuaded out of her chamber so seldom, and he did want only to do her good. Surely he should have taken her instead to the cheerful back parlor this afternoon, where the servants' children came and went? Or perhaps the billiard room?

But it would have made little difference. These days Charlotte seemed alien everywhere, surrounded by unspoken terrors. For a time he had thought they were self-invented or exaggerated in order to punish him for what had happened to her here in his fine America. But now, as he lifted her up to carry her, he had almost to pry her thin fingers away from the arm of the sofa, and through her blue silk bed gown he could feel against his chest the real and terrible battering of her heart.

It was no illusion. The fear was real, and it tied him to her.

Four years, he thought. *Already there have been four years of this slow torture. How many more?*

Did he wish for Charlotte's death? No. No.

Christ Jesus, did freedom always come wrapped in grief?"

"Oh, my dear Mouse," he said softly. "I shouldn't have urged you to come down and join me." He allowed his lips to brush against the child-soft tendrils of her hair, for he was fond of her. Another kind of man, who knew himself less well than Daniel Josselyn—and who had never known Hannah Trevor—might still have thought he was in love with Charlotte.

When they married, twelve years ago at his father's estate in Herefordshire, she was pale blonde and handsome in the way of idle girls bred to sketching and needlework and modest fortunes. She was twenty, then, and he was thirty-one, just back from a tour in India. No doubt she had married him expecting a house in London or Bath, plenty of servants, and a secure, fashionable, independent life with a husband away in the army and too busy making a success of his career to bother her.

It had begun that way, but in the end, his sense of justice—the same one that bound him to her now—had betrayed Charlotte's expectations badly, for as she never failed to remind him, he was, after all, the third son of Charles, Lord Bensbridge. And third sons were army sons.

First son, squire. Second son, vicar. Third son, captain. That was how the saying went.

Oh, he had been a captain, that he had. Not in one army, but in two. In the first, his father had bought him a fine commission, and he had risen in it. Captain, the Honourable Daniel Josselyn, Esquire, of the Bengal Rifles and then of Gentleman Johnnie Burgoyne's Third Horse in America.

That swaggering, blood-minded fool Burgoyne, who thought he could trust his Indian allies to fight like little gentlemen while he sailed off to London every autumn for a winter at the gaming tables with a society trollop on each arm.

It had been on his way from Boston to Canada to join his regiment at the siege of Quebec that Daniel had first seen the Manitac country. It seemed to cut a kind of clearing in his mind and let in light and air, the cold, silver finger of the broad river that reached up among the high bluffs thick with spruce and pine and tamarack. He lived in the thought of it then, all during those months of dirty siege, just as he lived now in the memory of Hannah.

But he stuck it out.

And then, suddenly, after the fight at Trois Rivières, he had ridden calmly away from the British camp, changed from a red coat to a blue, and become an American. He had first seen scalping at Trois Rivières. Gentleman Johnnie's Indians had gotten out of hand at the sight of a foraging party of two hundred Americans. Hungry men, they were, that was all. Woodsmen and farm lads, seeking no engagements with the British troops. Two hundred of them, shot down from ambush. Scalped. Their noses, ears, penises cut off for souvenirs.

Burgoyne himself, it was murmured, gave the order to attack. Though of course he deplored the results.

But Daniel had seen a few red coats bent over the bodies, too, and mad eyes in English faces. There was a line you could not cross when you were fighting in wilderness country, where everything was alien to you, to what you had been bred to and taught to believe. There was a madness that came with waiting and marching and foraging, with never quite winning and never quite losing. You could lose your self instead, and never find it again.

Wars should be fought for causes. Freedom. Justice. The Rights of Man.

All the proper rhetoric was on the American side, it seemed. So he became Lieutenant Daniel Josselyn of the Continental Army.

The Americans gave him a rank equal to his original British commission. But they didn't trust a turncoat, and why should they? So he had gotten the worst of it, the commands nobody else wanted, rearguard duty herding the mob of Loyalist prisoners and their wives and ragtag children. Their numbers swelled and declined as the men were sent off to prison ships or work camps. Sometimes there were as many as a thousand, half of them dying of the fevers that ran wildfire through the troops. Food and doctoring came last of all to prisoners, and were scarce enough even for officers.

It was among those prisoners that Daniel first realized the irrelevance of causes, even when they are good.

Women and children, potbellied and starving. Husbands and fathers executed as traitors. In one mass grave in a forest clearing, he had seen four hundred Loyalists buried, some of their bodies still jerking with what might have been life. It had been thought a kindness to kill them, since they would otherwise starve to death.

Lone women, too, abandoned, husbands fled to Canada or England to save their own necks. Nearly a thousand once-respectable housewives had followed in the wake of Burgoyne's army, and when the troops, too, discarded them out of boredom or want of provisions, they drifted. Driven out of their decent homes by patriotic neighbors. Begging. Whoring for troops in any uniform in exchange for food or a night out of the cold in a warm barracks bed. Scrubbing uniforms. Cooking. Often they lugged bits of their old lives with them. Teapots. Silver candlesticks hidden under their rags of gowns. Dragging their blank-eyed, bewildered children by the hands.

One summer morning, Daniel had found an emaciated boy of five or six on the roadside, almost dead, his mouth full of the grass that was his last vain hope of living. He didn't know that grass could not be digested. If you were well fed, it only made you vomit. If your belly was empty, it made you retch until you hemorrhaged and died.

He shot the boy in the head and buried him. So much for the Rights of Man.

But he had gone on fighting. Shot other boys.

It was at Ft. Ticonderoga that he had stumbled onto the Rufford company—Will Quaid, the blacksmith; jovial Josh Lamb; the badly-matched Siwall brothers, Ham and Artemas. Soon after came Saratoga. He had stayed with them, and felt at home at last.

Until Webb's Ford. He had lost God and two fingers of his left hand at Webb's Ford. Now—almost always—he wore a glove on it, even here in his own house.

After Webb's Ford and its horrors, he negotiated a private peace with the world. Unfit for duty and of course unwelcome in England, he let big, gentle Will Quaid take him back to Rufford.

It seemed the War had scarcely touched the place. Nobody knew Daniel but the few fighting men who were his friends. They understood the blood behind his eyes when he closed them, and nobody else saw it. There was a cleanness about his alien state that calmed him. He lodged above Will's smithy and went to work stoking the forge, mending wheels, shoeing horses and mules. Gradually, during that slow year of healing, the place became more his home than his father's great house in Herefordshire had ever been.

The broad, navigable finger of the Manitac River that burrowed its way inland. The steep, rock-faced woods so thick you could hide in them from almost anything except your own rattling brains. And the wide sea nearby, that he always came back to.

Endless, backbreaking work.

And Hannah. Jesus. Hannah.

And then, when she had finished with him, he went back to the War with the others, having nothing more to lose.

Yorktown, almost the end of it. He was Captain Josselyn again, and then Major.

When it ended and he found he had not managed to die, he went home to Rufford. Where else did he have to go?

He found letters waiting at the forge. An edict from his elder brother, Geoffrey, the new Lord Bensbridge, telling him he would be shot on sight if he dared to return. A quiet note from his newly-widowed mother containing a draft on a London bank and a letter of introduction to a certain Frederick Worth of Philadelphia, head of the Bristol Land and Trading Company, a British firm that had managed to transfer its vast holdings of timber and farmland to American silent partners just before the War broke out.

And a letter from Charlotte at her father's house in Kent. As the wife of a traitor to the British Army and King George, she was no longer received in decent society and she preferred to join him in America as soon as possible. Where exactly was this Maine, could you get there by post chaise from New York Harbor? Should she have her spinet and her porcelain shipped, or would they be able to purchase articles of equal quality in the city of Rufford? She presumed one of his servants would meet her ship.

Your obedient and affectionate Wife, etc., etc.

Then, of course, he'd had no servants, nor much else, neither. But now, only five years later, an inheritance from his grandfather and his shares in Bristol Trading had already made him rich. There was a fine house, Mapleton Grange, at the edge of the vast tract of woods he and Siwall argued constantly about. A sloop of his own, the *Lark*—iced in, now, of course, in the slip down by the ferry, but fast and bright when he took her down to Boston on the spring tide.

Prosperity. Servants—even Charlotte had all she wanted. Men to command—he had been asked to train and supervise the Rufford militia.

Nothing. To him, it was nothing.

Daniel closed his eyes and buried his face in Charlotte's soft hair.

"Are you cold, Mouse?" That was twice today he had used the old nickname. He seldom called her by it, though he knew it pleased her.

"I am always cold in this terrible country," she replied in the thin, sulky voice with which she punished him. "I only came down because I thought it might please you, Daniel. You know I wish very much to please you."

"Of course. You do, Lottie. Always."

"I should not have thought so, indeed. Whenever I'm here, you spend all your time over those silly account books with John English, or having endless debates with Mr. Siwall, or else staring out the window as if you could make the ice melt by looking at it. I don't see why we can't live in Boston, at least. Or, better yet, Williamsburg. I'm told the climate there is mild, like Devon."

She sighed. And then, as though punishing him had worn her out, Charlotte lay back against his shoulder and pretended to drift off to sleep.

He carried her up to her room and left her to be fussed over by Abby and by Mrs. Twig, the housekeeper. For a moment or two he waited in the hall outside his wife's door. But there was nothing more to say. There never would be. He went back downstairs to his desk again.

Hopefully, Daniel looked out the window once more, but the two women on the opposite bank were long gone. There was not even a speck of red fading into the distance for him to close his eyes upon and keep.

There was only a small boy on wooden skates gliding in perfect ellipses on the face of the frozen river. The flattened circles grew smaller and smaller, until at last the boy spun like a small brown top, the toe of his blade cutting deeper and deeper into the ice. Finally he fell, red-faced and wailing.

From the window glass, Josselyn's reflection superimposed itself upon the figure of the fallen skater. He pulled the heavy curtains shut.

FIVE

THE FEARFUL IMPERTINENCE OF WOMAN

Hannah Trevor's only surviving child, Jennet, had been born a dubious number of months after James's flight to Quebec as the Revolution intensified into civil war. The best thing he had ever done for his wife was to provide Jennet with an official father. According to the legal records of Rufford, she was perfectly legitimate, and there was no proof to the contrary—though there was plenty of gossip.

It was fueled by the fact that the little girl was born deaf and mute—as indicating the Finger of Divine Retribution. Worse yet, she had straight red-brown hair that drifted across her forehead exactly like that of Daniel Josselyn and deep-set hazel eyes that blazed like his when she was crossed.

But whatever the old biddies found to cluck about in private, they could prove nothing, and Hannah had gradually become indispensable to many, for she was good at her work. In the six years since she had taken over most of her Aunt Julia's practice as Rufford's chief midwife, she had delivered more than a hundred babies and lost only six, and none of their mothers at all. In part, this was due to her ability to put two and two together, to piece symptoms and superstitious fears and their common remedies together like the patterns of her quilts. But she also made a constant and unflinching study of anatomy, and she observed, at the behest of a natural fastidiousness, standards of hygiene then only beginning to be practiced by the Great Men of medicine.

It was one of these worthies, a certain Dr. Samuel Clinch, who rode spitting, farting and snorting out of the February fog, across the flat expanse of the Training Ground of Daniel's militia, and straight toward the small, weather-beaten house of Mr. and Mrs. Phineas Rugg that Valentine's Day.

"Go home, Madam!" Sam Clinch bellowed as he heaved his well-stuffed yellow breeches out of the saddle and caught sight of Hannah in Mrs. Rugg's untidy back garden. Hannah had just tossed out a pail of murky scrub water onto the mess of muddy ruts and packed snow, and was hauling another bucketful up from the well.

It was iced-over except for a small open triangle at the far side, and even when she managed to find the water, the bucket came up only half full. Like everything else at the Rugg farm, the well had been hastily made and neglected for years, and now it was nearly blocked from the bottom with water weeds and sticks. But Phineas Rugg didn't seem to consider it man's work to bother where the water came from. When he wasn't in the Debtor's Jail at Salcombe, he was down at the Red Bush tavern.

Rum and skittles were the limit of Phinney's ambition. Man's work, indeed.

Hannah looked around at the tipsy outhouse and the claptrap barn, where one scrawny cow lowed forlornly through the half-open door, and sighed. She didn't grudge her services to those who couldn't pay. But her rational principles nagged at her. What virtue was it to bring another life into such a hopeless muddle? Perhaps she should leave them to Samuel Clinch after all.

"Go home!" he brayed, puffing heavily as he clumped through the mud in her direction. His servant, a tall black man with twice his master's brains and a constant look of veiled amusement, dismounted from the white mule he rode and led the two animals aside to hobble them with Aunt Julia's mare.

Clinch emitted a Vesuvian belch. "We want no scrubwomen here today, Mistress Trevor! Today we want alacrity and despatch, Ma'am! Alacrity and despatch and the scientific mind. All qualities of the male, Ma'am! M-a-l-e. Can you write, Ma'am? Can you spell? 'Course you can't! Not expected! Qualities, and so forth, d'ye see? Go home and Godspeed! Not needed here."

Hannah let the wellsweep snap back so smartly that the balance end of the long pole almost knocked the old fool down. Without replying, she unfastened the bucket from the rope and settled it in her left hand. Then she turned to Clinch and smiled, the cool smile of benign disinterest she knew infuriated him.

She practiced it sometimes, in front of her mirror.

"Good day, Master Clinch," she said quietly. "I was not aware you had been sent for. I'm quite sure Mrs. Rugg does not require you."

"Mrs. Rugg? *Mrs.* Rugg?" Clinch snorted and pulled a silver snuffbox from somewhere inside his blue cloak. He laid out a careful pinch along his index finger and sniffed it back with a brisk whistle, then squinted and held his breath, waiting for the relief of the sneeze. It did not come, and his face turned beet-red with frustration.

"I beg your pardon, Ma'am," he blustered. "Rugg himself bid me attend her. Rugg himself. Horses are not the best judges of their own fodder, Madam! Women are not the best judges of their welfare, else what are husbands for, eh? What are they for?"

"This small house is home to eleven children at present, sir, the eldest not yet fourteen." Hannah's smile did not alter. "The fact offers some proof what husbands *may* be for. But oddly enough, I seldom see a one of them at any wife's bedside during travail. Even the best husbands lurk in barns and cold parlors at such times, looking costive and liverish. Possibly the sight of blood and afterbirth dismays them."

The black servant, a freeman called Caesar, was unstrapping a wooden contraption from the back of his mule. It was an unwieldy cross between a stocks, an antique ducking stool, and the kind of chair into which mad King George was strapped to be blistered back to sanity.

Hannah recognized it as soon as she caught sight of it. A birthing chair, and obviously invented—like the ducking stool—by some Great Man.

"I waste no more time on you, Ma'am!" huffed the good doctor. "You ain't worth fiddle!"

Samuel Clinch was one of the old breed, a barber-surgeon who did things as they had been done by such men since the Middle Ages. Cupping, bleeding, blistering and purging were his stocks-in-trade. For the shingles, he prescribed cat's blood. For the colic, he recommended the drinking of freshly-passed urine, mixed with licorice and honey.

He was an old man, not far past sixty, tall and heavy, with puffy eyes and a look of bloating about the belly. His wig was old and moth-eaten, and tufts of uncurled hair stuck out like bird's wings at uncertain intervals, as though the bird himself partook of too much rum. His tricorn sat permanently askew, his yellow calamanco breeches were splashed with mud and his double cloak had a heavy border of horse dung at the hem. He drank and whored and gambled heavily on his horses, which he raced till they were too worn out to stud and brought no price at the spring horse fair, leaving him deeper in debt than ever. In addition to a weary wife and five silly daughters, he was forced by law to support one or two witless bastards gotten on the tavern maids.

And there was one thing more about Clinch, which Hannah knew by the pricking of her thumbs. Like most men who insist upon the inferior qualities of women, Samuel Clinch was secretly terrified of every last one of them.

She stood her ground, blocking the doorway. "You may leave the birthing chair outside, Caesar," she announced quietly as the servant approached her, his back bent under the heavy contraption. "Mrs. Rugg is in no need of more furniture."

The black man paused but did not lower the chair. There were no slaves in Rufford, but even free servants may be beaten and turned off, and servants' wives and sons may starve.

"Inside, sir!" commanded Clinch. He aimed a muddy boot at Caesar's breeches, pushed past Hannah, and strode into the house like Garrick the actor making an entrance in one of Mr. Congreve's plays. He stood there, blinking in the near-darkness, as Hannah slipped past him into the room.

It stank of smoke and rancid tallow, and of urine dried in diapers and woolen blankets that would not be properly washed till spring, but just now most acutely of the panful of turnips abandoned to burning on the hob when Mrs. Rugg's water broke just before the noon meal.

A huge hearth filled one whole side of the small, square kitchen, and although a fire blazed and sent sparks far beyond the andirons, two feet from the flames it was colder than the out-of-doors, for the shiftless Phinney had taken no trouble with the angle of the flue. The windows had been hung with quilts to keep out drafts, but they were worn so thin as to be of little use.

Still, thought Hannah, casting her eye over them, the patterns were well worked out and the stitching was careful. Even faded and threadbare, the tiny squares and triangles of the eight-pointed star pattern were clean and perfect. Northumberland Star, they called the design. Mrs. Rugg had been born in Northumberland. Probably the quilts had come with her to America when she was a bride, their colors still bright and hopeful.

They could no more have predicted their fate than could their owner. And they had scarcely less chance of doing anything about it.

Marriage was marriage, and Phinney Rugg was Phinney Rugg.

But the quilts still had a ghostly beauty, and they endured, like their mistress.

They did, however, make the small room very dark. The clapboards of the inside walls had once been whitewashed, but now they were stained and smoked and hung thick with bunches of herbs and dried flax that rustled softly in the drafts. Hannah had looked for a candle when she and Julia arrived, but there was none to be found. Instead, an aged and rusty betty-lamp hung from an iron hook beside the fireplace, dripping its hot, smoky grease onto the flagstones in slow and regular rhythm. But its feckless flame gave precious little light.

On the rough pine table in the middle of the room, the remains of the breakfast oatmeal still lay half-frozen in a clutter of wooden trenchers. There was a settle at one side of the hearth, and Julia had made it comfortable with folded quilts and one or two worn cushions as soon as they arrived. Mrs. Rugg, a long-boned woman with thinning, mouse-brown hair, pale as the faded quilts, lay back against them, dozing, waiting, the worst of her labor not yet begun.

"What is this blabber of a chair?"

Aunt Julia suddenly rose up like a well-stuffed black woolen tea cozy from behind the settle, her arms loaded with the clean sheets and linen they always brought with them to be sure of a supply. She shoved the Great Man aside and began to lay a birthing pallet a safe distance from the fire.

She glared up at him. "Look to your boots, Sam Clinch! We've been an hour scrubbing that floor so as to make her a decent bed. Don't stand here rumpussing! And we'll have none of your contraptions, if you please!"

Caesar had just brought in the ridiculous birthing chair and put it down beside the settle. Mrs. Fortunata Rugg opened one baleful eye, looked at the thing, gave a thin wail and closed her eye again. Across the room eleven pairs of smaller eyes—all, amazingly enough, masculine—opened wide from under and upon a half dozen unmade beds and trundles and cribs and cradles. Eleven shrill masculine voices gave eleven wails.

"You children, there!" honked Julia, spying them. "Did I not send you to bed?"

Eleven pairs of eyes closed tight again and eleven masculine heads dived under bedclothes to keep warm.

"What has scrubbing to do with it, Ma'am?" roared Clinch, finding his wind again. "This is a sound scientific device!"

Hannah strode across the room, sat down in the oddly-tilted chair, and pulled her skirts tight across her hips to reveal their position. "Look there, sir," she said, staring the old man down. "See the angle of the pelvis? Too flat on the buttocks, the weight of the child too much smashed down upon the birth passage. A woman cannot possibly bear down properly."

He spluttered. "Buttocks, indeed! Have you a knowledge of science? 'Course not!"

"Have *you* given birth, sir?" Julia advanced a step. "Are you a prodigy? Hunh! Prodigious noodle!"

"Ma'am! Ma'am! I shall endeavor to overlook—"

Hannah's dark eyes widened. "I daresay. Oh, I do dare say. And have you endeavored to overlook the matter of Major Josselyn's lady, whom, with the help of this monstrosity, you have left damaged and sickly for life? Whose first and only son you dismembered in order to deliver it, rather than take my aunt's advice and my own in safely turning it? You cut off its head, if I remember, and both arms, did you not? Or was it an arm and a leg? I assure you, neither the lady nor her husband has overlooked it, nor ever shall. Thanks to you, they buried their only son in pieces."

There was a silence.

Clinch took out a rumpled square of silk and mopped his face, wiped his lips. "I deplore the loss, but I trust I am not morbid, Madam! A doctor ought to feel no guilt on such unfortunate occasions. We take risks, and some of the risks prove, and some do not."

"Are you describing a horse race, sir? You play with lives."

"I sleep soundly, Madam, which is more than you should do, from what I hear of you! I shall be forced to report you to the magistrate's court, Mrs. Trevor! You are insubordinate! You take liberties! Have no doubt, Mr. Siwall shall hear of this! I shall have you struck off and fined!"

Across the room, Aunt Julia held her breath for the explosion.

Hannah's eyes closed for a moment behind their spectacles, then opened again, the anger quelled in favor of a sweeter vengeance. She drew a deep breath and stood up from the chair.

"I do beg your pardon, Dr. Clinch," she said in her softest voice. "I should not have quibbled with a man on such a charitable errand as your own. Do, pray, forgive my impertinence. I beg you to stay and deliver the child yourself. Come, Aunt, we shall go and leave this good man to his unpaid labors."

Something like an oink issued from the depths of Clinch's stock-tied throat. "Un-*paid?*"

In the far corner, Caesar's smile grew a fraction wider. Julia sailed out of harbor and, seizing Clinch's arm, dragged him out of the hearing of Mrs. Rugg, who was whimpering softly now and then as the pains became more frequent. Or was it at the echo of the word *pay?*

"Clinch, look around you," hissed the old lady. "Where do you see money within these walls?"

He gaped, small pink eyes blinking.

"Do you see a rack of good pewter dressing those shelves? Do you see porcelain bowls and silver candlesticks?"

"I scarcely understand—"

"What is your usual fee, Clinch?"

"Fifteen shillings, Ma'am, as you well know. If it's any blasted business of yours."

Julia Markham folded her arms across an expanse of white linen apron. "Then what are you thinking, sir? My niece charges six shillings, the same as I did myself. And we can be paid in wood ash for making soap-lye, or in comfrey roots for our medicines, or a bag of sewing scraps for colors in a quilt."

Hannah smiled her most infuriating smile. "Perhaps your own creditors weave, sir? Or do they quilt? Or spin?"

The only sounds were the drip of grease from the lamp and the scuttle of rats' feet in the storeroom above their heads.

"Caesar!" roared Samuel Clinch, and he turned with a sniff and clumped out. "Follow me, sir!"

The servant's shoulders shook with silent laughter as he moved to follow, but he paused, remembering the offending chair.

Hannah laid a hand on his arm. "Will you leave it, if you please?" She pushed up her spectacles and smiled at Caesar. "I perceive we are in need of firewood," she said, and picked up the ax from the hearth.

When the birth of Rugg Number Twelve had been safely accomplished and mother and child put into a clean bed, Hannah at last had time to wash her own hands and forearms properly in the damp cold of the yard.

She had not come to Maine by choice, and she had never wished to be at home there. But the long sweep of the river and the sudden lift of the wooded hills made her breath come easier whenever she saw them, and the smell of the cold itself affected her like salt on tasteless food. She took a deep breath and plunged both arms into the pail of icy water.

"Will you leave us, Niece?" demanded Julia's voice behind her. "Will you go sensibly back to Boston and marry again?" She laid a hand on Hannah's shoulder. "You go to waste here, my girl. Waste is a mortal sin. Or if it's not, it should be."

Julia Markham had made up her mind to part with her niece. Hannah was not too old to settle into a decent marriage with some manageable widower—the Reverend Rockwood of Boston, perhaps, who still wrote to her. Legally, a woman had no rights without independent property; she could not survive without a man to act as her guardian. If she were married and unhappy and lived apart from her husband by her own will, the law could drag her back to him, no matter what he had done. If she had children, they belonged to their father, not to her. If she had bastards, a man must be accused during the worst pains of her labor—when she was supposed too desperate for her own life to tell a lie— and afterwards he was given the rule and support of them whether he married her or not.

Julia closed her eyes and drew a deep breath of cold air. Such was the insolence of man's office, and she meant to see her niece protected from it. For a time, so long as her uncle was alive, she might be under his official protection and legal control.

But Henry would not live forever. The farm and the mills would go to that rogue Jonathan and Sally, his fluttery child of a wife. They would take the house-rule from Julia and she herself would be left with only her dower rights—a single sleeping chamber, her linens and clothing, a few sticks of furniture specified in Henry's will, and the gracious use of her own kitchen and privy. It was the way of widows, even widows far richer than herself.

And for Hannah and Jennet there would be no room at all. Even if appearances were true—and Julia had never asked—there was nothing Daniel Josselyn could do for her unless Hannah accused him, had him arrested for fornication and adultery. And that she would never do.

Julia took her niece's shoulders and turned them to face her. "*Will* you go sensibly to my husband's sister in Boston and let her help you to a marriage of your own, or won't you?"

Hannah didn't answer. A lone gull wheeled above the river houses in the town below them, hoping for scraps thrown out in the yards to rot. A horse made its way across the frozen river at Lamb's Inn landing and turned in at Will Quaid's forge. Smoke spiraled slowly from the forge and from the dozen or so shops and houses clustered round the meetinghouse and the town jail.

All but one. No smoke issued from the chimney of one particular house, painted the omnipresent red-brown they called Indian red. Its whitewashed shutters were closed, and outside in the small yard a nondescript black dog prowled back and forth, stopping now and then to scratch at the closed front door and whine and howl.

Inside the house, the beaten and strangled body of Anthea Mary Emory lay naked and half frozen in the cold darkness. On the previous night, the eve of St. Valentine's Day, she had been raped for the fourth night in succession, as the letter left under the pewter salt cellar on her kitchen table would testify. She prayed, she said, that God might strike her dead, although she had no particular hope He would oblige.

"Look there, Aunt! I perceive that little fool Nan Emory's let her fire go out," said Hannah, as she turned toward the house again. "I'll go and fetch her down some coals."

So, thought the old woman, there was her answer. Hannah wanted no second marriage. And what Hannah did not want, she would not hear of.

"Waste," said Julia softly, and did not know how true she spoke.

PIECING THE EVIDENCE:
Letter of Mrs. Anthea Mary Emory,
Dated February 13, 1786

To My Beloved Husband, Mr. Dunstan Emory

My Heart—
As I do not think I shall live beyond another night, I write to say good-bye.

Having broke the lock of the door and found me disordered and almost to bed, they have all three forced me to adultery and done me great hurt with fists and with fire as it pleased them, these three nights past.

I thought best to tell no one until you returned, for shame of myself and with respect to your honor. I have trusted in God, but He has abandoned me. I am out of sight of the mercy of God and of men.

The third will come again this night silently, the lock being already broke, and says he will have my life as he has had my body, for fear of his wife's knowing, lest I should charge a rape against them all.

I believe him, for in my sight he did wring the neck of my cage-bird, Trinket.

May God take my life before he does, for I am afraid of his hands.
I have sent Polly and Jotham to Mrs. Dowell till you come for them.
                              Your Affectionate Wife Nan

To this letter she added three names, in the uncertain spelling of the time.

Lambe Sewwall Josyellen

Mrs. Emory's handwriting was unpracticed, and the quill with which she wrote had not been sharpened in some months, nor was the ink of the best quality. The paper was the back page torn from an account book of the Bristol Company, her husband's employers.

The second name, *Sewwall,* had been partially scribbled over, and William Quaid, Rufford's constable, was unable to determine with certainty whether it read Seward, Stewart, or Siwall.

SEVEN

WHAT THE CONSTABLE FOUND

" 'There was a rich lady lived over the sea, And she was an island queen . . .' "

The song reached Hannah through the open street door of Quaid's Forge. Even in the damp February cold, the heat of the great brick firepit struck her a blow in the face, and she blinked, eyes watering.

"Will!" she shouted.

" 'Her daughter lived off in the new coun-te-ry, With an ocean of water between. Wiiiiith an ocean of water between!' "

"Will Quaid!"

When Constable William Quaid sang at a frolic or a cornhusking, the codfish heard him out on the Banks, so it was said, and took to step-dancing with the lobsters.

He hadn't heard her, but he stopped for breath and bent to pound out the perfect curve of a sled runner over a carefully rounded oak log with an iron sleeve. He had made the shape himself for the purpose, and he took great pains with his blades. The sleighs and sleds of Rufford were unique, and already known as far as Montreal.

Will caught sight of Hannah and lowered the hammer. The broad back straightened, the leather apron creaked. He plunged the half-shaped blade into a wooden tub of water beside the forge and grinned his gap-toothed grin at her, raking back his stringy dark hair with a seared and sooty hand.

"Well, Hannah-girl? Phinney Rugg's latest here already? Too soon by half, you know. He's not had near enough of Bill Edes's rum-and-lemons yet to bear the sight of another'n." He cackled and nudged a three-legged stool in Hannah's direction. "Have a chair, now, my dear. I've good cider in back, if you'll take some?"

Even before James's departure, Will and his wife, Hetty, had been Hannah's friends, and she was always certain of a welcome at the forge. But the place had shadows in it for her, it made her remember what she could otherwise deceive herself she'd forgotten. This was where she had first met Daniel, and for the most part, she stayed away these days.

But today her errand was more important.

"Could you spare me some coals in this fire pan, William?" she said. "I brought some down from Rugg's, only I was too long on the way, and they've gone out now, most of them."

He raised a singed eyebrow, rubbed the back of a big hand across his stubbly moustache, and eyed the long-handled carrying pan she'd set down on the floor. Then he went to his forge, worked the huge bellows a few times, and reached in with his tongs for a half-dozen glowing coals, red at the heart and edged with deep blue. They turned ice blue, and finally were cloaked with white ash as the air surrounded them.

"Don't tell me your cooking fire's gone out while you was up yonder at Rugg's?"

The big constable frowned. There were usually three or more hired girls at Two Mills to keep things going when Hannah and the old woman had a birth or a dying to trouble with elsewhere. A cold hearth at the Markham place—at any place in Maine in the middle of winter—meant trouble. Will Quaid dropped the coals into the pan and opened the louvers in the lid to make a draft. "Not like your auntie to let a fire go untended," he said.

"Oh, no, they're for Nan Emory," replied Hannah. "There's no smoke at her chimney, I could see it from up at Phinney's."

The blacksmith raised an eyebrow. "Been sickly, has she?"

"Not that I know. But she's young. And she's alone these months past, since her husband went off."

"And you feel for her. Well, now." Will crashed his fist through the skim of ice on the leather fire bucket at the doorway and splashed his sooty face, then scrubbed at it with a huckaback towel.

"Anybody with a lick of sense would've let surveying till the spring," he said. "He's a damn fool and no mistake, is young Emory, going into the Outward that time of the year. Weather only gets worse in November, and that's near three months now. If he's not back in a fortnight, I misdoubt he'll come back at all."

The Outward was the name they used for the huge, trackless forest of pines, hemlocks, and spruces that began to thicken to a labyrinth no more than a mile beyond the town. A precarious lumbering road ran north and west from the edge of the worked fields and gardens at the back of Daniel Josselyn's brick manor house, and here and there squatters and settlers and charcoal-burners had hacked out small clearings and tried to hold their own against the trees.

But even the lumbermen despaired of roads after a few miles, and dragged the felled trees two or three at a time with oxen as far as the river sluice, then pegged them into rafts and rode them on down to Henry Markham's mill with the current. There they were cut into lumber and rafted downriver to the yards at Wy-brow Head, where the huge cargo vessels called in for them.

On the Two Mills side of the Manitac, where there was more cleared farmland, a township road ran south and west, climbing along Maid's Hill, past the Markhams' sugar bush and the falls on Blackthorne Creek. It led eventually to the county town of Salcombe, and from there it went on south to meet the Boston post road.

But behind it all, like the shadow of some old blood-life will-fully discarded but too strong and proud to accept its own defeat, the dark trees crowded in again as soon as they were cut. Settlers disappeared in them and were never seen again. Hunters and woodsmen ventured in alone and came back a year, two years later, blank-eyed and silent and out of the habit of their own humanity. Somewhere among the trees, the remnants of the Manitawan tribe drifted like harmless ghosts. And even in the roughly-cobbled main street of Rufford, the scent of pine lay always, sharp and rich upon the cold air and mingling with the smell of river ice and not-far-distant sea.

If the Outward was the heart-blood of the Manitac country, then ice was her cold, sweet bones.

In spring, you could sink to your horse's neck in mud in the forest. In summer, it was almost impassible with shoulder-high ferns and wild berry bushes, and, worse yet, it buzzed with hordes of insects that nearly ate surveying parties alive. In dead winter, the snow and the fierce North Atlantic cold could come crashing down in an hour and last a month or two, snowing you in until provisions were gone and firewood dwindled. The weather made it a mortal risk to venture even a quarter-mile into the Outward from November to early March. It was safest and easiest to go when the deepest of the cold had ended for the year, while the snow still had a hard crust that would hold up a man's weight on snowshoes and the barely-visible Indian trails were hard-frozen enough for the feet of a horse or a mule.

Dunstan Emory, Anthea's husband, was an independent surveyor employed by the Bristol Company to lay out lots for sale among its vast holdings and to mark sections for the logging crews to cut during the warmer months. He had gone out in late November, just after Thanksgiving, with a party of four men up from Salcombe. Now it was February, and none of them had returned.

Anthea had been alone with her two small children for almost three months.

"I haven't seen her since the quilting party we had at New Year's. I meant to call on her sooner." Hannah frowned, punishing herself. "I was worried when I saw the chimney stack was cold. I thought she might have come to you for coals already, or sent a neighbor."

Will shook his head. "No, my dear, nobody's come. Now I think on it, I've seen nothing at all of the girl for a week since, nor the young ones, either. Thought nothing much of it. She's not inclined to visiting herself around."

He passed a hand across his dark blue eyes, sorting out what mattered from what did not. His mind was not swift, but it was strong and keen. "But, wait now!" he said at last. "When I rode the bounds before daybreak, I did mark that old dog of hers prowling about, though as a rule she keeps him inside with her till first light. And he was out last night, too, come to think of it, before I handed over the keys to the Watch."

He turned towards a curtained-off doorway. "Dodger!" he roared. "You're wanted, Dodge!"

In another moment, a diminutive old man scuffled into the Forge from Will's living quarters at the back. He wore brown breeches, a homespun shirt that reached below his knees, and a sleeveless blue jacket with most of its tarnished buttons missing. On top of his head, which was no bigger than a good-sized turnip, he wore a perfectly-groomed and recently-powdered campaign wig of the pigtailed sort, with loose puffs of hair over the ears. At the very top of everything, perched like a flag upon a mountaintop, sat a rusty black nightcap with a long red tassel that swept his shoulder as he trotted along.

Although Mr. Dodger had lived at Will Quaid's house ever since the War, neither Hannah nor anybody else knew exactly who he was or where he had materialized from.

"Who was the Night Watch last night, Dodger my dear?" asked Will.

There was a clicking sound as Mr. Dodger's jaw snapped shut and another as his eyes snapped wide open.

"North Bank. Ticknor, Ephraim W.," he said in a sweet, dry voice like old pages turning. "Ticknor and Jaybury, North Bank. South Bank, Upper, Fellingham the First. South Bank, Lower, Fellingham the Second."

"Anything amiss at Emory's, Dodge? Three houses past Lawyer Napier's place, this side the river. Anything reported?"

The old man seemed to scan some distant prospect for a moment, one hand across his mouth. Then he returned to earth and spoke from behind spread fingers, and when he spoke, he drew very close to Will, as though he needed shelter.

"Dog howling at large before sunrise, sir," he said softly.

"That'd be old Toby. What else, my dear Dodge?"

"Sounds, sir."

"Sounds?"

"Sounds was reported quite distinctly."

"What kind of sounds, Dodge?"

The small black eyes opened wider. "Sorry sounds, William," said the sweet voice. "Female sounds." Tears began to roll down the papery old cheeks and wet the crimson tassel. "Fellingham heard them. I took note of them."

"Screams, was they? Shouts? Swearing and blaspheming, Dodger?"

Mr. Dodger's two hands in their fingerless gloves darted out like claws and gripped hold of William's sleeve.

"Sounds like the heart cracking," he whispered. "Sounds like giving up and giving out and giving over. Sounds."

Will flung on his blanket-cloak and pulled a knitted cap over his ears. "Blast it, now! Why the deuce didn't you tell me, Dodger?"

"Your pardon, sir, was I properly bid? Was I bid, sir?" sobbed the old man. "I am to watch and listen and present observation when called upon. I am to take note and depart. I do stay in the back parlor unless I'm bid, you know. I wasn't never bid till now."

Toby, Nan Emory's old black dog with the one white eye patch, lay whimpering nervously on the stoop when Will Quaid, with Hannah mounted sidewise behind him, rode up the pounded path to the front door.

She slipped her arms from around him and slid easily down, and she could have been at the door long before him. But suddenly, as though they had come at him with a club, the old dog was up, snarling, lunging at them.

"Look out, now!" Will grabbed Hannah's arm and jerked her sharply away from the bared teeth. He picked up a stick from the woodpile in the yard. "Now, Tobe," he said. The constable reached into a tow sack on his saddle and pulled out the remains of one of his wife's pork pies. He let the animal smell the food.

"You know me, now, Tobe, don't you? Come, you rascal. Yes. Come on. That's right."

Will tossed the pork pie a few feet away and Toby raced for it and wolfed it down, then trotted back for more, tail wagging eagerly. Will scratched him behind the ears and patted his quivering sides.

"Not been fed in some while," he said softly. "Feel his bones, poor old hayrake."

He walked to the front door and rapped on it. No one answered and he tried the thumb-latch. The door swung open. He looked round at Hannah and frowned.

He wanted to be rid of her and she knew it. If there was death in Nan Emory's neatly-kept cottage, he could meet it alone well enough. But he might flinch with anyone's eyes on him, especially a woman's.

William was not at all ashamed to weep, but he preferred to do it alone.

"You take the horse, Ma'am, if you will," he told her formally, as though what was inside the house had suddenly made strangers of them. "Fetch me young Peter Fellingham, if you please. He'll have been past here with the Watch at least twice last night. We shall need him."

Hannah set down the all-but-forgotten bucket of coals she was still balancing. "I fancy you'll need me more than you need Pete Fellingham," she said, and marched stubbornly ahead of him through the open door.

NTHEA

Sounds like the heart cracking.

That was what Dodger had said.

Looking down at Nan Emory's body where it lay sprawled on the quilt-covered bed in the downstairs chamber, Hannah Trevor could hear those sounds clearly. They made her dwarfed and cold and battered, as though a hopeless wound had opened inside her own body.

Anthea.

Hannah said it aloud, and her voice was angry.

It was a strange, fanciful name. Her uncle had named her, the girl had once said, and he was a schoolmaster and knew some Greek. The name meant *like a flower.*

So she had been, as though she grew to order. A pale flower with a dark center. Anemone, perhaps, or gillyflower.

Her father was dead now, she had told Hannah one day when she came to Two Mills for a quilting. All her own family dead.

In the War, was all she would say when you asked her. The War had been her childhood. She hardly remembered anything before it, or cared for anything since.

Nan Emory had married at no more than seventeen, somewhere in New York State, if Hannah remembered rightly, and had still

55

been a year shy of twenty-one when she died. Though her eyes were a dark brown, she had fair hair, reddish-blond, and a pale skin flooded with freckles.

Even her small breasts were lightly freckled. Hannah let a fingertip stroke the fine skin below the nipple gently, as if the fragile nerves were still alive there, and might feel it and be comforted.

Then, remembering the rule of reason, she stuffed her hand into her apron pocket and began to take an inventory of the corpse. She would be called to the inquest at Wybrow, where the borough court sat, and her report must be true to the last broken thumbnail. She would give old Clinch—alas, the borough coroner—the satisfaction of nothing less than icy professionalism when she presented her statement.

It was dark in the room, and there was no fire yet to light the stub of candle. She pushed back the linen curtain from the small window and bent close to the body, so as to be sure of missing nothing.

Nan Emory's face and breasts and belly had been battered with fists, but not recently. The bruises looked half-faded, as though they were some days old, perhaps even a week or more. Where the blows had broken the skin, it was almost healed.

Besides the bruises, there were burns. They were oval, no more than an inch at the center, and newly-suffered, just long enough before her death to blister. He had wanted to watch her suffer pain before she died, to feel his own power through her defeat.

Each time he grew more as she grew less. Each time the fire touched her. Each time he slammed himself inside her.

By the time she died, he had usurped the throne of God.

Hannah looked closer, ran her finger around the edge of one of the blistered patches. The burns were not random. They formed a kind of pattern, moving down from the girl's throat to the cleft of her breasts to the base of her belly. He must have used a candle flame, for there was tallow dripped onto the skin.

Anthea's legs were still spraddled from his last use of her, and below the concave navel, the belly and the inner thighs were smeared with his seed, still only half-dried and vaguely glutinous. He must have arrived near morning, perhaps even been here inside the house at the same hour Will passed by on his watch outside and saw old Toby, the dog.

Slowly, like the piecing of one of her quilts from scraps and patches—like the quilt she had named Hearts and Bones, for it seemed almost a human thing—Hannah began to rebuild the last scene of Nan Emory's life.

The girl was alone, expecting the return of whatever man had beaten her a week ago. Peter Fellingham had heard her sobbing as she waited, but he'd passed by, perhaps embarrassed, perhaps discounting the just causes of women's tears. If you stopped to question every wailing woman, you'd never see your bed.

So. The man had waited until the Watch was gone, its last round made at four in the morning. Will didn't ride his morning round till nearly six, for not much trouble erupted in Rufford once the two taverns closed their doors.

He had two hours, then. He knew the girl was expecting him, knew the door lock was already broken. There was no wooden bar and cradle on the inside, but she had tried to latch it with the contrivance of bent nails and leather thongs that now dangled from the door frame.

It was no proof against him. He had anticipated her flimsy defenses and brought a chisel with him, to pry the nails loose from the wood. Inside, she must've heard him working. The dog barking, howling. Her children gone. Did she sit down and wait for him, unable to think of anything else? Perhaps she had fought him off before and been beaten for her trouble. Perhaps if she accepted him, he would come easier to her, wouldn't crash open a great, howling hole in which he could bury himself.

Or perhaps she had no will left in her to fight. There were no signs of resistance. Aside from the body itself, the place was amazingly tidy, even the bedclothes not so disarranged as you might expect after such a battle.

Hannah looked away from the body, focusing on the darkness

in the corners of the room, focusing on the clothes-chest, the black-oak rocker, the scrap of mirror on the wall beyond the bed. Focusing anywhere but on the dead. Her mouth was parched and her tongue felt swollen, as if she had been walking through a desert for a long time. She forced herself to swallow several times, painfully. It brought saliva back into her mouth, and she wet her lips with it.

Her work was not finished. She looked at the body of Anthea Emory again.

So then. The nails gave way on the door frame, the leather strap hung flapping. He opened the door. The dog came at him, but he was ready for it. Perhaps he had brought it food, like Will's pork pie. Once Toby was safely outside, he pushed the door shut, propped a chair against it to keep it shut.

He knew he had come to kill her, but he let her hope for a while. She lay down with him willingly. Still hopeful of life. She led him with the candle into the cold chamber. He seemed to want the light, kept it burning all the while. There was no more than an inch of the tallow left, and the wick was untrimmed, all but drowned.

She undressed as he watched her. He let her take her time. Her gown and petticoats were folded neatly on the chair beside the bed; over the ladder back of the chair hung a handsome crewel-work pocket with ribbons to tie round the waist. A delicate circle of briar roses and oak leaves, worked in soft yarns and bits of silk thread for contrast, the whole marred only by a dark smudge of what looked like grease, or perhaps soot, near the edge. Aside from the quilt, it was the only bit of beauty in the room, and she was careful with it.

Only her shift had been carelessly left upon the floor.

She lay down here on the bed to wait for him then, watching in the ring of candlelight as he stripped off shirt and breeches. Some men like to be watched.

Was it then he had taken up the candle to burn her? Or had he begun with her arm? The left one was broken, a piece of the bone sticking out through the skin. Great handfuls of her hair had been pulled out and some stuffed in her mouth to gag her.

Perhaps by that time it had been growing late, people in the nearby houses beginning to rise and stir their hearth fires, light their lanterns, and stumble out to milk cows. He could not risk being heard. While he took her, while he burned her, he must have needed silence. Above the grotesque mouth, the girl's wide brown eyes still stared into the dimness of the room as though she were looking for someone.

Inside her own pocket, Hannah Trevor's hand made itself into a fist. Although she had intended to touch nothing, she reached out and closed the staring eyes, then put her hand back into her pocket again. Once more it became a fist.

The quilt under the girl's body was perfect and beautifully made, of the pattern called Job's Trouble. No blood stained the finely-stitched bits of fabric. He had shed none of her blood.

It was the quilt they had stitched together at the New Year's party at Two Mills. Hannah remembered the girl's face, looking down at the colors as they came slowly together in the piecing, the deep green and dull golden brown and buff, and then the amazing bright crimson of the center squares. With such a color, you would hardly have noticed if there were blood. Hannah wondered if he had thought of it, once he had killed her.

By then it must have been nearly six, and time was short. After her terrible punishments, Nan Emory had been neatly and efficiently strangled.

The marks of it, like so many dimples in a loaf, lay along the two sides of her neck, and Hannah put on her spectacles and bent to examine them. A broad hand. Five fingers spread wide on the left side of the throat. Three fingers on the right. She moistened her lips and counted them again. Not five. Three. A man with a ruined hand.

A wave of dizzy sickness flooded over Hannah, but she fought it off.

The hands. The hands, she thought.

They would be opposite, of course. The dead woman's right

was her murderer's left as he crouched over her. He had only three fingers on his left hand. A thumb, an index finger, and a small finger. Between them, two useless stumps no longer than the first joint.

Daniel.

Once Hannah had allowed the name to reach her rational mind, she could not remove it. It lay there like a burden of ice.

Upon the picture she had drawn of the last night of Anthea Emory's life, the face of Daniel Josselyn gradually imposed itself, and would not be erased.

What the Letter Told Them

Until Will Quaid's heavy body brushed against her, Hannah did not realize she was shaking. She locked her two hands together under her cloak, but they would not hold still, and the cloak itself shook. She slipped her left hand out and gripped the bedpost with it, digging her nails into the wood until they pulled away a bit and bled. The pain reached her and the shaking stopped. She forced herself to straighten, to stop leaning against the strength of the man beside her, even though he seemed to want to lend it to her.

"I've got a fire going," Will said, looking only briefly at the dead body. As constable, he would have time enough with it before they were done. "Come out of this, my dear," he said softly, "and breathe free."

Hannah made herself stand very still. Inch by inch, muscle by muscle, staring wide-eyed at the slim, ruined shape on the bed, she battled the invisible presence of Daniel Josselyn and believed she had won.

Daniel, whose hand was missing two fingers. Daniel, who had touched more than her body—though that would have been enough for her. Even now, at night before she slept, she lay very still in the bed, with Jennet snuggled up beside her, reinventing

61

the memory of that mangled hand, the delicate remaining finger-tips mapping the territory of her flesh.

"You are made like your quilts," he had said softly. He let his index finger trace the circle of her nipple, drift softly down the ellipse of her already-swelling belly and then to the triangle below it. "Strange geometrical hinges."

She had laughed at him. Daniel was a great one for books, and words took root in him, spilling out at the most inappropriate moments.

"You are my quilt," he said, and kissed the hollow of her shoulder. "Beautiful pieces in a perfect pattern."

"Some of the pieces have been roughly used," she told him, "and are a little worn."

"But pieced together, they are strong enough. Quilts must have names, though, must they not?" He propped himself on an elbow, studying her by the candlelight. "Daniel's Delight?"

She had laid a hand on her belly and smiled ruefully. "Pay the Piper, more like," she told him.

"I have it," he said quietly. "Hearts and Bones. For I shall never get you out of mine."

That night, she had decided to leave him, and she had done it. Coldly. Harshly, so as to make him turn his back on her. If he had killed, now, with those mangled hands that had loved her—

If Daniel Josselyn had killed the poor lonely girl who lay on the clean quilt, it was because of her, Hannah knew it. Because he could not get Mistress Trevor out of his bones.

She stared at Anthea's body for what seemed like a very long time, getting control of herself. Only when she was convinced she felt nothing but a perfectly rational sense of outrage did Hannah allow the constable to lead her to the kitchen, sit her by the fire, and give her a tankard of rum.

"Wrong you should see that," Will mumbled, staring at the floor.

"Why? I have seen death before."

"This is no ordinary death, and well you know it!"

"No death is ever ordinary, William. I won't wilt and flutter, you ought to know that. I attend at every autopsy Clinch and Cyrus Kent perform here, the law requires it. I've watched many dissections these past years."

The presence of a woman at such official performances was thought to be needed to ensure a proper respect for the dead. Left to their own devices, male physicians had otherwise been known to drink and place wagers on the internal condition of the cadavers they investigated.

"I'm not afraid of death—or what causes it," she told him.

Will was still concentrating on her face.

"Then what set you shaking like a cat in a windstorm in there, if you're not afraid?"

For a moment she wondered whether to tell him about the marks on Anthea's throat, the man with two missing fingers on his left hand. To tell him that it wasn't *what* had caused the girl's death that troubled her, but *who*.

Again the name assailed her. *Daniel.*

"It was a long walk from Rugg's," was all she said. "I'm not as young as I was. I'm weary, that's all."

For a long time Will Quaid was silent. "You don't cry, do you?" he asked her suddenly. "Not ever?"

"No. But you are welcome to."

Will stood up and kicked a stool out of the way. "Christ, girl, can't you take a little comfort, not even from me? You never stop doing battle."

"If I stop," she said softly, "I am finished. That is how it is with women. If you don't believe me, go and look in the next room."

The constable said no more, only picked up a scrap of paper from the table and handed it to her.

"What's that?" she said.

He scowled at her. "Now, how should I know? I can't read writing, as you damned well know. I found it under the salt cellar."

Hannah read the letter aloud, and when she had finished, she folded it, removed her glasses, and sat silent. For a few moments there was only the sound of the fire snapping, sending up squibs of burnt pitch, and of the dog whining once more to come inside.

"Josh Lamb?" said Will at last, stunned. "Siwall?"

"Or Stewart. Her hand is very unsteady."

"Ralph Stewart's in Salcombe jail for a debt of fifty pound and has been since just past Christmas."

"Seward, then?" She peered again at the crossed-out letters. "Only there's no Seward here in Rufford, unless the killer came all the way from Wybrow or one of the farther towns, or from the Outward."

Will shook his head. "Not likely, all that way and gone without a trace by morning. My shilling's on Siwall. But not the magistrate. Young Jeremy, his son, that's more likely. Boy's wild, Hannah, and he fancies himself with women. Been in my jail for drink more than once this year, too. If he took a fancy to the poor lass, and she'd have none of him . . ."

Hannah did not wait for William to move on to the last name on Nan Trevor's bill of accusation. "And Daniel Josselyn," she said, clearly and carefully.

"Oh, now. That I *don't* believe. Not in a thousand year."

Hannah's voice was steady, but it seemed to her to come from a great distance away, as though the words were an echo of somebody else's speaking. In her wish to face the worst of it, she must become a woman who had forgotten Daniel's hands upon her, and the sound of his quiet voice.

"Why should she write such a letter and lie, William?" she said sternly.

"I don't know," he cried, suddenly angry. "I know it's not sense and facts, and I know the law eats facts and doesn't care a bloody damn for people. But I *know* Dan, and I know Josh Lamb, too! He's your cousin's husband, and a kinder soul never drew breath!"

"She says they broke the lock of the door. The lock is broken."

"Daniel's hard at times, I grant you. But still . . ."

"She says she was raped," Hannah went on. "Look at her body."

"Forced three times by three different men on three nights running? I don't believe it."

"She says the third man—the man she knew would come last night—has a wife he dare not trouble. Josselyn has a sickly wife."

"Daniel, take her by force?" He stared at her, his dark blue eyes like the hearts of the forge coals, boring into her skull. "If Dan wants a woman, my dear, there's a half dozen serving maids up at the Grange. And that housekeeper, Mrs. Twig. She's been willing enough with one or two others, by all accounts. And why should he kill the girl, if he *did* have her?"

"Why should he send her husband into the Outward at the most dangerous time of the year, except to get him out of the way?"

The great fist crashed down on the table. "I don't know! You have reason to grudge him, I know that, Hannah, but—"

"I grudge nobody!" She almost shouted.

Another silence. When Hannah spoke again, her voice was calm. "Nan Emory was a careful, quiet girl. A little sad, I think. But she had no name for lying."

"No. She did not." He spat into the fire. "I'll have to charge them," he said softly. "All of them. Won't I?"

"The sheriff will, certainly."

"Hah! Old Marcus Tapp? The Siwalls bought him a county, he'd be snake-bit before he'd charge one of them with so much as sweating on the Sabbath, let alone rape and murder." He stood up and folded Anthea's letter, then put it inside his shirt. "No. If it's to be done, it's myself must do it. I'll go up to Mistress Dowell's place, where she says her little ones are, see if they can tell us anything. But first I'd best send for old Clinch to certify her death." He skewered her with a look. "So, Hannah. If you had a mind to do any errand in the neighborhood of Dan's place just now . . . A man ought to know what's coming at him."

Will would most probably have gone to warn Daniel Josselyn himself if he weren't a constable. He was asking her help, and she stood thinking a long time, deciding—rationally, she supposed— whether to give it or not. Though she saw Daniel often enough, it was always at a distance. She had not spoken to him since the night of his son's death four years ago.

In a wicker cage at the edge of the firelight, the goldfinch Anthea Emory had once named Trinket still lay dead, his feathers ruffled by draft from the chimney flue. Hannah reached into the cage and let her fingers stroke the small stiff body as she had done the girl's, as though she might somehow stroke life back into it.

"I won't go to Daniel," she said at last. "I cannot. You must do that yourself."

The truth was that Hannah was afraid to see him. If she went to him now, he would take it as an act of affection. And its price was too high. She had learned well enough that she could not afford it, and she did not mean to risk it ever again.

Let Daniel Josselyn look after himself. She felt only the need to know the truth, she told herself, and to make some sense of things in Nan Emory's stead.

Hannah took the dead bird from the cage and threw it onto the fire. It made little impression upon the flames.

WHO THE DEAF CHILD WAS

Snow always drifted heavily into the north-facing back garden of Two Mills Farm and stayed till spring. This year there was a deep, soft heap of it banked against the neatly-stacked woodpile, and Jennet Trevor, age seven and a half, had found the perfect use for it.

She was small for her age and looked delicate, but she was almost never subject to the childhood complaints of her few play-mates, and instead of making her afraid or shy, her deafness had made her fearless. The silence that ruled her was that of the immense dark stretches of the Outward, where trees sprouted, grew, rotted, and fell beyond the hearing of a single human ear. Jennet had its darkness, its wildness, and its secrecy.

Hannah had never been altogether sure how deaf the child really was. Perhaps, as it seemed, she lived in a world in which her own footsteps made no more sound than the falling of snow. Or perhaps she could hear a little—muffled noises, faint echoes of human speech.

In either case, Jennet wore a cloak of invisibility, and it gave her—at times, at least—a freedom of movement her mother en-vied. You were liable to turn at any moment and find her wide, amber-colored eyes watching from a corner or peering out of a clothespress or a store cupboard at you. Often she slipped into her mother's bed and sat there crouched inside the closed curtains, still watching when Hannah woke.

Jennet went where she liked, and no grown-up held his tongue on her account or left off doing what he might have hidden from a child who heard and spoke. Around the farmhouse, the barn, the sheep meadow, and the mills at the foot of the slope, she ventured everywhere, trailed by her ginger tomcat, Arthur, and three or four of his harem of barn cats.

Just now, the lot of them were climbing the woodpile. Though it was smaller than it had been at the beginning of the winter— it required forty or fifty cords of wood to keep Two Mills's four big hearths blazing until the chill went off, around the middle of May—the pile, covered with a blanket of snow, was still a formidable mountain for an eight-year-old.

At each plateau where the stack leveled off, the little girl stopped, hiked up her long, sodden skirts again, and looked to see if the cats were keeping up with her. One or two of them had already tired of the game and gone to look for mice in the deep banking of straw and old cornstalks piled up against the barn for insulation.

But Arthur had persisted, as usual. When they reached the topmost level, he sat down, wrapped his tail around him, and calmly began to wash his one remaining ear.

Though he could not see the orange cat, Daniel Josselyn could see his daughter Jennet clearly as he crossed the frozen river on the jam of last fall's logs and headed for Henry Markham's lumber mill. The child spread her arms wide, blue cloak flapping, turned round with her back to the snowdrift, and let herself fall. In a minute she had begun the long climb again, her back crusted with snow.

When he reached the mill landing, Daniel paused, watching her. It took him a minute or two to realize that he was smiling.

"She's a clever child, like her mother," said Henry, leaning in the open door of his mill.

He was a thickset old man, fond of his wife's baking, and he was seldom seen without a long-stemmed clay pipe sending wreaths of tobacco smoke into the air around his head. The pipe had almost gone out, now, and he strode outside to meet Daniel as he sucked powerfully at it to set the bowl smouldering once more. He wore—as he always did—a knee-length homespun workman's smock to keep his clothes from harm when bits of burning ash flew up from the pipe and landed on him.

"A good girl, too," he went on, glancing at Josselyn, "though she's wild as a deer. I had an uncle born deaf, and he ran mad, with no language and nobody able to instruct him."

"Able? Or willing?"

"Bit of both, I expect, and on both sides. But Jennet watches and does what her mother shows her. And she's better than a monkey at aping what she sees, or at making up her own games and such. Look there."

Up in the house-yard, Jennet balanced precariously on the woodpile, spread her cloak again, like dark blue wings, and took another fall into the snowdrift.

The old man chuckled. "Oh, now, I was a great lad for snow angels as a boy," he said. "That and coasting. Had a sled before I had breeches, indeed I did." Henry was a second-generation American, from the hill country of Massachusetts. "Not much snow where you come from, was there, sir? England's a warmish climate, I understand."

Daniel smiled again, remembering. "Oh, there was usually snow enough. My father's house stands very near the Welsh border. But my brothers and I had to go for miles to find a proper hill to slide down."

"A long walk, was it, Major? But then I expect the servants took you in your father's coach and made a picnic-party of it."

The words were more sneered than spoken, and Daniel knew without looking to whom the voice belonged. He turned to face Jonathan Markham and met a pair of black eyes always on the look out for something or someone to resent.

"What do you want here?" said the young man, rather as though

Daniel were a dog that had broken its leash and gone sheep-worrying.

"Weather's warming early, Johnnie," he said, determined not to be goaded. "I saw you both up at the pond earlier, thought it might be time to talk business. This mess of logs wants dealing with soon."

"Looks like early thaw, maybe," said Henry. "Early freeze, early thaw, that's the way of it. Lot of fog here lately, too, ever since Candlemas. February fog means March rain. River'll break up fast in a rain."

Jonathan, dark-haired and sharp-faced, was handsome, Dan supposed, in a petulant kind of way that some women saw as a challenge. He was Henry and Julia's youngest son. The eldest, Eben, had been killed shortly after Saratoga, and the two others, Ben and Jared, though they helped out at the mill when they were needed, had no mind to give their lives to the work. Like Henry's three married daughters, they lived in Rufford or in the other small settlements that sprawled away down to Wybrow Head, where the Manitac emptied into the Atlantic between steep granite bluffs. They were townsmen, and would be merchants one of these days, keeping only enough land to subsist on when the times were bad.

So the mills and the Markham farm would come by default to Jonathan, who knew it and had made no effort in any direction of his own. He seemed to find nothing to his liking, and grew sullen.

"We'll have a good two month of freeze yet," he growled. "No need to get in such a twist."

Jonathan scowled in Dan's direction and began to work a whetstone over the blade of a pit-saw, removed for sharpening from its place on the huge bed above the bearings worked by the ponderous water wheel in the millrace. The wheel was locked down and silent in the winter months, but for the rest of the year its constant turning made a sound like slow, steady breathing that could be heard for nearly a mile around. Daniel, supervising the loading of milled boards or walking in his garden, paced himself by it and felt oddly damaged and bereft when it was silent, as it was now.

"If the river should break up suddenly," he said, "we'll need men to clear these logs out of the channel before the jam floods the low fields." A sudden thaw could heave up chunks of ice as big as houses onto the banks, and late-winter floods were commonplace and usually devastating. Daniel had no wish to be the cause of one. "I can let you have all the men you need to clear them," he said. "The crew's been wintered-in up on the Trace these three months. They'd welcome a trip to town, I have no doubt."

"We know our own business well enough," Jonathan snapped. "What needs doing, we'll damn well do ourselves."

Daniel's hooded eyes seemed to withdraw an inch deeper into their cave of skull, and there was fire in them. But he said nothing, only drew a breath and looked up the hill path for another sight of Jennet.

She had given up on the woodpile and the snowdrift now, and was leading the old mare, Flash, toward the stable. So, then. The old lady, old Julia, had come back. And Hannah, too, must be at home, or would be soon, for he had seen them set off together to some birth or other.

What Daniel did next came without conscious thought, but only because he had been planning it all day.

"Your good lady was coloring some wool for my wife's embroidery, Henry," he told the old man. "I may as well go up and see if it's ready."

It was a lame excuse, for Charlotte usually sent her maid to fetch things. But it was all he needed. He paused, glancing at Jonathan, who was bent over the saw blade.

"If you've no objection," he said, "I'll find my own way up."

"None in the world, sir," replied Henry, puffing harder on his pipe to hide his amusement. "Perhaps you'll take a cup of tea or some spiced cider from my wife and my niece before you return!"

"I thank you," said Daniel, and strode solemnly away up the

icy path, whistling softly under his breath. Young Markham spat into the snow and wiped his mouth on his sleeve.

"We're no part of England now, old man," growled Jonathan. "There's no need to pull your forelock and kiss His-bloody-Lordship's arse for him every time he does us the honor of passing by our door."

Henry turned methodically, took the pipe from his mouth, and tapped out the ash on the flat of his hand. He dusted his palm on the seat of his breeches, strode over to his son and, without so much as an intake of breath for warning, landed a powerful blow along the side of Jonathan's head. The boy—he was barely twenty—lay flat on his back in the muddy snow at the doorstep, dark eyes lit with rage, blood trickling down his temple.

"I kiss no man's arse, sir," said Henry. "And I take no scorn from any man, neither, and well enough you ought to know it, for you got your hot head from me. Dan Josselyn has more money than I have, but he's offered me no impudence in all the time I've known him. I wish to God I could say as much for my youngest son."

"And where do you think his money comes from?" hissed the boy. "Profiteering! Buying up land poor men can't pay the taxes on and selling it back to other poor men at twice the price, while them that have worked it and built on it and poured blood into it sits in Debtor's Jail in Salcombe, and their wives and children goes without!"

"You're talking of Ham Siwall, now, not of Daniel," the old man told him. "Josselyn came here poor, for all his high birth, and near to broken by the War, and he bought his land at fair price, same as any other man."

"With the Bristol Company behind him! They can buy all the land they need and they lay down the law to the poor hereabouts. The War's changed nothing, not for the poor. You may talk of freedom and independence, but it's money makes you free, and nothing else."

"Well," said Henry, "whatever Daniel's got, I reckon he's paid dear for it, one way or the other, and there's no going back to

England, not for him. And when he buys, he pays a fair price, whatever the money's worth."

During the War, nearly every township and borough had issued its own paper scrip, and now it was all worthless and the country millions of dollars in debt. New taxes on land had been levied, and between the rocks of taxation and the hard places of a devalued bank account, many a Rufford man had already been ground to pieces. Some turned to barter, subsistence farming, and piecework or day labor, and survived, as Henry and his wife had done.

But most men balanced constantly on the edge of ruin, no matter how hard they worked. Some grew bitter, made a run for the woods and turned outlaw—or went to sea and turned pirate—drank smuggled rum, and festered.

A few, like Hamilton Siwall, cultivated the new leaders in Boston, New York, and Philadelphia, traded favors, and got rich and fat and greedy for more.

Henry said nothing else, only sighed and held out a broad hand to help the boy up. But Jonathan refused it. He scrambled to his feet and stood there, hands balled into fists and half-raised, as if he might return his father's blow. Then he spun on his heel and stalked off in the direction of the village, hatless and cloakless in the cold, his dark hair escaping its black ribbon and falling across his shoulders like a girl's.

"Your work's not finished, sir!" Henry called after him. "I don't pay a wage for nothing, and you have a wife now to feed and shelter!"

"You and your wage may go to the devil and take Sally Jewell with you!" the boy shouted over his shoulder, and broke into a loping run across the snow.

It was hard, thought Henry Markham as he picked up the whetstone and began to work it along the teeth of the blade. Hard to be young and already boxed and crated, with a wife you never wanted and a son you never bargained for on a soft night in a warm featherbed. Hard to see no more ahead of you at twenty than a lifetime of sweat and scratch.

No wonder Johnnie resented Dan Josselyn, who had done much the same and come out scot-free and thriving. But Hannah was no Sally Jewell, to tumble a man for the sport of it and act the innocent afterwards, as if she'd had no notion she might end up with child.

And there was an ache, too, and a danger in Daniel there would never be in Johnnie, for all his spite and the rum he fed it with. Henry sighed, relit his pipe, and went in from the cold.

ELEVEN

A Family Portrait, or, What the Deaf Child Heard

When Hannah reached Two Mills, she came in through the back garden as usual, straight into the wide lean-to that ran the full width of the saltbox house. Even more than the kitchen, or the stillroom where she made up her syrups and decoctions and poultices, this room was her home, for it was the daily workroom, the women's kingdom. It belonged to them and, for the most part, the men kept their distance from it, sitting in the warm kitchen just beyond like kindly, awkward guardians.

The loom and the great walking wheel for spinning wool and the small flax wheel were all in the workroom, and the quilting frame. So were the rods on which they tied the wicks for candle dipping, and the great iron pots to boil the soap in spring from the winter's stored-up tallow. A wooden pole was suspended from two chains in front of the fireplace, hauled up and down by a wheel and crank; on the pole hung Lady Josselyn's softly-colored crewel yarns in several shades of rose and indigo and green and gold, still drying from yesterday's dye pots.

For whatever reason, almost everyone in Rufford called Charlotte Josselyn "Lady," as though her husband were still a nobleman and the War of Independence had never happened. Perhaps they knew that, for her, it never had and never would.

At first, Hannah did not notice Daniel standing with Jennet beside the quilting frame. It was only when she heard his fists strike his chest that she realized he was there.

It was a strange gesture, and he repeated it, the right arm crossed over the left, the fists striking the upper chest together, eyes fixed on the child.

He put a hand on Jennet's hair and stroked it, long smooth strokes, with his fingertips. Finally he let his hand brush her cheek. So far as Hannah knew, it was the first time he had ever touched his daughter.

"Friend," he said, speaking very softly and precisely, and made the strange motion again, arms crossed, fists striking his chest. He glanced over at Hannah then, gave her a slight nod of greeting, and turned back to the little girl.

Next he pointed to Arthur, the tomcat, now sprawled full-length on the hearth, and Jennet's wide eyes followed him. Her face, as always, was stoical and without emotion, impossible to read.

Daniel put the thumb and finger of his right hand together and touched the end of his nose with them, then moved his hand straight ahead in midair, a space nearly the same as Arthur's length from nose to tip of tail. He walked over to the cat, demonstrated the measurement, then went back to Jennet.

"Cat," he said quietly, pointing to Arthur. He made the sign again. Jennet watched, but made no move to imitate him. He took her hand in his and led it.

Jennet only stared. From her place by the door, Hannah said nothing.

"Cat," Daniel said again, and made the sign.

Jennet's small hand moved slightly, and for a moment it seemed that the lesson had had some effect. But she reached instead for Josselyn's leather-gloved left hand. She laid it flat on the patch-work surface of the quilt in its frame beside them and let her fingers trace around his own thumb and index finger. When she reached the stumps of his missing fingers, where the glove was sewn down, Jennet stopped. She looked up at him, her face expressionless as always.

That was all.

Ignoring both the grown-ups, she went to a box of quilt scraps in the far corner and began to lay them out by colors—dark reds, indigos, greens, browns. Arthur the cat got up, arched his yellow back, yawned, and went to rub himself on Jennet's feet.

Daniel turned to Hannah and shrugged, a smile playing around his mouth. "Indian sign," he said. "I thought it might be some use to her."

"I hope it may be of more use than it has been to the Indians," she said. The native Manitawans had almost disappeared from that part of Maine, except for the occasional stray who came out of the woods to barter or take casual work on the farms.

Just then Kitty, one of the hired girls, sailed into the room, caught sight of them together, and sailed out again. From beyond the doorway came eager whisperings and an occasional repressed giggle.

"I'd like to teach the child," Daniel said, ignoring them. "Not just hand signs. Words. If Jennet could learn to read—"

"To what purpose?"

"She could write, Hannah. Say what she wants, what she thinks."

"And be as much a misfit as her mother? Do you imagine anyone is likely, sir, to be much interested in what she thinks, or if she thinks at all? And God forbid she demonstrate more talent for it than most men. No, sir. She is better as she is."

He moved a few steps, needing to break his anger before he said something he did not mean to. Carefully, he matched her own formality. "You are telling me to mind my own business, Mrs. Trevor?"

"If I think it well for my daughter to learn how to read, Major Josselyn, I am able to teach her myself."

Daniel picked up his tricorn from the settle. "I've waked bears in the woods and been kinder welcomed. Good day to you, Ma'am."

"Wait." Hannah moistened her lips, then went to the fireside and began taking down the hanks of dyed wool that were dry. "You came for these, I think. They are ready."

"Very well." He stood silent, angry with himself.

Hannah wound the skeins lightly, putting them into a basket by the hearth. "I spoke harshly," she said at last. "I ask your pardon."

Daniel shrugged. "You wanted to be rid of me, as you tried to be eight years ago. I have not disappeared, and I shall not. The child has a father. I mean to let her know it."

"James is dead." She finished with the yarn and stood quietly, hands limp at her sides. "I had a letter."

Daniel drew a breath and sat down on a joint-stool, watching her. "Is it certain this time? There have been other rumors."

"My friends in Boston are certain. He died last summer, of the cholera. In Quebec. This time there is no mistake."

He sat thinking, but said nothing more for a few moments.

"James may be dead. But the child has a father, when there is need. I would have you remember that."

Hannah continued to evade the point. "My aunt advises me to return to Boston and marry again."

To this, Daniel made no objection. Had she hoped he might fall at her feet and beg?

"Why should you not? You are still young," he said softly. "And you look—very well."

It was too much for Hannah.

"Did you think I was an unhardy apple, sir," she snapped, "and would not keep once I had borne fruit?"

Daniel stood up again and fastened his cloak. "You are in a mood to wrangle and I have no skill at it. We two cannot talk without drawing one another's blood, it seems. I won't come again."

"Did you kill Mrs. Emory?"

It struck like a blow, and he was so still that for a moment she could not tell if he was breathing. "Dunstan Emory's wife, you mean?" he said at last.

"I've just seen her. She's dead."

He turned, his cloak wrapped tight around him as though he needed it to keep from flying into pieces. He moved a pace or two back into the room. "How?"

"Raped. Beaten. Burned. Strangled."

"Which?"

"All."

She watched him closely. Nothing appeared in his face that she might read as fear or guilt. His features were blank as those of the child laying out colored scraps in the corner. He sat down wearily on the settle.

"Christ. She was only a girl," he whispered.

"You do know her, then?"

"I've seen her. In the village. Her husband has been surveying lots for us, you know that."

"Why did you send him out at the worst time of the year?"

"I didn't send him, he contracts with us, with Siwall and me, that's all, he's his own master."

"You might have stopped him, but you didn't. You knew he might not come back. Perhaps you did not wish him to."

"Hannah—"

"Perhaps she was your mistress. Did she anger you?"

"No!"

"Did she threaten to tell Charlotte? Or Judge Siwall?"

"Hannah, you're mad! Have I the name of a brute in this town? Or even a womanizer? If so, it is with no one but yourself, and that was eight years ago and during a desperate war, when I was—" He stopped short, and when he spoke again, his voice was barely audible. "Why should you think I would kill her? And in so cruel a way? Surely you know me better, even now."

"She left a letter, accusing you. You and two others."

It was another long moment until he replied. "Who else?"

"Joshua Lamb and one of the Siwalls. She gave no Christian name. She said the three of you came these past three nights and used her by force, and that the last man said he would return and kill her. She is dead, and your name was last of the three."

"How do you know it was even she who wrote the letter? *Could* she write? Sweet God, Hannah, anyone with the skill can write a letter, even a murderer!"

"There is more. She was strangled. With a pair of hands, sir."

"And?"

"With your hands, sir."

"You ask that as a question?"

"I saw the marks. The left hand was missing two fingers. The same two fingers as your own."

Daniel looked up at her. "You really believe this, Hannah? Of me?"

"I have seen the girl's body sprawled dead and used on her own clean bed. I—"

"That is not what I asked, and you know it. I asked what *you* think of *me*. What you remember."

" 'I am afraid of his hands,' her letter said. I've seen the marks of your fingers on her."

"Are *you* afraid of my hands, Hannah? When these same stubs of fingers touched you, was it by force? Did they leave marks then? Or are you afraid to remember?" He laid a hand on her arm, the touch so deft and delicate that Hannah scarcely felt it. "There," he said softly. "Is it so terrible?"

She stood very still for a moment, then ducked away, suddenly sure of nothing that five minutes ago had seemed true. "You said yourself! That was eight years ago! We were different."

"And you suppose I've learnt to rape and strangle in the meantime."

Hannah looked down at his face. He was three-and-forty now, and began to be tired of the sheer effort of living, as most people did when they had passed four decades. It was an act of the will to continue in the face of what had been lost or stolen or thrown away. Pain took you over in sleep or weariness, and death never quite left the waking mind.

She remembered something he had told her once, one night as they lay quietly together in the long grass of the sheep meadow on the Common, the cold March stars reeling above them.

"There is a line," he had said, "that a man dares not cross. Nor a woman, neither. No matter what the orders are. A thing you must not do, because if you do it, nothing will matter afterward."

"Killing, you mean?" she had asked him. She knew he had killed many times in the War and relived it constantly. In his sleep he sometimes screamed like a woman being violated.

"Worse than killing," he had replied. "I can't say what. But after it, you're beyond saving. You can do anything to anyone and feel nothing at all."

"And did you cross the line?" she had said.

"You never quite know," he had told her softly, "until the next time you reach it."

"Where is Will Quaid?" he said at last.

"I left him at Mrs. Emory's house. He may be there still, he said he would send for Clinch."

"I must go, then. I want to see her. There'll be a dissection?"

"Of course."

"Then I must see her now, before Clinch muddles things up."

He stood up to go. Hannah did not speak until he had almost reached the door.

"Will hadn't noticed the finger marks, Daniel," she said suddenly. "I doubt if Clinch will, either. "

"But *you* noticed? And said nothing?"

"I am no sheriff. Let them see for themselves."

He paused, holding the door open and letting in a rush of cold air. Over the river, the fog was thickening again as the afternoon drew toward evening.

"Hannah," he said. "You have not answered my question. Do you really think me guilty?"

"You have not denied the charge."

"No. And I shall not. I'll send someone else for Mrs. Josselyn's wool," he said, and closed the door determinedly behind him.

Hannah turned back into the workroom just in time to see Jennet, fists clenched, arms crossed over her chest. She was making the Indian sign for friendship to Arthur, the old yellow cat.

Certainly the sight of her daughter's first effort at any form of human language was no reason for Hannah Trevor to accompany Daniel Josselyn back into the village, to face once more the terrible sight of Anthea Emory's body.

But that is what she did.

THE WITNESS OF THE DEAD

Samuel Clinch, the Sussex County coroner, was just huffing away from the Emory house as Daniel and Hannah rode up to the door—a fortunate chance for all concerned. Since the death of his son, Josselyn had seen the old butcher only twice, and had had all he could do on both occasions to keep from being charged with common assault by bashing Clinch's skull in. And one small dose of Sam Clinch a day was quite enough for Hannah.

In the gathering dark of the short winter afternoon, Will Quaid met them on the doorstep, followed by the old dog, Toby.

"Daniel," said the constable quietly, "I fancied you'd be here. Best come in."

Josselyn gave his friend no greeting, only bowed slightly in respect to Quaid's office and strode past him into the kitchen.

Mr. Dodger, who was never far from Will and functioned as his clerk when there was need of one, had installed himself at the table with a quill and ink pot and a heavy leather-bound record book.

"You are a contrary creature, Hannah Trevor," muttered Will as she passed him in the doorway. "Thought you wasn't meaning to speak to Daniel."

"I only met him by chance, William, and so I told him. I saw no harm in it."

"How much does he know?"

"Only that she's dead, and that he and the others are accused."

Will nodded and went on into the kitchen. "Well, as you're here, Major, we may as well get the questions over with. Will you have a chair?"

The formality of this speech startled Hannah, even though she had observed the constable at work before. Where the law was concerned, William Quaid had no friends to serve and no reprisals to fear. So it was *Major* now, and not *Dan*.

"I should like to see her body first." Daniel's voice, too, was cold and formal. "Before we speak of it."

"Well, now, I don't know, sir."

"I'm told she accuses me in a letter. A man has a right under the law to confront his accuser, William, alive or dead. Does he not?"

"He does at that," said the constable softly. "Dodge, my dear! Light!" he announced, and the little old man lit a second candle from the hearth fire, then trotted before them into the chamber where the woman's body lay.

They had covered her with a linen sheet, and Mr. Dodger pulled it back so that Daniel could see her face. At a nod from Will, he folded it carefully, all the way back to her feet.

Until the autopsy had been performed, they would make no effort to wash her body or interfere with anything that Science and Reason might observe about the deed. Medicine, especially in the hands of men like Clinch—or even his competitor, young Cyrus Kent—could not be relied on. Aside from careful observation by largely untrained sheriffs and constables like Will Quaid, there was little else but logic.

So Daniel saw Anthea's body, that late afternoon, much as her killer had left it.

The snarl of her hair was still stuffed into her mouth and the burn marks were clearly visible.

He had seen worse, and not only in wars. In the dockside hovels and the gin alleys of London and New York—and even of Boston—young women died of worse brutalities almost every day. They had been dead long before their hearts stopped beating. Nobody mourned them. Scarcely anyone noticed that they had ceased to exist.

But in time, the world wasted for the lack of them. His forefinger reached out of its own accord and traced the bird's-wing arch of Mrs. Emory's cheekbone.

There was no sound in the room but the rhythmical wheeze of old Dodger's breathing. Perhaps, thought Daniel, they expected the body to bleed in his presence, since they suspected him of murder. It was an old superstition, going back to prehistory, and had been practiced in Massachusetts as late as the beginning of the present century. The Witness of the Dead, it was called, and men had been hanged on the strength of it.

But Anthea did not bleed when he touched her. Daniel took his hand away.

Where the sheet fell back, he could see the crazy angle of her arm and the bone that protruded from it.

"Was she found here, William? On the bed, just as she is?"

"We didn't move her till Clinch arrived."

"And the rest of the house—was it like this? Nothing disarranged, I mean? No chairs upended, or—"

He glanced at the clothes carefully folded on the chair, the crewel-embroidered pocket with its wreath of roses. His eyes closed and his body swayed slightly, like Dodger's candle flame.

"Seems all the fight had gone out of the poor lamb," said Will. "Why do you ask?"

"Look at the angle of that break in her arm," said Josselyn, pulling himself back to the point.

"I see the break. But what of it?"

"Think, Will. He couldn't have done it here on the bed unless he was strong enough to take her arm in his two hands and snap it like a stick." He looked up at the blacksmith. "And you're the only man I know who could perform such a feat, at least in Rufford."

"He's right, William," said Hannah. She moved a step closer to the bed. "And how did he manage to break it, here on the bed, without spoiling the bedclothes? The skin's broken. Was there blood when you and Clinch turned the body to examine her?"

"Not a drop, now you mention it. To say the truth, I'd wondered about that." Will Quaid frowned.

"No sign of any blood elsewhere in the house? The kitchen?"

"No, sir," piped up Mr. Dodger. "No blood, sir. The dog has been in the kitchen this hour. A dog will smell blood, sir, even a single drop. The dog shall witness it. No blood."

"Unless I miss my guess, that arm was broken after she was already dead. And contrary to legend, the dead do not bleed. Am I right?" Dan said, looking at Hannah.

"For the most part," she replied, "you are. There are exceptions. A body can sometimes hemorrhage some hours after death, providing the conditions of temperature are right. But for the most part, no. A wound inflicted upon the dead occasions no bleeding, because the heart no longer pumps the blood."

Daniel took the candle from Dodger and held it close to Anthea Emory's throat. "Mrs. Trevor, if you please," he said, and Hannah took it from him and directed the light where he bade her. Once his hands were freed, Daniel placed them where the murderer's had been—though he did not actually touch Anthea's throat.

"The heels of the hands push down, so, on the windpipe," he said, "and the fingers grip the wall of the throat below the ears."

"You seem too well acquainted with the way of it, Daniel," said the constable, frowning.

"I was commissioned in His Majesty's army at twenty-one, my friend," Josselyn replied. "There are few means of taking life that seventeen years of war on two continents do not teach you." He demonstrated. "The man must have bent above her, so. The killing force is in the heels of the hands, as I said. Large hands. Broad." He looked up at the constable, eyebrows raised. "I trust you've noticed the finger marks on her neck. That two fingers of the left hand are missing, or at least have left no marks?"

Will Quaid looked back at him steadily. "I'm not a fool, Daniel."

"No. You are not."

"I seen the marks there: Clinch seen 'em, too, and unless I guess wrong, he's halfway to Judge Siwall's by this time, crying you up a murderer." He waited for a denial, but got none.

"Come here, Will, and look at these marks again. Remember what I said about most of the pressure being on the heels of the hands?"

The constable sighed. "Look, Dan, just reckon I'm simple, like poor old Reuben Pomfrey, and spell it out clear, will you?"

"Don't you see, Will?" Hannah caught hold of the big man's arm and led him very close to the bed, where the candlelight fell onto Nan Emory's throat. "The windpipe is smashed, just as Daniel says it should be, and the skin is bruised from the pressure. But if he was pushing down with the heels of his hands, why should the marks be even deeper where his fingers gripped her? There might *be* marks, but not so distinct, and not necessarily a complete set."

"Why, you're right, indeed!"

"Those finger marks are there," said Dan, "because somebody wanted them to be seen."

Will sounded relieved. "Damned if I don't think you might be right! Troubles my mind some, too, why a murderer would walk away and leave a letter naming him behind on the table, lying there plain as day."

"Unless, of course, he couldn't read," said Hannah.

Will's face turned a brilliant rose color. "But Daniel *can* read, and so can the Siwalls."

"And Josh Lamb. Though he can't *write* more than his name."

"So then, it would seem there's somebody wants Daniel, here, on a gibbet up in Salcombe with a good hank of hemp around his neck, don't it?" The constable rubbed both permanently blackened palms on his breeches and stared into the candle flame. "Who you been vexing, Dan? Whose nose you put out of joint lately?"

"No one I know of."

William glanced over at Hannah and grinned. "Nobody new, any road." He looked back at the body on the bed and the grin faded. "Well, then, just to keep me in humor, lay your fingers against her throat, Daniel, if you please. I'd wager the marks don't even match, and you've been troubled for nothing. Still."

Josselyn did as he was bid. The indentations made by the murderer's fingertips in the throat wall of Anthea Emory fitted his mangled hand almost perfectly, with only a fraction of an inch to spare.

He removed his hands and stood for a moment, looking at the dead girl. She had not been especially beautiful, except for the universal beauty of a life not yet past twenty, still capable of a hope that revives endlessly, without effort or discernment or even prayer.

Something about the girl was familiar to Daniel, and he stood for a long moment more before he realized what it was. Except for the freckles, her pale skin reminded him of Charlotte's. He let the sheet fall back across her face.

"If you don't mind, William," he said, "I'd like a moment alone with her. To say a prayer."

Will Quaid studied his friend for a moment. Then he nodded. "I'll wait outside," he said. "Come, Dodge. Leave the candle. Hannah, my dear."

She hesitated. Unless eight years' loneliness had made him pious, the idea of Dan Josselyn saying a prayer—even in such a case—was astounding. Hannah lingered in the doorway, but at last she had to join the others or explain herself.

She did not see Daniel draw the heavy draft-curtains across the doorway, go to the chair beside the bed, take the embroidered pocket from where it hung, and hide it away inside his shirt.

THIRTEEN

PIECING THE EVIDENCE:

The Enquiry into the Guilt
of Major Daniel Edmund Josselyn

Made by William Quaid, Constable
Recorded by Cornelius Dodger, Esq., Clerk

QUESTION: Have you two fingers missing from your left hand?

JOSSELYN: I have.

Q: Which two fingers, sir?

J: The second and the third finger, the ring finger.

Q: How did you come by this injury?

J: I was thought to be dead after the Battle of Webb's Ford. My fingers were cut off by scavengers. Such things were kept as trophies, and I was wearing my wedding ring, which was gold.

Q: How do you explain that the finger marks on the victim's throat match the configuration of your missing fingers?

J: I have no explanation.

Q: Were you acquainted with the dead woman, Mrs. Anthea Mary Emory?

J: We met once or twice. Our acquaintance was in no sense personal.

Q: Do not answer questions that have not been put to you.

J: What?

Q: Answer only such questions as you are asked, sir. Do not qualify your answers.

J: I am sorry.

Q: Have you ever visited Mrs. Emory in her own house?

J: Once. When I agreed to employ—

Q: Do not volunteer information, sir!

J: I am sorry. Once.

Q: On what occasion did you visit her?

J: I have no record of the date.

Q: Can you approximate?

J: Sometime last August. Toward the end of the month.

Q: What was the purpose of your visit?

J: To contract with her husband, Dunstan Emory, as surveyor for the Bristol Company, of which I am the manager and a shareholder.

Q: Was her husband present on that occasion?

J: Certainly.

Q: Have you ever visited Mrs. Emory in the absence of her husband?

J: Never.

Q: Have you met her elsewhere with no other person present?

J: Never.

Q: Where, to the best of your knowledge, is Mrs. Emory's husband now?

J: Mr. Emory went into the woods last November with a small survey party. He has not yet returned.

Q: Would you agree that it was foolhardy, at the very least, to send a man into the forest at the beginning of winter?

J: I would, yes.

Q: Was the decision your own?

J: I believe it was Mr. Emory's. He is an independent contractor and does as he pleases, so long as the survey maps are supplied when they are needed.

Q: What is the purpose of these maps?

J: Our lumbermen use them to mark sections of trees to be cut during the summer.

Q: When was Mr. Emory required by your contract to supply these maps?

J: The first would not be needed until April. Two months from now.

Q: Would he have had sufficient time to complete a map within a month or two?

J: With clement weather and vigorous assistants, certainly.

Q: Then why did he go into the woods last November?

J: I have said. He made his own decision.

Q: Did you in any way induce him to decide on this dangerous course, which left his wife alone and unprotected for nearly three months?

J: No. I did not.

Q: He was new to the Manitac country, was he not?

J: I believe so. He arrived sometime last spring.

Q: So this would have been his first experience of a Maine winter. Did you warn him what to expect, or advise him to wait for spring?

J: I did. He chose to ignore me. He was—is—very young.

Q: Major Josselyn, where were you on the nights of February the tenth, eleventh, twelfth, and thirteenth?

J: I was—at home. At my home.

Q: I perceive you hesitated before completing your reply. Why did you do so?

J: I—was at first uncertain. I wished to be precise before I answered.

Q: And are you certain now?

J: Yes. I was at home.

Q: On all four of the nights in question?

J: Yes.

Q: Can your lady confirm that you were present in the house all during those four nights?

J: I— My wife is ill. We do not share the same chamber.

Q: For how many years has your wife been unable to fulfill the duties of the marriage bed?

J: That is impertinent and irrelevant.

Q: Mrs. Emory was, according to the witness of her letter, raped on the three nights preceding February the thirteenth, and again on the night of her death. You accept this as a fact.

J: I have been told so.

Q: Then the question is not irrelevant. Did you rape Mrs. Anthea Emory on the night of February the twelfth, threaten to return and kill her, lest she might tell your wife what you had done, and did you then return on the night of February the thirteenth, rape her once more, and strangle her?

J: I did not.

Q: Can you give the name of anyone who might testify you were at home on the nights stipulated?

J: No one. I— No one.

Q: Until the Sheriff arrives from Salcombe and further evidence is taken, Major Josselyn, you are advised to remain within the bounds of Rufford Township, and to give surety of your good faith in the sum of a hundred pound to the clerk. Please pay Mr. Dodger, sir.

IRE AND ICE

"Ride to the Falls with me."

Daniel spoke so softly that Hannah almost failed to hear him through the muffling wool of her hood. Will's questions had taken a good while, and by the time they rode away from the Emory place it was almost dark. The fog was pulling itself up from the Manitac like a great blanket smothering the two banks, but through it shone the faint flickering lights of Rufford's scattered houses and shops, and the brighter ones of the two inns, Lamb's and the Red Bush.

"It's late," she told him. "I've been too long already."

It was, of course, only an excuse. Hannah made her way to births and deaths and sickbeds largely unmindful of darkness and such trifling inconveniences as fogs and snowstorms. And no one at Two Mills expected her at meals on time.

The truth was that she did not trust herself with him, and that keeping intact the chilly barrier she had built against him had begun to cause her pain. But that, of course—being Hannah— she could not admit.

"I suppose the Falls is nothing out of my way," she said suddenly—lest he might think her afraid of him. "Yes. I'll ride with you."

They turned their horses south and west, up the gradually climbing terrain that grew abruptly steep once you crossed the Salcombe Road. They walked their horses in silence, Flash, the round little mare, and Daniel's big sorrel gelding, called Yeoman. The fog was slowly closing around them, and the horses followed by instinct the ruts of sleighs and sledges inscribed in the narrow snowy track. As they neared the Falls, Hannah could just make out lights in the kitchen at Two Mills, which lay below them, perched upon the slope.

Blackthorne Falls was hardly worthy of the name, a small spill of water on the creek that bordered Henry Markham's property and emptied into the Manitac just below the mills. At the edge of the woods, the granite core of the Maine earth jutted outward, then sheered off suddenly, forcing the water to fall perhaps twenty or twenty-five feet to the gravel creek bed below. It was unspectacular, but not unhandsome.

This time of year, of course, it was frozen solid, the falling water caught in midair and turned to parallel ice columns of irregular lengths and thicknesses. They shone in the near-dark like polished glass.

The two riders sat their horses quietly. The fog hid the Grange from sight altogether, and even the closer lights of Two Mills were almost invisible now, as the night drew in.

"I asked you before, Mrs. Trevor," Daniel said at last. "Knowing what you know of me, do you really think I am a man to rape and strangle girls?"

"No, Daniel," she replied quietly. "I do not."

He drew a long breath and Hannah could see it as he breathed out, like smoke in the deep cold. "Thank you for that," he said.

"But still," she went on, "you lied to Will. Did you not?"

"Good night, Ma'am," he said irritably, and turned his horse's head toward the river crossing as if he would ride away.

If he wanted an unconsidered loyalty, she would not give it. "You were not at home these last four nights. And you did not stay behind in the girl's room to pray, either. Did you?"

He paused. "You said you believed that I had done her no harm."

"So I do. But you make yourself look guilty. I think Will believes as I do that someone wants you not only disgraced, but hanged. Only you cannot defend yourself with lies and evasions, even those you may think are prudent. Go to Will and tell him plainly where you were. If he finds you've lied on one count, he may misdoubt the rest of your story." She paused. "Daniel. If you were with some girl or other on those nights, my dear—"

"There was no girl. Christ, Hannah, I'm three-and-forty. I'm long past girls."

"Woman, then."

"There is a lady. In Boston. She's practical, kind-hearted, and completely unsentimental. I see her now and then. We take one another for what we need, no more."

Hannah bristled. "And have you asked the lady what she needs?"

"Oh yes. Long ago."

"What was her answer?"

"A simple one. Money. She has a house and position but no wealth. I provide it. We enjoy each other's company. It's uncomplicated."

"Oh, most. And, I should think, unsatisfying. From what I know of you."

His eyes blazed for a moment, wolflike. "You are unkind to remind me. Yes, you do know what I am. I've not changed. But you know nothing of what my life has been these years. I take shabby half-measures because I have no others left me. Perhaps I am myself shabby and half-made. But I try not to do harm. Don't presume to judge my conduct until you have been elected God Almighty."

"I do beg your pardon," she said softly, knowing he was right. "And God's."

After the terrible birth and death of his son, Daniel had been told by the doctors that he could not share Charlotte's bed again. Intercourse, even with such precautions as were possible, would almost certainly result in another pregnancy. If she tried to give birth again, it was unlikely she would survive, and even the conjugal act could prove dangerous, so damaged was her body.

Some husbands would not have hesitated to enforce their rights, risk or no risk. But Daniel was no such man. And arrangements like the one he had just described were common in hopeless marriages, especially when there was money enough to buy a sophisticated discretion.

Besides, if Hannah were the rationalist she professed to be, the satisfaction of mutual needs uncluttered by the baser demands of passion should have appealed to her.

But reason had little to do with it. The fact was that she hated to think of Daniel with some predatory Madam in a fashionable Boston neighborhood, forced to endure talk of ruffled ball gowns and new bonnets. A sickly-sweet confection of a woman, all froth and no substance, like a bad meringue.

Hannah shook herself, forcing her mind back to the subject at hand.

"But," she said, "you were not at home for these last nights, and you were not in Boston, either. The road has been snowed shut for a month, and the first boat came in at Wybrow Head only yesterday, after six weeks of gales."

She was watching his breath in the cold dark, a veil across his motionless features like the fog over the columns of ice. His gloved hands gripped the horn of his saddle.

"No, Hannah," he said quietly. "I was not at home. I'm seldom at home for all of any night. God knows, you should remember that."

He picked up the reins and would have ridden away from her then. But there was one last thing.

"There's a deed in my bank in Boston," he said without looking at her. "Three thousand acres of timberland. It's Jennet's. Don't let Siwall take it from you if I hang."

He dug his heels into his horse's sides and in a minute the fog had swallowed him.

*   *   *

Hannah did remember Daniel's wanderings. He had slept little, and even when his nights of screaming eased and his memories and his battle-guilt became less vivid, he had no rest. Often she would wake and find he had dressed in the dark and left her, unable to lie still and feign sleep even for her sake.

Oh, they had both become good at tricks and evasions during that first long winter and spring. There was a small storeroom on the upper level of the sawmill, and Hannah brought a brazier of coals and made a bed of old quilts there, folded and laid on the straw-covered floor each night and hidden away among the piles of rope and scrap wood during the day.

For the most part she lay still when Daniel left her; she waited, and at last he would come back, soft-footed as a forest cat. Hannah trained herself to hear the sound of his feet on the narrow ladder even above the grating of the mill wheel and the splash and roar of the race. Once or twice she had grown curious and followed him, dodging the Night Watch with almost as much skill as he did.

But there was nothing to see. He only walked, often by the river but sometimes venturing a little way into the woods. They had reached farther toward the town then, the land he had since turned into fields and gardens.

After a while he would turn and walk back, sit by the frozen river or, as the spring came, by the moving water of the millrace, then slip inside again and up the steps to their bed-place, shooing the venturesome mice away with his boot as he entered. He lay down beside her and in a few minutes more she would feel his hands drift along her body before he came inside her, as though he were learning her, training his mind to remember her. To remember her pattern of hearts and bones, when she had left him.

For by then, Daniel had learned how tightly she clung to her delusions, how fiercely she meant to protect herself from the threat of his love. What she was and what she believed herself to be were two different things. For the first, he would have done anything. The second had driven him away.

*   *   *

The fact was that Hannah Trevor had expected her husband James to leave her and flee to Canada, that she prayed for it and rejoiced when it occurred and she was free of him.

That for several weeks before his departure, she conducted a careful survey of the entire male population of Rufford, determined to select a lover who could help her to conceive another child. She was unwilling to do so with her husband, and—being a midwife—she had had the skill and means to prevent herself from becoming pregnant ever since the deaths of her three children in Boston some years before. She wanted a last child that would be hers and hers alone.

That she met Daniel Josselyn at Will Quaid's forge soon after the two men returned from Saratoga, and decided he would do nicely. He was educated, gentlemanly, physically attractive, and healthy, except for his bad hand and his battle-nerves. She cultivated his acquaintance and made him at ease with her for several weeks before James's departure.

That as soon as James had gone—for the child had to be conceived soon enough to be passed off as legitimate—Hannah became Daniel Josselyn's lover. He had told her plainly that he was a married man with a wife in England, not knowing that that fact was one of his best qualifications. Even if James were caught and executed by the Patriots, there would be no wrangling over whether Daniel ought to marry her, and Hannah was determined never to marry again.

That once the child—Jennet—had been conceived, in early spring of 1778, Hannah informed Daniel that his purpose in her life had been served and that he could have no claim upon her child or upon herself. She denied having loved him, and repeated it so often to herself in the eight years that followed that she almost began to believe he had been no more than a means to an end.

Almost.

Once Daniel had ridden away toward the Grange ford, Hannah slipped down from her horse and let her boots sink into the deep snow, needing the strength of the cold and its hardness. She had been nine-and-twenty when she went to Josselyn's room at the forge and lay down on his bed to wait for him.

Now she was eight-and-thirty. Only Jennet's small, tense body came near her these days, lying warm against her side like the sleeping cat who shared the bed with them. Otherwise, Hannah had almost forgotten until Daniel touched her what human hands felt like, man's or woman's, whole or mangled. Even the births of her four children had impressed themselves only faintly upon her senses, so that she did not remember the extremity of pain or anything like the joy motherhood is supposed to bestow. Instead, her mind recalled having felt at each and every birth a strange perception of the end of something, of balancing on a frail ledge that was crumbling apart by inches under her feet, and then the vivid sensation of falling weightlessly into blank space.

She felt nothing now, not even when she watched other women give birth. She was through with all that, she told herself. She was neither man nor woman nor anything remotely human, for human things may be broken, and Hannah did not mean to break. She was a thing that worked and reasoned and consumed itself by each day of struggle it measured, that would melt slowly like the columns of ice into the stream of things and disappear, leaving no trace behind her.

Hannah Trevor had reclaimed her sovereignty of herself. The secret places of her body belonged only to her, though what they were worth she could not say.

Those of her mind were another matter.

PIECING THE EVIDENCE:
Constable's Enquiry into the Guilt of
Mr. Joshua Perkin Lamb, Esq., Innkeeper,
Lamb's Inn and Ordinary,
The South Common, Rufford

QUESTION: Mr. Lamb, you have been informed of the accusation against you, made in a letter left by the victim, Mrs. Anthea Emory?

LAMB: I have, sir.

Q: Have you anything to say in reply?

L: I say, bosh, sir. Plain as that. Bosh, I say.

Q: Were you acquainted with the victim?

L: Saw her once or twice at Meeting. My Dolly knowed her some, sat up with young Jotham when he was ailing last spring. Cut his foot on a rock, up by Rugg's, I believe. You ask Hannah, she'd know. Phinney ain't never got the rocks out of them bean fields. Never will, not till rocks is rumpots. Ha-ha!

Q: But you yourself have no closer acquaintance with Mrs. Emory?

L: Well, now. What Dolly knows, I do know, too. That's all. She

101

never come into the Inn parlor, not the kind for much socializ-
ing, Dolly says.

Q: Are you acquainted with Dunstan Emory, then?

L: Oh, aye, that I am. Fond of a nice glass of flip, is Dunny
Emory. My Dolly mixes the best quince flip in four counties.

Q: Please answer only the questions you are asked, Mr. Lamb.

L: Oh, bosh, Will Quaid.

Q: Now, you listen here, Josh Lamb, you—

L: Well, I declare. Bosh and bother.

Q: Did you rape Mrs. Anthea Emory in her house on the night
of February the tenth?

L: Me, tumble a rickety young thing like that when my sweet
plump Dolly's lying warm in my own featherbed? No, I did not,
sir, not on the tenth, nor on no other night, neither!

Q: Where were you on the nights of February the tenth, eleventh,
twelfth, and thirteenth?

L: Will Quaid, I shall lose my patience directly! I was here, is
where I was. Right where you'd see me, if you wasn't such a
pumpkinhead! Dolly'll tell you. I've been in my bed since a
week Saturday, han't I, with one of Hannah's mustard poultices
on me and sneezing fit to blow— Fit to—to—to—

Q: Bless you, my dear. Excused.

SIXTEEN

$\mathcal{P}$IECING THE EVIDENCE:
What the Neighbors Said

She come here once or twice, to be sure. Last spring when we boiled up the soap, and again at brewing time in September. A good worker, she were. But she kept secrets. I'm no gossip, mind. Only I can't abide a secret nature. 'Tis unnatural, 'specially in a woman.

—Mrs. Dorcas Holroyd, *neighbor*

Q: Did you hear a woman's cries coming from the house of the dead girl on the night she was killed?

A: Oh, that I did. I made my round as usual, didn't I, and when I passed her place I heard her in there, sobbing fit to bust. Worse than crying. She had a way of wailing like the damned, that girl.

Q: Did you investigate?

A: I didn't, sir. She were at it most nights when I passed. First time or two, I rapped on her door and asked if she was harmed, or feared anything.

Q: And what did she say?

A: She come to the door and opened it a bit, and I could see her face by my lantern, though there was no light in the house. "You all right, Missus?" says I. "Quite well, Watchman," she says, and shuts the door again. And before I'm on my horse, I hear her wailing again.

—*Peter Fellingham, Night Watch, South Bank*

Her husband come back and done for her. Mark my words. Some say she were mad, but he were a plain fool, and that's worse. He done for her, all right. Poor lamb.

—*Mrs. Ruth Dowell, neighbor*

Q: Did you ever stop at the house again when you heard her crying?

A: I did, sir. Once. She answered my knock, just like before. She had her little-un in her arm.

Q: Was there any sign that she had been beaten, harmed in any way?

A: None. Red-eyed from crying. She had that look women get when they've wept too long. Empty, you know. Dead behind the eyes.

Q: Was this after her husband left for the Outward?

A: No, sir. He was still in the town then.

Q: And yet she herself answered your knock, you say?

A: I asked after him. "My husband is sleeping," she said.

Q: And did you believe her?

A: Well, hadn't I just seen Dunny Emory down at the Red Bush, with Bella McKee in his lap and drunk as an admiral on Edes's best scotch whisky?

Q: So you knew Mrs. Emory was lying to you. Did you challenge her word?

A: No, sir. For I could see she knew well enough where he was, and I left her her pride.

Q: And when you heard her crying again?

A: I didn't bother her after that, sir. I left her alone.

—*Peter Fellingham, Night Watch*

Dunny Emory? A plain fool, out for the quick chance. Easy money. Kill her? Why, Dunny hasn't the bottle to kill a rat with a musket, let alone a woman with his bare hands.

—*Willoughby Francis Edes, tavern keeper*

I said when her husband left, "Nan, my dear, bring the little ones and come and stay a month with me. You shall help with the flax-breaking and the hetcheling, and I'll pay you nine shillings for the work." For Sally Jewell had just left me to marry Johnnie Markham, and I had only Black Caesar's wife, Tirzah, and though she's deft and willing, there's too much for the two of us, at my age. But Mrs. Emory took it amiss. "I've a house of my own to keep, and I'm nobody's servant," she told me, and I saw no more of her until she brought the children to leave them.

—*Mrs. Ruth Dowell, neighbor*

She was thoughtful of her children, that I'll say. Good with a needle. A beautiful, fine quilter, she was, near eighteen stitches to the inch. Most women boast to manage fifteen, and if they told the truth, 'tis nearer ten. An eye for patterns, too. Colors and shapes, and that. She took pains at most things. It takes some wit to keep a house well, as she did, whether a man believes it or not, and it's hard work. She wasn't used to the winters here, she came from New York, I think, or thereabouts. The War was hard on her. The night I sat up with her boy, young Jotham? She lay down to sleep, and at first I heard her breathing, steady and clean. But in a while she began to cry in her sleep. Not sniffles and whines. She cried like a dog we had once, got smashed by a sledge. Not human, that crying. I lay down on the bed with her and held her, but she didn't quiet. Finally I had to go outside, just to get away. I thought of her husband, how it must have been to lie every night with her. It's no wonder he stayed away. I think she was too much for him.

Like her? Yes, I suppose I did, well enough. I suppose I did.

—Mrs. Dolly Lamb, wife of Joshua Lamb

Could she read and write, sir? Now that I can't say. Though perhaps she did, for she kept a book of sermons at home. I taxed her, you see, because she went but seldom to Meeting of a Sunday, though she lived but an easy walk from the Meetinghouse. She said she did not sleep well and often felt ill of a morning, and she had the Sermons of Dr. Athanasius Bedford at home. A paltry contrivance, I told her, and no substitute for the good instruction of Mr. Reverend Waite. But she was proud and she lacked a proper discipline of spirit. To say the truth, I did not like the chit.

—Mrs. Dorcas Holroyd, neighbor

Now, Will. Old Aunt Dorcas drinks a quart of rum a day, and has done for the last twenty years, and she hasn't been to Meeting herself in— oh, well, I don't know how long. Besides, she likes nobody, she's famous for it! But I must not speak so ill of her. Only young Mrs. Emory, I think, was too much alone, and if she was proud, she had little else to protect her. It pains me to think how she died.

—Reverend Timothy Waite, minister

A woman living alone is a damned unnatural thing, sir, and unnatural things invite trouble. She knew what to expect, with her husband away. Why did she not accept the hospitality of friends, sir, or put herself somehow out of the reach of harm? No, sir. Her very existence enflamed the man, whoever he was.

She made an attraction of herself. She expected it. She invited it. She got what she deserved, sir. Got what she deserved.

—*Samuel Clinch, physician and surgeon*

She brought the children to me six days ago, on the eighth day of February. Said she felt unwell and had no one to watch them while she took to her bed. I offered to send for Mrs. Trevor, but Nan wouldn't have it. I'll keep them now, young Jotham and Polly. I'm past any more of my own, and I'm used to the racket of children in the house. And they like me, I think.

—*Ruth Dowell, neighbor*

Do I credit Daniel could've killed her? Why, bless you, I'd just as soon think you would, Will!

—*Henry Markham, miller*

Josselyn? Murder the girl? Well, now, I don't know. He's been a decent master to me. Treated me evenhanded. Hired me to run his place though I'd lost my own to Mr. Justice Siwall for debt. Trusted my judgement and honored his own word.

But I believe he had a worse war than many, including myself. And war's like fever. There's a time, after the real heat's broke, when the heart has to settle down to beating true again, and the brain must come out of hiding, and the eyes must see clear what they look at. For some men, it never happens. They don't die. But they never seem to find a way to live. And sometimes they do great harm in the world.

—*John English, Steward, Mapleton Grange*

SEVENTEEN

TRIANGLES, CIRCLES, AND SQUARES

Hannah stayed a long time watching the fog climb the hill to the Falls after Dan Josselyn rode away from her, and when at last she reached home in the six o'clock darkness, she found an anxious Will Quaid in front of the kitchen fire, as Julia and the hired girls, Kitty, Susan, and Parthenia, fussed over the supper of mutton stew, applesauce, new-baked bread, and cucumber pickles.

"I was just on the point of going out looking for you, my dear," Will said, taking her cloak and hanging it by the fire to dry.

"Has something else happened?" Hannah began to take down the pewter from the dresser and hand it to Jennet, who had been waiting as always for this nightly ritual between them to begin. "Have they set a time for the dissection?"

"Noon tomorrow at Cyrus Kent's surgery. He's in Wybrow today, and I had all I could do to hold old Clinch off from doing it alone tonight, just to get one up on the competition."

"A fine lot you'd learn from that." Hannah smiled, watching the child set the long trestle carefully with plates, tankards, knives and spoons. "But you *did* hold him off."

"I did. If the body has anything to tell us, we'll more likely hear it from Dr. Kent."

Henry Markham, still in his working smock, sprawled on the settle, his feet out before him in danger of being trampled by the women bustling back and forth from table to hearth. The old man had removed his periwig, as he always did, the minute he came through the door, and perched it on the newel post at the foot of the stairs, where it now hung, neatly red-ribboned and rocking slightly in the draft. Under the wig, Henry kept his head shaved absolutely bald, and at home he wore a knitted smoking cap to keep off cold. Now he stood up, pulled his cap down another inch, and braved the crush of busy women to reach for his tobacco box on the mantel shelf. He sat down again, stuffing his pipe contentedly.

"Will's been telling me the tale, Hannah," he said. "It's a wretched, bad business, this with Mrs. Emory."

"I've talked to Josh Lamb, and he's been sick abed this week. Well, you know that, I expect. Dolly swears up and down he hasn't been out of her sight for an hour. So he's proved innocent, at least," said Will Quaid.

"That's well. I thought he might have been up by this time." Hannah smiled. "A few more sneezes are a small enough price to pay to be out of this muddle."

"I'll talk to the Siwalls in the morning," Will told her. "But knowing Josh is clear puts the whole business of that letter in doubt, do you see? It's a right old puzzle, and no mistake. All shapes and no pattern, just odd corners and chasing your tail in a circle." He paused. "Do you think Dunny Emory could've come back himself and killed her, Hannah?"

Will was right about one thing. Dunstan Emory might be able to answer any number of questions, if only they could find him.

"Has anyone seen him in the town?" she asked.

"Not that I know. But he might've come at night, I expect, and gone back into the woods before morning. If he killed her, that is."

"Were there footprints in the snow? Or hoofprints?"

"That snow's packed too hard for boots to mark it. Fresh horse droppings in the stable out back. But you can't tell a man's name from what his horse leaves behind, more's the pity."

"Nothing inside the house? Mud on the floor? Wet boots leave puddles on a hearthrug."

"I saw no dried mud, and there was plenty of time for a hearthrug to dry before you and I come in and found her." Will sighed deeply and accepted a pull on Henry's pipe.

"Did the neighbors see anything?" asked Hannah. "Did you speak to Mrs. Dowell?"

"I did, and that's another puzzle. The old lady says Nan brought her the young ones six days ago, and that's two days before the letter puts the first rape. Did she *know* they'd come then? Two days' warning, and she made no move to save herself?"

"Maybe there was some other reason she wanted the children out of the house."

"She told Ruth Dowell she was feeling badly and wanted to take to her bed for a few days. But the house was neat as a pin, the work all done up proper. And as for taking to her bed, it was still made up, even after he'd finished with her. You saw as much yourself." Will shook his head. "Neighbor women called her proud and secret, stubborn. Dunny didn't do well by her. Spent his money and his nights at Edes's, cuddling Bella McKee, by all accounts. And half a dozen others."

"When does the sheriff come?"

"Two days. Maybe three, depending on the weather. This fog'll bring snow before long. Could be a week or ten days before Marcus Tapp can hold his inquest." He sighed. "I tell you, I see no way out of it. Discounting the letter, there's only one piece of proof, and that's Daniel's finger marks on her throat."

"Or somebody's." Hannah helped her aunt dip the stew into the great pewter serving dish.

"They matched *his* fingers, my dear. Marc Tapp will take one look at matters and have Daniel in my jail and charged before we can blink."

"Oh, fiddle, William Quaid!" hooted Julia as she sailed past with the platter. "I could name you a half dozen perfectly respectable ladies in Rufford who would lie down with Daniel Josselyn on a snowbank if he so much as winked at them! And glad of it, too, husbands or no husbands!"

There was still, of course, a law against adultery, but nobody had taken it seriously for almost a hundred years; these days it was mostly used for leverage by very pregnant young ladies like Jonathan's Sally to induce a respectable marriage in the nick of time.

Henry laughed and puffed away at his pipe. "Mother's a shameless old fox, but she's right about one thing. What need has Daniel to take to a sorry little thing like Nan Emory, when he could have his pick of hearty girls? There's a dozen servants at the Grange, and John English has two fine daughters nearby." He did not mention Hannah, but she caught the look that passed between her uncle and Will.

"No," said the constable. "It's not Daniel's way. It doesn't make the best of sense, to be sure."

Henry blew out a puff of smoke thoughtfully. "But I'll tell you what does, though. Land and money."

"Did the Emorys own their land?" asked Hannah. "Surely they hadn't enough money to buy property, young as they were."

"Maybe so, maybe not," said the old fellow. "But he drew the boundaries of Daniel's land. And Ham Siwall's. And young fellows with their bellies full of Edes's rum can be talked into most anything."

Will considered. "It's worth looking into, I suppose. Only what's it to do with rape and murder?"

"That I can't say," replied Henry. "But when there's a human price paid dear for something in this world, it's been my experience the thing that's paid for is most likely either land or the money that goes with it. And land and money is power. Used to be you was born to power, like the Josselyns was in England. Now the only way to get it is to buy it, and have money enough to keep it. You have to have money, at least enough to look like you've got more."

"You're meaning the Siwalls, Henry?" Will studied the old man's face in the firelight.

"I say no names." He sniffed and knocked out his pipe on the hearthstone. "Only this I will say. I lost a son to the War, you know that, and I'm no Tory, like Hannah's James. But nothing's what it promised to be ten years ago. Oh, we're rid of the mad old king and Parliament. But if they send somebody to speak for us to the Congress, it won't be Dan Josselyn, for all his high principles. It'll be Ham Siwall. Because he's grabbed all he could get. You can die a hero for noble talk, like my poor Eben did. But a politician would sooner die rich, no matter how he does it."

MISTRESS AND MAID

At a little past seven that evening, about the time Will Quaid was leaving Two Mills after supper, Charlotte Josselyn was told by her housekeeper of the charge against Daniel.

The housekeeper, Mrs. Arabella Twig, was plump and fiftyish, her greying hair dyed a muddy shade of greenish-brown with black walnut shells soaked and boiled to an essence.

Mrs. Twig had prodigious bosoms and was possessed of two small brown moles which she considered her most alluring features. One of these was located on her left cheekbone, and she had developed a habit of smiling in order to flex her cheek and show off "Nature's Embellishment," as she called it.

The smile arrived without warning, vanished just as suddenly, and then came popping forth again, and it was apt to give anyone who did not know Mrs. Twig the impression that she was suffering a fit. Her eyes were small and yellow-green and piggy, and the barrage of smiles made her blink like a hibernating creature just ventured into the light from underground.

As for the second of Nature's Embellishments, it was located just at the cleft of her billowing, lavender-scented bosoms, and it was for this reason that Mrs. Twig's kerchief—which should have been pinned at the back of her neck, then crossed and

115

the ends neatly tucked inside her bodice—was for the most part untucked, and flapped like an unrigged sail at either side when she marched in close order along the halls or descended the great staircase.

"I took it upon myself, Ma'am," she said to Charlotte. "I dearly hope I am no gossip, but I took it upon myself to inform you, seeing as how someone else was bound to blab it in the course of time." She sniffed and patted her crocodile tears with the tail of the kerchief. "I sorrow for you, Ma'am," she said, and ventured to lay a hand on the lady's shoulder. "Indeed, I mourn most pitiful."

Aside from her desire to display a becoming sympathy, Mrs. Twig had a rather more particular reason for spreading the news. Though she was aging, she was by no means beyond desire. Indeed, she could be positively frisky when the mood struck her.

And Major Josselyn was a man, was he not? He was denied the comfort of a wife's bed, was he not? What could be more natural than that he should turn to the good and willing Mrs. Twig for solace? After all, she was not without attractions. Had she not skill? She had profited, she hoped, from her life's experience. Had she not ripeness?

In the course of time, she determined it was her duty to offer him the comforts only she could provide. Twig hinted. She blinked until her eyes watered. She flapped, and flapped again, contriving situations in which the flapping and the paste-white, fragrant bosoms could not be missed. Upon one or two occasions, she even undressed to her tentlike shift and left her door ajar when she knew Daniel would be passing.

But the man was more than human. Major Josselyn began to disappear from rooms unaccountably as soon as her footsteps could be heard approaching. When she hove into view, he averted his eyes. No, no. The man was not normal, certainly. He seemed to have no appreciation for Nature's Embellishments at all.

And Hell hath no fury, as Mr. Congreve *might* have said, like a silly old trout ignored.

"I hope I am not without compassion, Ma'am," she said stiffly.

"And if 'twere rape alone, I should wish to know further of the matter before judging, for there's a-many of these girls mistakes a good brisk wooing and fancies it too rough. Myself, if I may be bold, Ma'am, I take to a hearty fellow who does not flinch at grappling." She blinked, briefly, and then remembered herself and wiped her eyes again. "But murder, Ma'am! Murder's beyond the bounds. Indeed it is."

Charlotte pushed her tray aside. "Has Sheriff Tapp charged my husband?" she said quietly.

"The sheriff is expected, Ma'am. He cannot charge while he is but expected. But when he shall *arrive*—"

"Do not waste time babbling. Is my husband under arrest?"

"I am told he is under bond, Ma'am. He cannot leave the town bounds or he is deemed a confessed felon, to be hunted down." Twig gave a scornful sniff. "Constable Quaid, that undistinguished specimen, calls himself your husband's friend and is unwilling, I expect, to put him in irons in a proper cell." Remembering her position, she added quickly, "Though undeserved, I'm sure. Innocent of all wrong, I'm sure, Ma'am. Being your husband, as he is."

"Where is Major Josselyn now, Twig?"

"In his library, I believe, Madam. Come in an hour since, turned up his nose at my nice dinner of chops, he did, and went straight in to his books." She cocked her head at Charlotte. "*And* locked the library doors. Shall I fetch him for you, Ma'am?"

"No, Mrs. Twig. Lay out my grey silk, if you please, and then send Abby to me."

"Grey silk? But you cannot dress now, Ma'am! You'll do yourself a mischief by lacing and gartering at such an hour!"

Charlotte rarely gave orders, but now she was firm. "My grey silk with the embroidered stomacher, Twig. And shoes and stockings, and my jewel case, the small one. And then help me into the chair."

Mrs. Twig did as she was told and flapped off to fetch the maid, Abby, who found her mistress already elegantly dressed and sitting beside the fire by the time she arrived.

"Abby," said Charlotte, "please do up my hair."

"For bed, Ma'am?"

"Don't be a fool, dear. Am I dressed for bed?"

When the soft blonde hair had been brushed into careful curls and knotted up at the back, and a ribboned cap of Brussels lace pinned onto it with a silver pin Daniel had given her, shaped like a swallow, Charlotte leaned back in the chair, looking spent.

"You tire yourself, Ma'am," said the little maid softly, for she was fond of Charlotte and had none of Nature's Embellishments to make her jealous. Abby was plain and silent, and found the work here far easier than minding a houseful of babies back in Herefordshire. She could afford to be loyal to both master and mistress, and she was.

Charlotte smiled. "I shall rest while you're gone, Abby."

"Gone where?"

"First give me my work-box and my embroidery frame. That's it, just put them where I can reach them."

The maid opened the tapestried workbox and gave Charlotte her wools, crane-bill scissors, and needle book, then pushed the embroidery frame into position, the half-finished work suspended above her mistress's lap.

Charlotte put a hand on the design stretched in the work frame, letting her fingers stroke the smoothly-laid stitches of a briar rose.

"Now, Abby. I want you to go for Mrs. Trevor."

"Oh, Ma'am, you *are* ill, then! I'll call the master, shall I?"

"No! I'm no worse than usual. Take no one with you. You must go alone. And for God's sake, don't tell Twig. But fetch me Hannah Trevor. Now."

"Yes, Ma'am. Only it's very late at night, Ma'am, and there's bad fog on the river. She might not wish to—"

"She will come," said Charlotte softly, and began to thread a needle with a soft rose-colored strand of crewel yarn.

"Of course I will come," Hannah told the girl.

But for a moment she stood stunned and immobile. It was a meeting she did not relish.

Henry Markham, who had been dozing, received an elbow in

the ribs from his wife. He put down his pipe—long since gone out—and took his feet from the hob. "I'll go with you, see you across," he said with a yawn.

"Please, sir," Abby told him, "I thank you, but Lady Josselyn said I must go alone, and tell no one, and only bring Mrs. Trevor back."

So they went unaccompanied down the steep hill path, their lanterns bobbing in the darkness, slipping now and then and falling into the snow, their cloaks heavy and wet.

"Has something happened at the Grange, Abby?" Hannah's voice sounded very small to her, not like herself at all.

"No, Ma'am," replied the maid. "Nothing's amiss that I know. My lady only said she would speak to you, and she thought you would come."

"Could it concern the death of Mrs. Emory? You've heard what has happened to her, Abby?"

"Oh yes, Ma'am."

Abby paused, deciding how much she might say, and for a moment they faced each other, the small flame of the lantern flickering behind its punched-tin grillwork. The fog cast the light back at them as if from walls that drifted and moved and seemed almost to breathe as they did.

"Poor Nan," said the girl at last. "She was not careful, and a woman must be, married or not. I think it did not matter to her if she lived or died."

"You knew her well?"

"Not well, I shouldn't say. Some people do move through this world like shadows, and move out of it much the same. But Nan worked out—day work, you know—and brought her babies with her, as most women will. That's how I came to meet with her."

"She worked at the Grange?" Hannah held her breath, for if the answer were yes, it meant Daniel might have lied about knowing Anthea Emory.

"Not at the Grange, no," came the answer. "She worked for the Siwalls when Mrs. Kemp made her cheeses last summer, and so did I, and then again at pig butchering. My lady lets me take other work when I'm not much wanted and other folk have need."

Hannah let herself breathe again. "What did you mean before, when you said Nan was not careful? That she flirted too much, do you mean?"

"Oh, no. Only that she went everywhere alone. Not venturesome like you, I don't mean that. But she didn't seem to heed things. Other people. Oh, she was a hard worker, and she was careful with the little ones, and that boy, Jotham, would keep a saint from prayers. But— You know how it is when you have toothache?"

Hannah ran a cautious tongue over her own ailing molar. "Indeed I do."

"The way you live altogether in the hurt and nothing else seems to be quite real till your tooth stops aching?"

"And you think, 'if I were dead, at least the pain would stop.'"

"Oh, yes Ma'am. Except with Nan, it never stopped at all."

A WREATH OF BRIARS

The girl raised the lantern high as they picked their way across the log-jammed river and at last reached the sloping path to the big brick house. In deference to Charlotte's housekeeping and her own sodden condition, Hannah made for the back door, but Abby stopped her.

"Not that way," said the maid, taking her arm. "There's a way round the side."

So, thought Hannah, *I am not to be seen. Daniel is at home and I am not safe to be seen, lest I prove too much for him.*

She smiled in the cold dark. Did Charlotte think they would take one look, fall down, and bestride each other on the hearthrug?

On the other hand, the idea was not without its attractions.

"Very well, then," she said. "Round the side."

On the wall nearest the woods, a row of high windows ran the length of the house, forming a kind of long gallery. It was dark when they entered, but, her lantern still burning, Abby made her way to a table and lighted a silver rack of three thick tallow candles. By their smoky glow Hannah glimpsed dark paneled walls and the portraits that hung on them, sober faces frowning down.

"This way, please, Ma'am," said Abby, and led her to a passage-way and a narrow stair.

When they reached Charlotte's room, the maid opened the door without speaking and then slipped away into the dark of the long hall until she was only three distant lights flickering.

Hannah did not go in at once. She had been here with Clinch and her aunt when Charlotte's child was born dead, but very little talking had been needed that night. Otherwise, the two women had never met.

"Please come in, Mrs. Trevor," said Lady Josselyn without turn-ing to face the open door.

Hannah stepped into the room. It was small and warm, the fire burning brightly and many candles lighted on the mantel and the small tables, leaving a heavy smell of burning animal fat in the air.

Was Charlotte afraid of the dark, or only of Mrs. Trevor? Possibly neither, but she needed light to work.

It was a handsome place, full of embroidered cushions, hang-ings, footstools, bedcovers. Charlotte looked weary, but even now she persevered at her embroidery.

"May I see?" said Hannah, pushing her spectacles up on her nose.

"Of course. But do take off your wet cloak. There, near the fire, where it will dry."

While this was done, Charlotte studied the figure of her rival. Certainly Hannah Trevor was not what one was brought up to consider handsome. Her mouth was too wide and her teeth were far from even, and her eyes behind the spectacles, though they were large and lustrous and full of the cold darkness from which she had just come, did bulge a little and seemed too big for her face.

But her body moved with an ease and a pleasure in itself that tight laces and bone stays and Miss Bowker's School for Young Ladies had discouraged in Charlotte long before her illness de-stroyed it for good. For a moment her mind—which had been similarly laced, stayed, and discouraged—played with the image of Hannah, naked and unafraid in Daniel's arms.

It was something Charlotte had never managed—to be unafraid and naked at the same time, let alone in any man's arms. The thought did not arouse her, it only made her uncomfortable. She had never received her husband without fear and a touch of distaste she could not altogether disguise. Oh, he had been kind, and as gentle as he knew how, but when you did not fancy it, the act was by nature unkind. She had conceived his child because it was what you owed in return for a comfortable life and servants of your own and perhaps a carriage.

And she was fond of Daniel. If being fond had had nothing to do with his bed, she might have been his friend, and loved him as a friend, and been far happier. But as it was, how *could* she love him? His hard body had thrust inside her and as a result her own body was ruined. Oh, she did not consciously blame him. But secretly, she was relieved that her illness had ended the obligation to have him in her bed.

"Your embroideries are quite lovely," said Hannah, glancing again around the room.

"Do you not find them useless?"

"It is never useless to make beauty. When men make things that have no other purpose but beauty and pleasure, it is called art. When we women do the same, it's called a useless waste of time."

Charlotte almost laughed, but caught herself and merely smiled. "I perceive you do some needlework yourself, Mrs. Trevor. You defend it very well."

"Only quilting, for the most part, to use up old gowns and petticoats too good to throw away." Hannah bent over the work in the frame, and when she caught sight of the pattern, she had to bite her tongue to keep from shouting.

The design was a circle of briar roses in the classic style of Queen Elizabeth's day, woven close with oak leaves and tendrils—the very same design she had seen that afternoon on the embroidered pocket hung so carefully over the chair by Anthea Emory's bed. Hannah held her breath, gave herself time to conceal the shock, and went on.

"A handsome pattern," she said. "And unusual, like all of these. Are they sent for from Boston, or are they of your own devising?"

"For the most part, yes. These roses are my own. It is hard to come by decent patterns here. And I was taught at school to sketch a bit."

"You're very clever with the colors," said Hannah, "and you have imagination."

Clearly she had underestimated Charlotte. But how had that pocket come into Anthea's possession, unless Daniel had taken it from among his wife's things and given it to her for a lover's token?

"Oh, my imagination cannot amount to much," said Charlotte. "For you are nothing like what I had thought." She stuck her needle into the linen and closed the lid of her workbox. "Not so handsome, for one thing. And therefore far more dangerous."

"But you've seen me before, surely."

The other woman's eyes closed. "Ah. On that night, yes. It was the worst night of my life. Now I remember but little of it, except that there seemed to be blood everywhere I looked, and I could not imagine whose it was. I know there were women in the room with Mr. Clinch and my husband. I have always assumed you were one of them. But I have no memory of your appearance." Charlotte opened her eyes and smiled. "I do have a faint memory of someone hitting Clinch with a basin, and rather hard. Was it you?"

"I'm afraid so." Hannah gave her a rueful glance. "I thought it best to attack him with blunt weapons before Major Josselyn had time to go for more pointed ones. I would not have blamed him. No one would."

She reached out suddenly and took Charlotte's hand, held it tight.

"Daniel says it is largely thanks to you," said Lady Josselyn, "that I am alive at all. Is that true?"

"My aunt was there. If I know anything of healing, it is she who taught me. She saw you often during the worst days."

"But you brought medicines for a long while after."

"Yes."

"So. I owe my life to you." She freed her hand from Hannah's and let her fingers dally with the lace on her cuff. "I am not sure whether I should be grateful for it. But I thank you." Then she leveled her gaze at her rival. "The maids tell me you still bring me strengthening herbs for tisanes. But you never come up here, you always leave the things in the kitchen."

"I thought it best."

"Did you think I would fly at you and scratch your eyes out?"

"You have no reason." Hannah sat down on the sofa opposite. "Lady Josselyn, it grows very late, and—"

"And you have a small daughter to see to. My husband's daughter."

"Certainly not. Jennet's father is dead. I received a letter but today."

"Please Mrs. Trevor. That is a story you need not tell in this room."

"Very well." Hannah looked at her without flinching. "Daniel's daughter, then. I repeat, I am no threat to you. Men of his station often have bastards. You're a sophisticated woman, you're aware of the privileges of rank, even in America. I have asked nothing of him, neither acknowledgement nor support. I never shall."

"Do you love him?"

Hannah did not reply. "Why did you send for me now? You must have heard the gossip years ago."

"Do you love him?"

"You will think me hard if I say no, and a sentimental fool if I say yes."

"Oh, no. That is only what you will think of yourself, until you learn to know better. But I shall put it more plainly. My husband is accused of rape and murder. Will you fight for his life?"

"Will you?"

"That is what I am doing now." Charlotte sat with her hands

clasped in her lap. "I am clever enough at small things. Useless things. But I have not the wit nor the courage for this monstrous business. Even if I were well enough, I would be able to do little more than hold my head high in his company and pretend I saw no cause for alarm."

"Do you believe him to be innocent of the charge?" asked Hannah.

"Daniel can do violence, and I am sure he has killed men before," Charlotte replied unexpectedly. "But that was war. Though I am sometimes afraid of him myself when he is angry, he has never been less than considerate, even when I provoke him badly. He is not at heart a violent man. And I do not think he would intend harm to any woman."

"Did he know Anthea Emory?"

"Only slightly. I do not think he visits any woman hereabouts, not in the way your voice implies. Unless you—" She glanced at Hannah, then looked away again. "There is a woman in Boston. I have friends there, and they have written me of the affair. But even there, they say he is most discreet. And I do not believe it is an affair of passion. She would probably break off with him if she suspected that it had become so. She is a lady of fashion, and that precludes overmuch genuine affection for anything but one's own amusements, do you not agree?"

"But otherwise, he is faithful to you?"

Charlotte's blue eyes sparkled in the candlelight. "Or to you."

"To me? I spoke to him today for the first time in four years, Madam. Since that unhappy night we talked of earlier."

"Nevertheless. He is not a man to waver from what he loves." Charlotte paused. "Mrs. Emory was very young, was she not?"

"Yes," Hannah told her quietly, thinking of the ruined body on the bed. "Very young indeed. Constable Quaid and I have begun to think," she went on, "that someone wishes to destroy Daniel and has used the girl's death to do it. Has he any enemies that you know of? Anyone who might profit from his disgrace?"

"If he were hanged, you mean? Not enemies, precisely. He has done well since the War, and that is resented by many who haven't been so careful or so clever. And some of the young men resent him because of his father's title, though Lord Bensbridge was never rich and Daniel was disinherited years ago from what little would've come to him."

Hannah could not help thinking of her cousin, Jonathan, who assumed that a secret dragon horde of wealth went with even the most paltry claim to nobility.

Charlotte continued. "He's always at odds with Mr. Siwall, of course, over the timbering, but—"

"With Hamilton Siwall? But they are partners, are they not?"

"Yes. But they seldom agree."

"What is the cause of their arguments?"

"Oh, they wrangle over which sections of trees should be cut and the land sold. I cannot say more precisely, but John would know. John English, our bailiff. He runs the farm and handles the bookkeeping for the Bristol Company. You must ask John."

"Have the arguments ever grown violent?"

"Nothing beyond words, that I know." Charlotte frowned. "Surely Mr. Siwall would do Daniel no harm? He is a magistrate, a man of law. And most religious, too. The deacons have their prayer meeting in his parlor. How could he rape and kill?"

"I don't know that he has. But Anthea Emory worked for the Siwalls. Did she ever work here? Abby does not believe so, but—"

"Mrs. Twig does not always consult me about the girls she employs from the village if the work is below stairs or in the dairies or the washhouse. But the name would certainly be in her account books. Twig is most scrupulous in her record keeping. Why?"

Hannah did not answer directly. How could she? But if Nan Emory had worked here, had been in the house, she might have ventured into this room, seen that bit of embroidery lying about, and taken it. It might have nothing to do with her death or with Daniel at all. Still, Hannah had to know the truth of it. "Perhaps

Abby might get a look at the books, then?" she said. "And come and tell me what she finds?"

Charlotte nodded. "She's a good girl, and she isn't afraid of old Dragon Twig."

Before the next question, Hannah hesitated. It was the one point on which she had been able to get nothing like the truth from Daniel.

"Mrs. Josselyn, can you say for a certainty where your husband was last night and the three nights before?"

"I expect he was here at home. In his bed."

"But if he was not? Have you any idea where he might have gone?"

Charlotte looked at her, a soft smile playing around her mouth. "Have you never looked out your own window in the night, Mrs. Trevor?" she said. "When he goes walking, it is always your side of the Manitac, I believe."

TWENTY

THE JOURNAL OF
HANNAH TREVOR

15 February, the year 1786

Fog still heavy over the river. This day I go with Will Quaid to the Siwalls, where I shall be paid the fifteen pence owed for my baking. If there be a pattern of truth in this trouble over Mrs. Emory, God assist me to discover it.

Was called last night to Lady Josselyn. She is more than I thought, and braver than she supposes. May God comfort and sustain her in all troubles. She need not fear me with Daniel, for though I find myself fonder of him than I believed, still I am past needing men's bodies. Saw among the Lady's needlework the briar rose pattern, which she says is her own devising. Mrs. Emory could have come by it but three ways—by purchase, theft or gift. She had no money to buy, even if Lady Josselyn were like to work for gain, which she is not. And I do not think Nan Emory was a thief, for all her strangenesses. Unless I mistake, the pocket was a lover's gift. I shall ask Will Quaid to show me Mrs. Emory's pocket again, lest I have mistook it for the same design.

Was called on my return to see Edward Tobey at my Cousin Eliza's house. The child was far spent with a bad colic and could take no medicines.

I tarried the rest of the night and slept but little. About three o'clock, his breathing eased, and he slipped softly away. Life went out as a Candle at morning.

I did not weep.

Had no heart for sleep when I returned. Lay down awhile on my bed, but rose early and spun before breakfast, eight skeins wool and five of tow. Mended stockings and carded some lengths. Also stitched a while upon my daughter's quilt of Hearts and Bones, which comes up handsome. Piecework and appliqué. Plucked, dressed, and stewed six nice hens for fricassee with carrots and parsley-leaf, and saved back the broth for a soup, to which I shall make my mother's forcemeat dumplings.

Shall attend, at noon, the dissection upon Anthea Emory, whose soul had no peace in this world.

My Aunt now troubles me to marry the Reverend Rockwood in Boston, who is a decent man but not to my taste, fancying no more a wife than a table or a chair. Told her I shall not marry till she find me another like my Uncle is. I possess myself, and am glad. Though my tooth still pains me.

I am uneasy for Daniel this morning, and my head aches. I have no mind to write more until I have seen he is calm and well. God send he has done nothing rash.

I am in some fear for his mind, for men do grow desperate in too much trouble.

Here I draw out in part the pattern of briar roses from Lady Josselyn's crewelwork, which I saw on the pocket in Mrs. Emory's room.
It is a woman's kind of proof, but proof it is, and no man would think to record it.

TWENTY-ONE

THE SLUT AND THE HOUSEKEEPER

When Hannah called at Quaid's Forge for Will, she found his wife, Hetty, alone in the shop with a scrub brush and bucket, engaged in the hopeless task of cleaning the soot from the stone floor.

"Oh, Hannah, my love," she said, and stood up, her gown wet at the knees. "Will's late rising this morning, he slept straight through morning prayers. You know him, riding rounds half the night, and when he sleeps at all, he sleeps like Lazarus. It'd take Our Lord Himself to wake him." She laughed. "I just let him be till he rouses, and then shovel the breakfast in him!"

Hetty was a round, pink, persistently cheerful woman with bright black eyes and greying hair in a knob under her spotless ruffled cap. This object, which tied with pink ribbons under her chin, made her look deceptively like a well-fed baby with a new bonnet.

But her smile soon faded.

"He was up till almost morning, Hannah, worrying over Daniel. They was at Saratoga together, you know, them and your Cousin Eben. And at Webb's Ford, too." She paused and laid a soapy hand on Hannah's arm. "You look worn yourself, my love, and short of sleep. Come in and sit down and I'll give you one of my

133

currant buns and some hot, sweet tea. I'm a great believer in hot, sweet tea."

"Now Hetty, my old girl," said William, still buttoning his waistcoat as he ambled in. He was dressed in his best shirt and breeches for his visit to the Siwalls. "Hannah's the expert on what-ails-you, and if she needs dosing, she's got all them herbs and such up at the Mills."

Hetty tilted her dimpled chin and made a face at him. "I'm *still* a believer in hot, sweet tea," she said, and flounced off to brew some.

Oddly enough, Hannah felt better after a dose of Hetty's remedy, and as they crossed the river at Lamb's Inn Ferry and rode up the North Bank toward Burnt Hill, Siwall's impressive neoclassic manor house, she drew deep breaths of the cold, foggy air, letting it swell her lungs and bring her energy back to its highest.

Behind her, little Mr. Dodger rode along muttering, talking to himself under his breath as he often did, and ahead of them both the sturdy, reliable shape of Will Quaid led the way.

Most days, he would have sung as he rode, "Reuben Renzo" or "The Birds' Courting." But this morning he had no songs left.

Leaving William to question the Siwalls in the front parlor, Hannah made her way around to the back kitchen and was soon settled at the fireside with more tea—though this time she escaped the currant bun, since Mrs. Marjorie Kemp, the housekeeper, had still found no meal or flour for sale.

"I tell you, my dear," said the old woman, lowering her bulk onto a small joint-stool with the grace of an elephant balancing on a teacup. "If I wasn't such a noticing body, Mr. Siwall would have no food in this house at all till spring. And as for the Missus and Miss Caroline, why, they take no more thought for the housekeeping than if they lived in an inn the year around and paid rent by the week! And that Mr. Jeremy—"

She broke off suddenly, sharp predator's eyes aimed at a buxom,

black-haired girl of perhaps nineteen who was puzzling awkwardly over a bit of sewing at the window seat.

"Molly Bacon!" snapped the housekeeper. "Didn't I tell you to
stir that pudding, girl? Well, do a thing when I tell you! I don't
mind if you're Mrs. Siwall's housemaid, you can still take a blessed
stick and stir the everlasting pudding!" The old woman sighed. "I
don't know. When I was a maid in Philadelphia, before Kemp
and me married and come up to the Manitac, why, my lady would
have died of shame to keep such a slut as that Molly about the
place even slopping the pig, let alone serving at table." Mrs. Kemp
lowered her voice to a mumble. "Between us, Mrs. Trevor, the
reason she's kept on is plain enough. Young Mr. Jeremy's had his
hands inside more than one placket in this house, if you understand me. A charming enough rogue, he is. But when a girl's
no sense, a man in his position oughtn't to take advantage,
ought he? She'll have a belly on her by midsummer, or I'm a
flying cat, and you'll earn your six shillings from her before
the fall."

"I suppose Molly's not the only girl young Mr. Siwall fancies."
Hannah smiled and sipped her tea.

"Oh, lor', no! The boy's over at Edes's most nights, playing at
cards and shove-penny and skittles, drunk as a lord, and ending
it all in between some girl's legs."

"I wonder he doesn't marry. Surely he's of an age?"

Though Marjorie Kemp spoke of her master's son as a boy,
Jeremy Siwall must have been nearly thirty.

"Oh, aye, but Master fancies to marry him to a Philadelphia
family. A third cousin of Mr. Franklin, I believe she is, or a niece."

Hamilton Siwall had not merely gotten rich buying up de-
faulted loans since the war. He had used his money to buy political allies. And a connection to Benjamin Franklin, however
tenuous, was enough to gain him admittance to balls and card
parties and dinners where the decisions made over port and seed-
cake and a good cigar might determine the matrices of power in
America for centuries to come.

What they did to its thrashing, furious, roiling soul, still gasping for breath in the intense poverty and rootlessness that followed the War, men like Siwall cared very little, if at all. They acquired, they manipulated, they bred self-satisfied sons with small brains and no responsibility except to spend the new wealth as fast as possible and get more.

In the cities, New York and Philadelphia and Boston, these water-fly children were already consolidating their power, forming profitable political alliances by lucrative marriages and by a subtle bribery possible only among those who have in common an ethical system with only one Great Commandment: Get and Keep Getting. If you got more money than the next man, it meant you deserved it more than he did, or else God would not have let you pick your neighbor's pocket.

To many who had fought in the War and come out of it poor and uprooted, it seemed that the noble cause of Liberty and Justice had been betrayed already, that they had lost far more than they had won. It was by no means certain that anyone who did not own land would ever be given a vote, even if the Articles of Confederation were revised, as many wished. But they would certainly be taxed and taxed again to pay the huge national debt. In the dense forests, in tiny settlements hacked out of wilderness and tenuously held by men and women always on the edge of poverty, watching their lives slip down into a gaping pit of endless toil, anger was growing, rising like a swollen river to a flood that would burst the banks in another year or two, when the worst foreclosures were sure to begin and the new elections made it clear that, vote or no vote, only the rich would go to Congress, and only the rich were free.

But Siwall's son, Jeremy, was too busy enjoying himself to care.

"I am told that Anthea Emory worked for you, Mrs. Kemp," said Hannah.

"Once or twice, poor thing, so she did."

The housekeeper launched into a tearful discussion of the crime. Mrs. Emory was said by the gossips to have been decapitated and dismembered by that raving madman Major Josselyn, who had confessed and was due to hang in a day or so. "And may God scourge his black soul, the devil!" exclaimed Mrs. Kemp, and stopped to gasp for breath.

Hannah didn't bother to correct her, for gossips rarely believed anyone but other gossips anyway. "Did Mr. Jeremy Siwall know her at all while she was here?"

The girl Molly, still stirring the pudding to keep it from scorching, looked up and pushed her lank hair from her eyes. But again it was Mrs. Kemp who replied.

"She was a delicate little thing, in spite of them freckles of hers, and she had the look of a lady about her for all she was poor, and nice manners, too. Mr. Jemmy misses very little when it comes to our own sex, Ma'am. He has an eye, as I've said. And a pair of busy hands. Molly! Stop that stirring! You'll spill that pudding on the fire, a-whirling it about that way!"

"Why don't you ask *me*, then?" Molly dropped the wooden spirtle into the sink-basin and stood in the center of the room, legs apart, confronting them. Hannah could already see the swelling that almost kept her bodice from buttoning across the hips. "That cold, scrawny little thing! What would Master Jemmy want with her? Anyway, she wanted naught to do with men, that one. You just ask her husband! He was glad enough of a little kindness, I can tell you, and God knows where he's gone to now, likely scalped and picked to his white bones and froze in ice in the woods!" She began to blubber, a high whine proceeding from her pouting lips.

Mrs. Kemp picked up a heavy rounded stick that served the dual purpose of stirring the boiling laundry and beating the occasional unruly servant. She heaved herself up from the stool and toddled a few paces in Molly's general direction, and the slattern scuttled away out of range, suffering no more than a glancing smack on her tantalizing bottom which she rewarded with an outraged whoop.

"I'm too good to that girl by half," muttered Mrs. Kemp. "If it wasn't for me, she'd be one of them whores down at the Head, doing for sailors and rum smugglers, so she would."

Hannah silently observed that "doing" for smugglers would

probably suit Molly Bacon to a tee. But there was one more question she needed to ask before Will and Dodger finished upstairs and came to collect her.

"Mrs. Kemp," she said, "when you employ extra help for the cheese making or the candle dipping, how are they paid? I mean, does your master keep the accounts and pay them himself?"

"Bless you, my dear, he hasn't the time for it! He leaves all that to me, you know." The old woman went to a shelf beside the stairs and took down a large ledger. Then she lugged it to the table and opened it to a certain page for Hannah to see. "There you are," she said. " 'Owed to Mrs. Trevor, fifteen pence for baked goods, loaves and pies.' You see, I haven't forgot. Only just now, to tell the truth of it, there's no money in the house. No coin, that is, for the master was obliged to settle a bill yesterday for a box of fine chinaware that come in by the Boston cutter."

Hannah glanced at the page before her and let the old lady rattle on. Whenever an account was paid, it was carefully receipted, sometimes by means of signed bills pinned to the appropriate page, sometimes by the signatures of employees, itinerant workers, peddlars, and others who worked at Burnt Hill itself. Some signatures were proper writing, but many were marks, in various shapes and often more unique than the names.

"When did you last employ Mrs. Emory?"

"Bless you, not since last November, when we butchered the two black pigs, just before Thanksgiving."

"May I see the notation?"

Mrs. Kemp riffled the long, brittle pages. "There now," she said. "That's my own hand, if I am proud of it. 'Mrs. Dunstan Emory, three shillings, ninepence for services.' There's her mark."

It was a strange shape, like a circle with a line through it: Φ. A unique mark was the only way to prevent others from forging your name if you were illiterate.

"She could not write, then?"

"Why, no. Nor read, neither. When I paid her, she asked me

to read her out what she was owed. And then she made that mark, there."

"So she could not have written a letter! There was a letter found with her body and signed with her name, you see. Are you sure it was not merely that she had injured her hand, perhaps, and could not write on that particular day?"

"I do assure you, Mrs. Trevor dear," said the housekeeper. "Nan Emory could neither read nor write, and if she could leave a letter behind her, then I'm Molly Bacon!"

PIECING THE EVIDENCE:

Enquiry into the Guilt of
Hamilton Gerard Siwall, Magistrate,
and of Mr. Jeremy Winthrop Siwall,
Gentleman, Burnt Hill Manor,
North Common, Rufford

QUESTION: You have both said that you were not acquainted with the victim, Mrs. Anthea Emory. Judge Siwall, did you know her husband?

SIWALL: Only by name.

Q: He was employed by the Bristol Company, in which you hold a large share, was he not, sir?

S: I represent the Company in legal and financial matters. My partner, Major Josselyn, is responsible for the direct operation of the business. I had no dealings with Mr. Emory at all.

Q: Mr. Jeremy Siwall, do you know Dunstan Emory?

JS: Not to speak of.

Q: But you do know him?

JS: We had, do you see, interests in common. Flip and fillies. Hah!

Q: You refer to drink and women, Mr. Siwall?

JS: I refer to drink and horses, you ass!

S: My son has, I believe, met Mr. Emory at the spring horse fair races. Have you not, Jeremy?

JS: Took the packet down to Boston last season, did a bit of strolling, Dunny and self.

Q: Strolling, sir?

JS: Parading. Walking. Appraising the prospects.

Q: Horses?

JS: Women, you ass. The ladies. Dunny's, it seems, was a bloody bore. Couldn't stand her for more than a month at a go.

Q: Mr. Emory didn't get on with his wife?

JS: Oh, he got on with her. Two brats by her, after all, what? Got on all right. She bored him, was all. No conversation, you know. Hadn't the wit to keep a man guessing. That's the sort of gal a fellow likes, you know. Kind that keeps him guessing.

Q: Did he confide in you his reasons for going into the forest in late autumn, when he would almost certainly be caught in the snows and stranded?

S: Constable, you seem to mistake my son for Mr. Emory's brother or his priest.

JS: Jove, yes! Old Dunny and I, never intimates, you know. Not the ticket, Constable. Doesn't do to cross the bounds, does it?

Q: What bounds would those be, sir?

JS: Well, now. Old Dunny's house is that side of the river, do you take me? And our house is this side. I mean to say, I may have met the rogue in the Red Bush now and again. But I didn't bring him home to warm his feet in my bed, what?

Q: Did you visit his wife when you knew he had gone?

JS: I did not, sir.

Q: Did you visit her on the night of February the eleventh, break the lock on her door, enter her house, and rape her?

S: Constable, I must protest!

Q: Answer the question, Mr. Siwall.

JS: No, I did not! What the deuce would I want with the wretched little cow? Anyway, I can never abide them.

Q: What's that, sir?

JS: Wailers. You know. Weepers. Wailers. Hysterical muffins. That's what Dunny told me. Had him half off his head with her wailing and screeching. Hard on a man like Dunny. Dreadful hard.

Q: And you, Judge Siwall? Did you rape Mrs. Anthea Emory on the night of February the eleventh?

S: Constable Quaid, I am a magistrate of this township!

Q: Not what I asked you, sir. Did you—

S: No, sir, I did not!

Q: And where were you both on the nights in question?

S: I was in my wife's bed, Mr. Quaid. We waste no candles at Burnt Hill. We are early to bed and early to rise, Honoria and I. After the hour of eight at night, during the winter months, once we have said our prayers, you will always find us abed with our curtains drawn.

Q: And you, Mr. Siwall?

JS: Why, I was here, too. Wasn't I, Pa?

S: To the best of my knowledge, yes.

Q: You retired early as well, did you, sir?

JS: Might say so.

Q: Can anyone give surety for it?

JS: Oh, yes. Molly. Nice little thing. Generous.

S: One of my wife's housemaids.

JS: Is she? I'd have thought kitchen. Smells rather of onions, does Molly. But as I say. Nice little thing. You ask Molly. She'll tell you where I was, all right.

TWENTY-THREE

PIECING THE EVIDENCE:

Statements of
Mrs. Honoria Lucinda Winthrop Siwall
and Molly Bacon, Housemaid

I, Mrs. Honoria Siwall, do give and depose that on the nights in question, my husband, Hamilton Siwall, magistrate of Rufford Township, was in my company abed from eight o'clock until past six in the morning. It is a habit from which he never varies. I pray God he never shall.

I, Molly Bacon, spinster, did lie with Jemmy Siwall, and have done every night he has been to home since Candlemas, and he was naked in my bed in the backstairs room on the tenth, the eleventh, the twelfth and on the night before Saint Valentine, when he did bring me candied quinces and a fine cone of sugar, and implored me to favor him once more, and so I did, too.

Don't you believe me, Will Quaid? For you ought to, I'm sure.

TWENTY-FOUR

THE MADMAN OF BURNT HILL

She had heard of him. His name was Artemas, and he was Hamilton Siwall's younger brother. Like Will and Daniel, he had been no boy when he went off to war as captain of Rufford's militia company. But he still seemed young to Hannah, and though he must have been past forty, the mad often do not age a year at a time like other men. They can grow old in a day and die in an hour, and never be missed.

When the heat of cooking and the clamor of Mrs. Kemp badgering the kitchen maids grew stifling, Hannah slipped out the back door to wait for Will and Dodger in the yard, and it was then that she caught her first glimpse of Artemas Siwall. She saw him first as a blur of pure energy passing in front of her.

But even before she saw him, she heard the clatter of his chain.

The back garden of Burnt Hill stretched up a slope to the woods, and beyond the vegetable and herb patch near the door a square stockade had been erected. It was made of saplings, peeled and sharpened at the tops and placed close together, about ten feet in height. There was a gate with a heavy iron bar across it. The bar could only be removed from the outside.

This was where they kept him.

Hannah moved closer to the palings and peered through one of the cracks to see. He was walking, moving steadily and very fast around a track his feet had pounded in the snow. At the center of the yard, a heavy stake had been driven deep, an iron ring set into the wood on a swivel bolt, so that the light chain they had fastened around his waist would still allow him to walk.

He was a tall, thin fellow, and he walked with his hands behind his back as though they were shackled, his long body bent almost double, eyes staring at the dirty snow under his feet. His hair was free of snarls and very long and dark, with almost no grey in it at all. He wore it untied, and as he walked it fell across his face like a smooth brown-black mask.

When he moved past her, Hannah could hear him talking, though she could not make sense of what he said. It did not seem to be words, or if it was he did not articulate them. She caught sounds that might have been syllables, no more.

Artemas made perhaps five circuits around the stake, his chain dragging on the snow and slapping against his legs. Then suddenly he stopped, moved to the stake, straightened himself against it, and put both hands across his eyes.

He stood very still for a moment. Then Hannah saw his body give three convulsive jerks, as though he had been struck by three successive bolts of lightning or taken three bullets from a firing squad. He slid down the stake and lay in the snow, arms locked around his knees and face buried. A soft sound came from him, something that could hardly be described as crying. It was as though his bones themselves were mourning.

He was the execution squad. He was the prisoner. He was the grief.

To a rational mind, the action was mad, it made no sense. But Hannah understood it perfectly. He was his own punishment, over and over again.

She slipped aside the iron bar from the gate and went into the wooden box they kept him in. She did not know why she did so. Perhaps because women know in their bones the terrible nature of boxes, and know they must somehow be broken, opened, their sharp walls kicked down.

She could only have said that as he lay there in the snow, she did not see Artemas Siwall. She saw Daniel, and he was chained and mad and dying of the box in which his hurt mind rattled, furious and trapped.

Captain Siwall must have heard her footsteps, for the snow was hard with ice and she was wearing her uncle's boots, which creaked with every step. But he did not move.

She had dealt with the mad before, of course, for even they grew ill and died and needed nursing. Most of them were not dangerous to anyone but themselves, not even old Dickie Bunch, who had hanged his nagging wife in 1766 and was still locked up in Will's jail. The door of his cell was bolted only when Sheriff Tapp was in town for the magistrate's court, and he often came out for a game of chess with the constable or to drink a cup of Hetty's hot, sweet tea. Once his wife was gone, Dickie had no grudge against anyone, and was no danger these twenty years.

But Artemas Siwall had no such freedoms, though he seemed well looked-after and his clothes were clean and sturdy. He wore no cloak in the cold, but the small cabin they had built him within the palings looked snug enough. Now and then, Hannah had heard, he managed to slip out and wander, but so far as she knew, he harmed no one.

Still, she kept her distance at first.

"Good morning, sir," she said quietly.

He did not look up, but remained locked in his fetal posture, the dark hair falling like a heavy veil around him.

"Captain Siwall!" she said sharply.

This time he looked up. "We will take no more than necessary, Ma'am," he said softly. "Forage and water and a little food for my men. We mean no harm to civilians. We will take—no— We will take—"

She could see his face clearly for the first time, and though he must never have been handsome, his eyes were pale blue-grey and might have cut through marble, and his mouth was soft and wide, the lips slightly parted. His voice had a sweetness about it, like a singer's who does not sing.

"Artemas," she said, and stepped close to him. "I'm Hannah."

She reached out a hand to touch him and he jerked away. He tried to stand—or perhaps to run—but the chain had tangled around his legs and he could not.

"Please!" she said. "Lie still. It's cutting you!"

Amazingly, he obeyed her. Hannah bent over him and gently lifted his ankle in her hand, then slipped the chain free. She did not get up from him but remained there, kneeling in the snow beside him. The iron chain had cut through his boot top and his stocking and left a deep gouge in his skin.

"Let me clean it," she said, and reached for a handful of untouched snow where no one had stepped. She applied it to the cut like a poultice, and when she took it away, the cut was clean and the cold had stopped the ooze of blood. It was all she could do.

His pale eyes studied her. "I am a prisoner here, Ma'am," he said. "You must not consort with me. Your friends will shun you."

"Such a friend was never a friend, and is no loss."

He put out a hand and touched her arm, let his fingertips travel upwards until they reached first Hannah's shoulder, then her face. She felt him trace the line of her jaw, then move downward to her throat. His palm lay against her windpipe.

"You are young," he whispered. "So young."

"Oh, no sir. But you are not old."

"The dead are young forever," he said.

Then suddenly he snapped to attention. Again he backed up to the stake and closed his eyes, his arms wrapped backwards as though he were tied there and waiting execution. Again the first of the convulsions rocked him.

Hannah went to him and put her arms around him until her hand grasped his locked fingers.

"Reprieved, Captain," she said.

He opened his eyes and his body seemed to fall onto her like a great weight, like a tree felled or a slide of rocks from a hillside, a thing beyond its own power to control. His arms gripped her very hard and they collapsed together into the snow. For a moment she was under him, his long dark hair falling across them both. His legs straddled her and she could feel the involuntary hardness of his sex, of which he himself seemed entirely unaware. She felt, too, the drag of his chain across her ankles.

Then he rolled aside from her and lay there. Hannah got up.

"Where are your men, Captain?" she said.

"All dead."

"Surely not."

"All dead."

"Ambush?"

"All dead."

"Execution?"

"All dead."

"What battle, Captain?"

"Men. Women. Children. God."

"Was it Saratoga?"

He looked up at her, the pale eyes as colorless now as ice.

"This place?" he said. "They call it Webb's Ford, Ma'am."

"The men and women and children there? Did *they* attack you?"

"She came out of the house. Her gown was undone. There was a baby at her nipple. I saw the baby bloom red, like a flower, and fall away, and the milk from her nipple was red."

"Someone had shot her?"

"They call it Webb's Ford, Ma'am. When it was a place on this earth."

"Did *you* shoot the woman and the baby, Captain?"

"I went into the house. He was with me. When we left, the knives were blooming. Red roses."

"Who was with you, Artemas? Was it your brother? Was it Josh Lamb? Was it— Was it Daniel?"

"All dead," he said.

He stood up and faced her, and Hannah knew that once, long

ago now, he had been a thing she might have loved. But he was nothing now, and nothing loved him. Even animals would want nothing to do with him. Artemas Siwall was more than a madman. He was a ghost.

His hands were on her throat before she could step away. They held her hard, she could feel the long, thin fingers dig into her flesh. She stood very still, her breath coming harder as the hands closed down on her.

Then suddenly he let her go.

"Reprieved," he whispered, and began to walk again.

She turned to go and saw Will Quaid at the compound gate, watching her. As she came toward him, she saw him draw a breath of relief.

"Hannah, you had no damn business in there!" he said angrily. "Artemas Siwall's mad as the moon, you know that!"

"He did me no harm at all, William. Stop fussing."

"It's nothing to take lightly! He could've snapped your neck like a stick with them hands of his. He's strong. Madmen and simples always are, seems like. Body makes up what the mind lacks, maybe. But you're not to go near Artie Siwall anymore, not without me or Dodger. He pays heed to old Dodge, don't he?"

"I do not fear him, sir," said the little man, glancing out from under the egret-plumed tricorn that replaced his nightcap when he was out upon the world. Whatever he had been in his long lifetime, certainly it had been more than a village constable's clerk. "And he does not fear me," said the little fellow. "I can lead him by the hand, you know, mad or not, and we do each other no harm in the world."

But William was insistent. "You promise me you'll not go inside that gate again, Hannah!"

"Very well," she said. "On one condition."

He frowned. "What's that?"

"I want a half hour alone in Mrs. Emory's house."

"What the devil for?" Will stamped his foot in the snow.

She considered explaining that she wanted to see the embroidered pocket. But he would ask too many questions that might be dangerous for Daniel. "Because I am your friend," she said instead, softly, "and I ask it."

He considered. "Well, then," he said at last. "I can't see the harm. I'll send Dodger, here, along with you. He's cheerful, is Dodge, and he has a quick eye for mischief."

Hannah took Will's big hand and held it for a moment. It was seasoned like iron from the heat of the forge, darkened with soot that could never entirely be washed out of the pores of his skin, and strong—hardly aware that it could snap a two-inch-thick pole without trying. The idea of Rufford without Will Quaid as its constable was unthinkable. No matter its confusion, the earth could not stop turning so long as William was somewhere on it, riding the bounds for wrongdoers.

He took his hand away from hers and for a while they stood in silence at the edge of Artie Siwall's compound, watching the madman on his sentry rounds. "Could he have killed her, William?" asked Hannah at last. "Could Artemas have slipped out of here and killed Nan Emory?"

Will took off his hat and scratched his ear. "Not likely. Possible, I guess. But none of the servants here at the Hill had anything to say about him slipping out, and that Mrs. Kemp keeps a close eye on the poor fellow. It would explain, though, why the killer didn't take away that letter. A man only half in his wits would hardly stop to read a letter lying about."

"William, Nan Emory didn't write that letter. She didn't know how to write. Mrs. Kemp told me. She used a mark, she couldn't so much as sign her name."

"But who, then?"

"Perhaps the murderer left it himself. Wrote those names to cast suspicion elsewhere."

"Hannah, for the love of God," he cried suddenly, "let it be, can't you? It's my job, let me tend to it!"

Will's big hands were shaking with sudden rage, and he stuffed them in his pockets. Mr. Dodger, who had been tightening their saddle girths before the ride back, came padding softly to the constable's side.

"Now, now, sir," he said, laying a fragile, papery hand on his master's arm. "The world turns, sir. Day follows night and the dead shall be raised incorruptible. I am here, sir. Be calm. I am here when bidden."

Will said nothing, only turned silently and mounted his big bay gelding. They rode out of Burnt Hill in a ragged procession and spoke little until they reached the crossing at Lamb's Inn Ferry. Dodger rode on ahead, his pony's hooves clattering on the ice, and Will was about to follow when Hannah pulled up her horse beside him.

"I won't go across with you," she said. "I'm called to Dr. Kent's, you know. The dissection."

William nodded. "I lost my temper back yonder. This is a hard business, and it gnaws at me. You'll let me know what you find?"

"Of course." He made a move to go, but she laid a hand on his reins. "William," she said, "where is Webb's Ford, exactly?"

He grew very still, the horse jittering under him to be gone.

"What makes you ask that?" he said sharply.

"It's where Daniel's hand was ruined, isn't it? And where my cousin Eben was killed?"

"Aye."

"And Captain Siwall spoke of it just now."

"Mother of God, he's mad, girl, he's like to say anything!" He paused. "What did he tell you about it?"

"Oh," she replied, "nothing very clear. Were you all there? All the Rufford company?"

"Things got muddled after Saratoga. Companies broken up. Men have to fend for themselves in a war, even if they start out in a regular army, you know."

"Is it near Saratoga? Webb's Ford, I mean."

"Up in the hills, along the Hudson." He studied her face. "What are you thinking, Hannah Trevor? What you chewing at now?"

She smiled ruefully. "I don't really know yet, my dear. Truly,

I begin to wonder if this is a business in which thinking will do much good at all."

Hannah turned Flash and rode away along the narrow road to Dr. Kent's surgery, and Will Quaid sat his horse at the edge of the river, watching her.

On the opposite bank, little Mr. Cornelius Dodger, Esquire, who could lead madmen by the hand, sat waiting until he was bid.

TWENTY-FIVE

ON THE DEATH OF THE SOUL

The night after they found Anthea Emory was the first night her killer—that was what he was now, though he still could hardly grasp it—was able to sleep. It was a long sleep, and deep, like a tree sleeping in the ground or a body frozen in the ice and waiting for the end of the world to thaw.

Then, when he woke, the magic was gone.

Ever since the War, he had felt there was a magic protecting him, that he could disappear whenever he chose and become invisible. He had lived inside his soul as a man walks through unmapped wilderness, returning to a small square of cleared ground where the sun penetrated. But the real boundaries were vast and secret and he did not know at what moment he might suddenly slip into the dark and be gone.

Now he *was* gone, and the magic had left him. Nobody knew him, no woman, no man. She had not known him, he had been nothing but an instrument for her use, as he was to all of them. So he had killed her, as she wished.

His father had been a religious man, a fulminating old hypocrite. But the old man had known things. As a boy, he had believed his father knew God.

One day he had asked him, "What is the soul, sir?"

"The soul?" said the older man. He was stacking some coils of rope in a storeroom, and he took one of the coils and looped it and threw the loop over a great beam above the boy's head. He picked the boy up and slipped the loop around his neck. Then he let go his hold on his son's body and the rope pulled tight.

He remembered the feeling clearly, although you are not supposed to be able to remember pain when it is over, or fear once the horror you are afraid of has taken place. As he swung from the beam, he saw the thing he was divide itself into two things. One of them was a boy kicking, flapping its arms, flailing. Trying to live. The other was calm and silent. Imperturbable. He could see this self at some distance from him, and even after his father caught hold of his thrashing legs and lifted him up to take the pull from the rope before it broke his neck, the secret self that was his soul remained distinct and visible to him. In the years since that day, it had never returned and yet had never left.

The thing his father could see was a small boy with a red welt on his neck from the rope. His body was shaking and he had wet his pants and shit was running down his legs.

But the soul that had left him was older than his father and older than his father's God. It hated them both and watched and was silent, and if it was sad it was a dry sadness, like old rocks crumbling, or like the skin a snake has left behind, sad and brittle-dry and beautiful.

That disenfranchised soul had kept him separate from everyone. He had been able to give them only so much of himself as they could see, a visible boundary, an illusion he managed, an honest fellow, kindly and generous to those he loved, honorable enough and open-hearted, able to fight back from anything and prosper.

His soul had been his magic, and he had lost it when he killed her. That was the last thing she had demanded, that night on her quilt-covered bed. It was why she made him rape her. She had to take the magic and break it. He had not thought she would succeed, but all during his deep sleep of that first night, he had felt himself falling, weightless, felt the illusion slipping away from him in pieces.

He remembered his father's sermons about damnation. Now he understood them. This was how it felt. Like freedom.

From where he was, he could see Hannah Trevor on horseback, traveling along the North Bank alone, her cardinal-colored hood falling down her back and her short brown curls tossed in the cold wind.

Now he was free. He could do anything now. After the madman and Daniel, she would be next.

PIECING THE EVIDENCE:

Results of the Dissection Performed Upon the Body of Mrs. Anthea Mary Emory, 15 February 1786, Rufford Township, Maine, Upper Massachusetts

Externally, the body suffered the degradation of various blows, perhaps a week since delivered. Burns traveled the length of the trunk from throat to groin, being small and egg-shaped and but newly received, and bearing the traces of tallow-wax and some small ash, as from a tow-fibered candlewick.

Compound or open fracture of left humerus or arm, just above the great joint or elbow. There was no observable bleeding, and the wound not being bandaged, it is supposed the bone was broken and protruded through the skin after death had occurred.

Hair was missing from the scalp, but the follicles or roots were still present in the scalp, and in some places the hair gave the appearance of having been cut, rather than pulled away by recent violence.

Death resulted from strangulation, the windpipe being smashed and the laryngeal area much damaged. Upon dissection, the vertebrae at the back of the neck were revealed to be broken also, and the spinal column severed giving evidence of great strength applied to the throat at the moment of death. There were marks of but eight fingers upon the two outer walls of the throat, and of the pressure of palms upon the larynx.

On the victim's right side, an inch and a half below where the marks of two fingers were missing, there appeared a depression or ridge upon the neck, about two inches in width, as though some unknown blunt object had borne down and left its mark below the marks of the fingers, as it were the edge of an object held under the hand and borne down upon during the killing.

When the body was opened, the organs appeared in perfect health, excepting the left lobe of the lights, or lungs, which was somewhat enlarged.

In the womb was discovered the fetus of a child unborn, grown to the size of perhaps two months' carrying, though this is no surety in time, for it was as yet very little grown.

To this we do give and subscribe as true.

Cyrus Kent, physician and surgeon
Samuel Clinch, coroner and physician
Hannah Trevor, witness

TWENTY-SEVEN

THE MEN SHE KNEW

When she left Cyrus Kent's surgery after the autopsy, Hannah was too busy puzzling over its results to go directly home. Instead, she rode a little way back toward Burnt Hill, along the North Bank. Daniel's bailiff, John English, lived just beyond, between the Siwall place and the Grange, and she might have had some idea of talking to him, as Charlotte had suggested.

But if she did, she never reached him. The fog had almost gone, and it was much colder, the sky heavy with snow. The clouds hung so low that noise rebounded from them as from a blank wall, and Hannah heard the shouting long before she saw the mob.

Some of them had muskets or swords, but most were farmers and their natural weapons were hayrakes, corn knives, pitchforks, sharpened pikes, axes. There were already nearly a dozen when she caught sight of them, and as they moved along the bank, others joined them, and more crossed from the opposite shore. By the time they reached the foot of Burnt Hill where it sloped down to the river, there must have been nearly fifty.

They were wild-eyed, furious, and now and then a fight broke out between knots of them. Hannah rode closer, determined to find someone she knew to ask what had happened.

"What do they care, the bastards?" shouted somebody.

"Aye, so long's they get what they want, and live fine and grand while other men sweat and starve!"

"They're all butchers! Think they're safe to do murder and run free!"

"They're no better than what we fought to rid ourselves of, that's certain, whatever color coat they did wear!"

"Aye, Josselyn's rich, and rich is bloody, and takes what it wants."

"If he's gone into the Outward, we'll play hell finding him."

"There's enough trees for a rope to hang him from, then, and we won't need Clinch and Siwall to give us leave!"

"Who's got a good rope now?"

"Here!" shouted a tipsy Phineas Rugg, and waved aloft a hank of new hemp—probably stolen from somebody else's barn.

He was not the only one drunk, though it was barely past two in the afternoon. The sober-minded, like Josh Lamb and Mr. Hobart, who ran the merchandise store, and Evan Wilkerson, the joiner, were still at their work, and for the most part these men were idlers, or laborers who drifted from job to job. Hannah recognized several who had lost farms to debt and taxes and seen them bought up by the Siwalls.

In the center of the group of angry men, she caught sight of her cousin, Jonathan. Some of the others lifted him onto their shoulders, where he could be better heard.

"Right then," he said. "We know what we must do, lads. He's taken two harmless lives already, and one of them a lone woman with two little ones. We can't leave it to Siwall. He's stricken, anyway, and can't think clear."

A broad-shouldered fellow with an arm missing below the elbow spat angrily into the snow. "I left my farm to go soldiering for Liberty," he shouted, "and when I came back 'twas no more mine, but Siwall's. I'll leave nothing more to Magistrate Siwall, if you please. Brother or no brother, he'll protect his own kind, and Josselyn'll go scot-free."

"Nor trust it to Will Quaid, neither!"

"Aye, that's right! Will's nothing but Siwall's monkey! Besides, him'n Dan Josselyn's friends, ain't they?"

"Aye, the law will do naught to punish the bastard! Aren't they partners, Siwall and Josselyn, and two of a kind? And the Siwalls own Sheriff Tapp."

Jonathan looked straight at Hannah, who was sitting her horse quietly a few feet from the edge of the crowd. "Brothers, it looks like Dan Josselyn's guilty. And we must find him and see him hanged," he said, "or no poor lone soul will be safe from harm in this place again. We fought a war to be free of lordships and tyrants. Now we must free ourselves and our women of fear."

Hannah dug her heels into Flash's sides and began to walk the animal through the crowd. As she passed through the mass of angry men, she could feel the heat that was on them. It was nothing so simple as anger. A cat out hunting at night feels no anger at the thing its claws tear the life out of.

They needed none of Johnnie's sullen rhetoric to turn them into a mob. It lived in them, in the anger that never left them, like a low-grade fever that dries the mouth and burns the eyes and makes the limbs ache for days and even weeks before the sickness really comes. They no longer cared who they pounced on. But they needed a name, and the name was Josselyn.

Though she knew most of them and had delivered sons and daughters for a fair share of their wives, their faces were scarcely recognizable to Hannah, as Flash walked steadily through the crowd.

Still, they moved aside and let her pass until she reached the center, where Jonathan stood on an upended cart, his eyes very bright and his cheeks flushed with the first real power he had ever had over men. His face was almost level with hers as Hannah pulled the horse up. Whether Jonathan really cared very much what happened to Daniel, or even what had happened to Anthea Emory, Hannah could not be sure. But he was certainly enjoying this.

"Good morning, Cousin," she said, her voice clear and loud

enough for the others to hear. "I must confess, it amazes me to hear you fought a war for anything at all. I had not known you were at Saratoga with your brother Eben, for you were but eight years old when the fighting began. Unless you mean that sweet war with Sally Jewell, which resulted in your son, Peter."

There was a soft riffle of laughter, but it did not break the mood of the men.

"You know about such wars well enough, too, Mistress," said Jonathan coldly.

He was no longer her cousin. He was power, and thought he had put her in a box and locked it on her.

"Aye, the whole town knows she's Josselyn's slut, and has been these eight years!" shouted somebody. Hannah recognized the voice of Phinney Rugg.

"And a Tory's leavings, to boot! Where'd you send that husband of yours, Missus? Running to King George for shelter? Or is his bones in the Outward, like young Emory's, with Josselyn's bullet in his head?"

"She knows where the murdering bastard is, all right! Riding to warn him, I wager, right now."

"We'll have that horse, Mistress!"

Hands began to tug at her, and Flash dodged and fidgeted. Somebody pulled Hannah off the mare and suddenly she was in the midst of them, smashed against faces she knew and did not know. Two men—only thick, hot bodies to her now—tossed her back and forth between them and she kicked and struck and bit when she could get a purchase on a hand or an arm.

But there were too many of them. Somebody cuffed her across the temple and she staggered back against the cart. A huge, white pain shot along her cheekbone and tears streamed from her left eye, so she could not open it. Hands gripped her, slipped inside her cloak and found her breasts, slipped down to her waist and below it. She could feel herself falling, and it seemed a long, silent fall, the faces of the men all around her. She knew they were shouting, but they seemed to her to make no noise.

Then suddenly she was down in the snow, kicking. She remembered biting someone's arm and tasting blood again. A heavy blow landed across her mouth and there was a terrible weight on her, a man's body. She opened her eyes and saw a face and thought she knew it.

Thomas Whitechurch. She had been kind to Thomas Whitechurch. Had forgiven him the cost of five nights sitting up with his wife, who had had a hard birth. Had brought his first son through alive when the child fell into the fire and was sorely burnt.

But now he was not Thomas Whitechurch. He was a box that locked itself down upon her body and could take whatever it wanted. And she was not Hannah Trevor, who belonged to no one but herself. She was a thing on a chain that could only march round and round in circles, and break itself with grief.

She could feel the man's hard body on her, pressing down on her belly and thighs, the others crowding in on them to watch, knowing already what the end would be, waiting their turns, perhaps. The man's breath was heavy on her and his hands clawed her muddy skirts out of the way. She felt cold air on her legs, and the rasp of his rough clothing as he crouched, panting, fumbling with the buttons of his breeches' flap.

When it's done, I will find them one by one and kill them all, she thought. *Every one of them watching, I will kill.*

There was more shouting then, and she heard the little horse scream.

Somebody fired a gun. Jonathan's voice. "You fools! Remember what we're here for! Get away! Get away from her, Tom Whitechurch, or I'll blow your brains out!"

The weight against Hannah's body eased and then was gone. She lay still in the snow, cloak trampled, skirts up to her waist, bodice torn.

The gun went off again.

A man's voice at the edge of the crowd screamed. "I'm shot! My arm!"

"Johnnie Markham, put the pistol away! And you, Tom," shouted Will Quaid's voice, "get the hell away from her, or I swear to God I'll put the next ball between your ears myself."

Where she lay, Hannah could feel the heat of the men draw away from her and the cold air strike her more sharply. She sat up and pulled her muddy cloak around her. There was a gouge on her cheekbone and her mouth was full of blood. The tooth that had been paining her throbbed as if they had driven a nail into her face.

She looked up and saw Jonathan above her. The dark eyes were no longer angry or even proud. They were ashamed.

William was there, too, and he tried to lift her up.

"No," she said. "Don't touch me!"

She slipped out of his grasp and scrambled to her feet. For a moment she hated him, too, because he had rescued her, and rescue was another kind of box.

"Harry Small!" Jonathan shouted. "Get your fool backside off that mare of hers!"

"We could catch Josselyn quicker on horseback, Johnnie," said the man Small. Hannah recognized him, a tapster at Edes's when he wasn't mending pots and kettles.

"Give the lady back her horse, I said."

Harry Small slipped from Flash's back and moved off to join a knot of grumblers. They had frightened themselves now, and were ashamed. None of them looked at her as she walked to the horse. Jonathan turned to help her mount, but Hannah whirled suddenly and raked her nails like a claw down his forearm. Blood began to seep from it, and the sight of it made her feel stronger.

"Go home, the lot of you!" William commanded. "There's a law in this town and the law will sort it out, murder and all."

"Oh, aye?" said one of them, a big man with a mop of greying hair. "Fine lot of sorting you've done so far, Will Quaid. Two dead already, and how many more before you catch him?"

"Two dead, you say?" Hannah spoke clearly, but her voice seemed to come as an echo, disembodied by the cold. "Who else is killed?"

Will looked up at her where she sat gripping Flash's reins in both fists. "My Christ, girl," he said under his breath. "Haven't you had enough yet?"

"God damn you! Tell me who else is killed!"

"Siwall's brother," he said softly. "Artemas Siwall. With Daniel's grandfather's saber. The one that hangs on his library wall."

TWENTY-EIGHT

THE DEATH OF A GHOST

It was the kind of blade they called a hunting sword. It was useless for fighting because it was too short, and the guard was decorative but of little use in protecting the hand. It was made for despatching foxes or deer or wild boar, once the hounds had run them down and torn them.

Still, the sword that pinned the body of Artemas Siwall to the post in the center of his fenced prison was strangely beautiful. It seemed almost to grow naturally from his chest, its slightly-curved blade glistening in the darkening afternoon and wavering a little in the wind, as though it danced.

The grip was silver-chased ivory carved in a twisting design, and the pommel was a swan's head of silver, connected to the quillion by a thin silver chain.

"I cannot believe it of Daniel," said Hamilton Siwall softly.

He was kneeling in the snow beside his brother's body as Hannah and William came into the yard, and when he heard them, he did not look up. He spoke more to himself or to his dead brother than to anyone else.

"It is certainly old Lord Robert Bensbridge's hunting sword," he said. "I've seen it many times, hanging over the mantel in Josselyn's library. It was part of the old man's legacy. But surely,

surely—" Suddenly he looked up at them. "We have had our quarrels, Dan and I. But they were business matters only, perfectly open, not secret festerings. Or so I thought. Surely men are not so false?"

Ham Siwall was stubborn, willful, inclined to resentment, defensive, proud. Perhaps even dangerous when angered or insulted. But incapable of concealing his passions, or so it seemed.

And for all his faults, he was certainly capable of love.

But even the worst of murderers and tyrants, thought Hannah, are so. And the best of men will turn to brutes at times.

She tried to open her swollen eye, winced, and made do with the other.

"Please, Constable," said Hamilton Siwall. His hand lay on his dead brother's knee. "Do what business you must with him, and take him down from there. I cannot bear to see him so."

"Dodge!" cried William, and the little man scurried up. His remarkable memory could be relied upon to record every detail until they reached the Forge, where matters could be written out properly for the sheriff—whenever he arrived.

Siwall stood up from the body and turned, and when he saw Hannah's battered face, he drew a breath and glanced discreetly away. "You are hurt, Madam," he said. "Step into the house and Mrs. Kemp will assist you."

"I fell from my horse. But I am well enough," she replied. "I am sorry for your brother, sir. And for you."

He nodded curtly. "I thank you."

"You are reluctant to believe that Major Josselyn killed him?"

"I can't credit it," he said. "They were friends in the old days. Even now, Daniel came often to see Artemas, and it was never pleasant for him. They— They had bad memories in common, I believe. But he came at least twice a seven-night, and my brother was often the better for it afterward."

"How better?"

"Calmer. Able to sleep, or sometimes even to read. He was a great reader in the old days, like Daniel. And when he'd seen Josselyn, he was not inclined to punish himself so. You saw him this morning, the servants told me. The marching. The mock execution to which he sentenced himself every hour of every day."

"What memories had they in common?"

"Oh, the War."

"Webb's Ford?"

"I believe so. Among other things."

"Sir, did your brother ever tell you what happened at Webb's Ford?"

"Not directly. And I— It made him worse, if he thought of the War. I could not ask him." Siwall stared at his boots and kicked a little at the snow under them. "I think I was afraid to know."

"You were not there yourself?"

"No. Our company became dispersed after Saratoga. Some few were wounded and taken to field hospital, Josh Lamb and some others. I, myself—well, truth to tell, I became separated from my friends and spent almost two weeks drunk as a lord with a company of Dutchmen. We thought we had something to celebrate."

"So you were with these Dutchmen when the others were at Webb's Ford. And did you ever speak of it with Major Josselyn?"

"No. We are business partners. Daniel shares little of his private history with me, nor I with him."

"So you are not friends?"

"I knew him in the War, of course. But he was, as I have said, more my brother's friend than mine. And I find it is better not to make friends in matters of business."

"I believe you disagreed recently over some such matters? The cutting of trees in some sections, how they would be parceled out for sale in the spring survey. Was the decision at all dependent on the survey maps Dunstan Emory went into the woods to complete?"

At this, Hamilton Siwall bridled. "If you recall, Mrs. Trevor, it is I who am the magistrate here, not yourself. I will answer the constable's questions gladly. But I do not need to explain myself to you."

He walked away, toward the small cabin in which Artemas had slept, and disappeared inside.

Will braced his feet in the snow and pulled at the sword. Its tip was driven deep into the post to which the madman was still chained. When at last it gave way, he pulled the blade out as cleanly as he could.

Hannah helped Mr. Dodger lay the body gently down onto the snow.

"Take off the chains, take off the chains," murmured the little old man. "Prisoner of war. Captured. Prisoner all these many years. Now he is free. Take off the chains."

"Here, Dodge," said William, and unlocked the heavy lock, then slipped the light chain from around Artemas's waist.

"Bury them!" cried the old man. "Chains want burying! Where's a shovel?"

He took the chain and the lock and gathered them to his chest in a bunch, then began to walk around the frozen yard as though an open grave might be waiting somewhere, a pit in which all locks and chains might be buried forever.

"What do you make of it, Hannah, my dear?" said William.

"Daniel could never kill a man in chains," she said.

"Oh, aye, that's love talking, and you know it as well as I do! After what just happened down by the river there, how can you say what any man would never do? Even Dan!"

But Hannah scarcely heard him. She knelt beside the madman's body, laying it out as she had done with countless dead before him, with babies and women and old men. With young men thrown from their horses, their necks broken. With woodsmen caught in bear traps, their legs gangrened and rotten. With her own three children, dead of diptheria all in the same week.

Hannah stroked back Artemas Siwall's long dark hair and laid it smooth as a girl's at his shoulders. His eyes were open, blank, but squinting slightly, as though he stared at something a great distance off and could not quite make it out. She closed them, let her hand lie on them for a moment.

Then she straightened his legs and let her fingers stroke them. She did not know why, but it was a thing she often found herself doing with the dead, as she had done with Anthea. They seemed to want touching, to be too much alone—though she knew it was for herself. With each of the dead, she had to let her lost children go again, and they must be bidden a gentle good-bye.

She did not realize what she was doing when she took up Artemas Siwall's dead hand and bent over it. She felt the pain in her face, but she had no idea it was because her battered eye complained when the tears came from it, because her sore mouth ached when she made it kiss the hand of the dead. She knelt there, bent almost double, her body shaken and jolted with something that did not seem like pain and could not have quite been sorrow for anyone except herself.

This was what it was to be alive. To live in a box and die on a chain.

"There's everything on earth but hope," she said aloud.

The words ended it. Hannah sat up, and Will and Dodger stood watching her as she laid Artemas Siwall's hand carefully beside his body.

Then she stopped. Something about the hand had felt strange to her even while she held it. Almost deformed.

When she looked down at it, she realized what her fingers had already told her.

The dead man's left hand was wearing a soft leather glove, and two of its fingers were missing below the first joint.

Hannah took up the hand again. The glove barely stretched over Artemas's broad palm, but she tugged at it and it came away. Will bent down to see.

Inside the glove, the madman's fingers were all there, whole and perfect as she had remembered them when they lay around her throat that morning. But the two fingers of the glove had been stitched down, as Daniel's gloves were. When a man with five whole fingers wore it, he had to bend his own fingers down against the palm of his hand.

The dissection had shown a ridge below the finger marks on Mrs. Emory's throat.

"William, don't you see! If Nan Emory's killer wore such a glove, he would have left marks just like the ones from Daniel's fingers. And if it were actually Daniel's own glove, stolen for the purpose, or found lying forgotten somewhere, it would explain why the lengths of the finger marks fit his hand so exactly. And if the killer *had* all his fingers, doubled up like Artemas's inside the glove, they would leave another mark as he bore down on her, just like the ridge Dr. Kent found on Anthea's neck. But I forget, you've not heard the result of the dissection. William, she was almost two months—"

He gave her no time to finish. "Daniel never takes off that glove, my dear, you know that."

"But what if he did? Surely he has more than one pair of gloves, Charlotte would see to that. He often came here to see Artemas, Siwall said so. He was kind to the poor soul. Perhaps he didn't feel he had to disguise himself with Captain Siwall. And if Artemas wanted the glove, if his hands were cold, then Daniel would give it. And, William. You know as well as I do that Artemas slipped out now and then when his keepers were off their guard or sleeping. Last Easter—"

"You're saying Artemas killed Nan Emory? Is that it?"

"You'd rather believe it was Daniel, would you? William, you are the most pumpkinheaded—"

"That I may be! But I don't have your reason for believing otherwise, do I?"

Hannah stood up, furious, holding her cloak around her. "I believe otherwise because these two deaths are connected somehow, and because it has been made far too easy to put Josselyn's stamp on both of them. There are too many pieces and they do not make a pattern."

"And it's too damn easy to blame a rape and murder on a dead madman! And if he *did* kill the Emory woman, then who killed him, and why?"

Hannah shrugged. "It would hardly suit a magistrate with ambitions to politics if his brother were discovered to have committed rape and murder, and blaming it on Daniel would be a convenient means of ridding himself of a troublesome partner. You heard him. They often disagreed."

"Nonsense. The man was grieving. Heartbroken. He didn't want his brother dead."

"I have no doubt of that. But it doesn't mean he didn't want him out of the way. And it doesn't mean he didn't kill him."

She turned and walked toward where Flash was tied, as Dodger spread a coverlet over the madman's body.

"Where you going, Mistress?" Will called after her.

"To get the truth out of Daniel," she said.

"Well you'll pay hell doing it," he said quietly. "I went looking for him early this morning, before ever we found Artemas. That's what's put the wind up Tom Whitechurch and Phinney and your cousin, Johnnie. Dan's up and gone, Hannah. Into the Outward, sometime last night or early morning. And now I must hunt him down."

TWENTY-NINE

PIECING THE EVIDENCE:
On the Nature of Damage

During the war I had a privateer. Sweet little cutter. The *Freedom*, she was called. In that ship, with the men I had, I could run any British blockade ever mounted. But that their guns were bigger, I'd be sailing her yet. They took us prisoner, to the Hulks. Prison ships, you know, anchored off Long Island. Eleven hundred men in the belly of a ship built to hold no more than four hundred. Triple the number of rats. Lice. And flies. I could never understand how the flies found us, there on the water, deep in the hold. But they did.

When we got food, it was half the Royal ration, and made up of what was too spoilt for their men to eat. Rancid bacon. Bread crawling thick with maggots. Our hair grew and our beards reached to our knees. Nothing but salt water to wash in, and it crusts the skin, you know. You turn a different color from a man. When you look at yourself, a man is nothing like what you see.

Madness. Half of us was mad, a hundred different ways. And smallpox. I pulled a nail from the hull and scratched some pus from a sick man and put it in my arm, a lot of us did. I didn't die. Got sick, but didn't die.

I remember the first day I came aboard, me and my boys. "Welcome to Hell," they said, and laughed and threw us down the ladder. I remember all those eyes below, mad eyes, and no light. No air. They sent a party ashore one time for work duty, and one of them brought back a clump of grass under his shirt. He took it around the men who were left and we all touched it. It was a holy thing to us. Grass. Some of us had been four or five years in Hell by then. Never a step that didn't rock under us. We kissed the grass and the roots of the grass and the mud that clung on the roots, and we dreamed we could feel the wind on us. We dreamed the smell of plowed ground. We dreamed the stars.

We paid a price. I'm not sure, now, what it was for. Things don't seem much better, so far as I can tell.

I lived through it. But I still see with their eyes now, sometimes. Dead eyes.

—*Captain Jonas Munday, the sloop* Belle Fleur

Before the war, my sister Elizabeth fell in love with an English officer, Frederick Parfitt, his name was. I think he was a leftenant, or some such. He was a nice boy, stationed in the garrison at Saratoga, and we lived a little way out of the town. Had a nice little farm, did my father, and we all lived there together. My brothers—I had three brothers. My father and mother. Two other sisters, and me. My older brothers and my father was Patriots, see, and they went off to fight. My mother told Elizabeth she ought to go into Saratoga, to stay with one of the officers' wives who was friend to her.

For the neighbors knew she would marry a British officer in the spring, and they spat on her once when we went out of church.

Once the men was gone, it was nothing but my little brother Joseph, and he was but nine years old. They came in the night. Dragged everything we had into the yard.

My loom, with the coverlet still set in it, half woven. My chest of quilts. My mother's dresser with all her pewter in it, and her six blue and white plates. The beds. My father's clothes.

They burned everything, there in the yard, and made us watch.

They burned the house. They drove the horses out and took the cow away and burned the barn.

And then they took Elizabeth. They cut off her hair and burnt it in front of her face, and my brother Joe fought with them and they hit him with the butts of their guns. I can still smell that hair, burning.

They stripped Elizabeth naked and painted her body with tar, and cut open one of our feather beds and rolled her in the feathers. She had a sweet body, my Elizabeth. Small-breasted and sweet and young.

And then they put her up on a wagon and hitched a horse to the wagon and drove it into Saratoga, where Frederick Parfitt could see her.

They hung a sign around her neck. KING GEORGE'S WHORE.

Elizabeth broke apart that night. She was mad, after. Women have borne worse and lived, but no two human things are made the same, and she could not live, after.

And I and my mother, who had only watched, we had no comfort. They had been friends, you see, them that did it. People we trusted. Women, as many as men. They didn't even bother to wear masks.

I think what they did was worse than killing. They took away the last thing there was to hold to. That if you were kind and decent and worked hard and honest, your life would have kind and decent and honest things in it. That you would get what you deserved in this life.

I don't believe that anymore. It's all lies. My husband's a decent enough man. But I don't love him. What's the use of it? I have no hope of anything. I have eight children, and another coming. Sometimes I smile or laugh, but the part of me that laughs is somebody else. I can see her face, watching me, and she doesn't look like anyone I know.

Mostly, I just go on. I'm not sure it's better than being dead. Elizabeth killed herself, swallowing lye.

I just go on.

—*Mrs. Ann Whitney, wife of Sylvanus Whitney,*
   bookseller and printer, The Rufford-Wybrow News-Letter

My Will struck an officer. British officer. In Boston, when he was a boy. They had him taken and whipped. Three hundred lashes. Three hundred. You can count the scars. Every one is hate, and every one is shame. He's a loving man. But something in him fears me and puts me away from him. The scars are a wall and I cannot climb it. He feels himself a different race from me. I have never been whipped, or even struck. Will would never strike me.

But even when he comes to me to do a husband's office in my bed, he never takes off his shirt, lest he should make me afraid of him. You can feel the ridges and the scars even through the cloth, you know. Dear God.

I have no wish to be disloyal. You know I love him dearly. But he has a hard time of it with women. There have been others, I know, though he loves nobody but me. He thinks he is too horrible, and it makes him end before he begins, most times. And when he fails, he rages. Because he cannot give me sons, you see. It pains him.

I am glad he has Mr. Dodger, for he looks to William's comfort when I cannot.

That's why we have no children, Will and I. Only scars.

—*Mrs. Hetty Quaid, wife of Will Quaid, Constable*

At Lamb's Inn

Hannah did not go directly home from the Siwalls'. Instead, she went to Lamb's Inn and allowed herself to be thoroughly fussed over by her cousin, the Markhams' oldest daughter, Dolly.

"Fell off a horse?" cried the innkeeper's wife incredulously. "Off old Flash? Why, you could ride her into Sunday meeting and she'd sit down on a bench and sing a hymn!"

Dolly, who was ten years older, was plump and greying, and the gown she had lent her cousin hung like a sack on Hannah. But it was clean and decent, and Hannah felt somewhat restored. She dabbed a cloth into cold water and laid it on her eye.

"That needs a comfrey poultice when you get home, my girl," said Dolly. "And don't you be like the physician who won't bother to look after healing himself! Does it hurt?"

"Yes. How could it not?"

"Good. Teach you not to take a mob of drunken fools lightly in future. Fell off a horse, indeed! Old Dodger come in here not a quarter hour before you did, told me the news and went paddling off again after William like the Devil's dogs was chasing him."

This last came from Josh. He was still wheezing mightily, but seemed happy enough to be back behind his bar again, white-aproned and busy polishing the rank of pewter mugs on their scrubbed-pine shelves. Now he stopped his work, poured brandy into a wooden cup, and brought it to the fireside, where Hannah had been installed on the settle with her feet on the hob and Dolly hovering by her side.

Josh plunged the poker into the brandy and it flamed up. He smothered the flame and handed her the cup of smoking liquid.

"You drink that up, chick. Don't burn your mouth, now."

He took the end place on the settle and for a while the three were silent, watching the fire. Gradually, Hannah felt an arm slip around her shoulders from either side, felt Josh's hand lock into Dolly's and the locked hands lie warm against the back of her own neck. Aside from themselves, the place was empty—a strange occurrence, for it was nearing suppertime, and Dolly's cooking was almost as famous as Josh's fiddling. But tonight they were all glad enough to be alone, to have only the primal comforts of fire and friends.

"We've heard about Daniel," said Josh at last. "Looks bad for him. Damn fool thing to do, that was. Taking off into the Outward, I mean."

"And Artie Siwall," said Dolly. "Can't help feeling it's something of a mercy to him, poor soul. Still, life's life. Who knows but he sometimes took some joy of the world, even as he was?"

"Sheriff Tapp's expected before the morning. When he comes, they'll all go after Daniel, the mob of them, not just Will. God send they don't hang him on the spot." The innkeeper shook his head and frowned. "Idlers like Phinney Rugg and broke farmers like Tom Whitechurch and a few young hotheads like Jonathan to rile them up. They was drinking half the morning down at the Red Bush, chewing over the death of Mistress Emory, and when they heard about poor old Artie, off they goes wild-eyed, and God only knows where they be at by now. Home, likely, cleaning the muskets they've left rusting since Yorktown."

Hannah found herself leaning against the steady weight of her cousin-in-law, for Josh Lamb was a man made to lean on. "Joshua?" she said.

"Chick?" he said softly.

"Did you know Nan Emory?"

"He didn't, my love, but I did," Dolly told her.

"Did you know she had a lover after her husband left her? She was almost two months with child."

"Ah. So that's how it was. Some man didn't want a living bastard, maybe."

Again they were all quiet. The clock in its polished black walnut case ticked steadily in the corner. It began to be cold in the big inn parlor, ice thickening across the windowpanes. It was growing rapidly dark, but none of them rose to light a candle.

"Daniel?" said Joshua into the firelit dark. "You think he was her lover, learned of the child, and killed her to stop it being known? If she threatened him—"

"I think he would not have minded who knew it. If he loved her," Hannah said.

Josh Lamb was implacable. True or not, the possibility had to be faced. "And if he took her without love?"

To this, Hannah did not reply. Instead she asked another question. "Where did she come from, Dolly? And how could she have gotten that letter written, the one Will found on the table? She couldn't even write her name."

"Well, that's easy enough," said Josh. "Travelin' letter writer. Dick Covington—you know Dick? Peddles a stock of ribbons, pins, buttons, pots and kettles? Writes a fine hand, too, a half-penny a foolscap sheet, if you haven't the skill of it. And knows how to keep his mouth shut afterward, too, I'll say that for Dick. He was in town last week, comes once a month, rain or shine or hailstones. Went off down to Wybrow on Thursday, but he was in here, at that table over there, writing letters for a dozen of my regulars. Wasn't he, Dolly? Spent a day writing at Edes's, too, and another day up at the Forge. Old Dick's got the rheumatics, so he mostly sticks where there's a good fire."

"Did you see Anthea with him? Did she come in last week?"

"Not that I know. Dolly, my love?"

Dolly shook her head. "I never saw sight of her."

"No reason she couldn't have gone to him elsewhere. Or maybe he come to her door peddling his gewgaws, and she had him in," suggested Joshua.

"Maybe," said his wife doubtfully. "Only—"

"Only what?"

"Well—I don't think she would. Do you, Hannah? I didn't read the letter, to be sure, but Will was here and told us what was in it, and—"

"You don't think Nan was the kind to tell such things to a man and a stranger?"

"Well, now. Would you?"

Hannah was silent. Dolly was right, of course. But Anthea had told no woman, either, or at least none that they knew of.

There was only the letter. A strange letter.

With respect to your honor, it had said to Dunny. But what honor had he? *Your affectionate wife, Nan.* Though she had carried another man's child inside her a good two months before the mysterious rapes. She had taken her lover almost as soon as Dunstan Emory left her, if she had waited even that long. And from what Hannah had so far heard, there had been precious little that could have been called affection between them.

It was not a thing she herself could have written to James, she knew that. And there was something else. The word itself.

Rape.

It was a word men used, in courts and questionings. But when it had happened to you, not once but three times in three nights, was it a word you would go calmly to another man—unknown, kindly, but still a man—and pay him to write down at your dictation?

Hannah remembered the weight of Thomas Whitechurch's body upon her in the snow of the riverbank. If it had not ended— If he had raped her, and others after him, gone wild as they were then— Would she have thought to use so formal a word, or any word at all?

She would have hurt, blindly, as much without words as Jennet was. She would have dragged herself away and howled such a howl that the world would buckle from it, and that Anthea had done.

And she would have killed them. It might take time, years even. But she would have found a way to destroy them one by one. Disgrace them if she might. Kill them, surely.

But write a formal letter? *Lest I should charge a rape against them all.*

It went against the grain. Legalistic. Formal. Much too rational. It was a word for lawyers, for Ham Siwall and old Napier, the solicitor.

"Nan never told you, Dolly, where they lived before they came to Rufford?" she asked her cousin. "The name of the village, I mean?"

"I'm not sure she ever said a name, love. Some place in New York, I think. Maybe New Jersey." Dolly suddenly got up from the settle and began to light candles, not just one but many, as though the room were full of customers. The light blazed up and made the darkness at the edges of the room deeper, angrier.

"Tell me what you know," said Hannah. "Please."

"It's little enough," Dolly replied. Josh drew her down beside him again. "Except she wept terrible. I've told you that. And she harmed herself."

"Harmed herself? How, my girl?" asked Joshua.

"When her boy was badly and I sat with him, she gave me supper. We had a candle on the table, for it grew late and dark. She put her hand into the flame."

"Go on."

"I screamed and pulled the candle away. She smiled. Just sat there, smiling. Her hand was burned, I could smell the burnt flesh. 'I can do anything,' she said. 'For the dead may do as they please.'"

Hannah had the strange sensation that she had heard the words before, though her mind was too tired and confused to remember where or when or in what context. But it was as though she expected what Dolly said next.

"She would cut off her hair and burn it in the fire. Cut great locks of it, short, so close against her head you could see the scalp underneath."

"Was she mad, then?" asked Joshua.

"She might have been. Who knows what is mad and what isn't? She had been somewhere terrible, that's all I know. And some part of her never came back."

"Like Artie Siwall."

"Yes. Maybe she would have been all right, in time. Maybe he would, too."

"Could *he* have been her lover, do you think?" Hannah asked him softly. "Slipped out of his cage and gone to her, and then done the same the night he killed her?"

"Artie?" Josh puzzled for a moment. "He was a handsome fellow once, and he liked the ladies. Manners like a duke, he had. I always liked Captain Siwall. Served under him, you know."

"At Webb's Ford?" The words were out before Hannah realized it.

Josh stared at her. "How do you know about that?"

"Why? Is there a reason I should not?"

"No, 'course not. Only—"

"Only those who were there made a covenant never to speak of it. Isn't that so?"

"No. Yes. I don't know!" Joshua got up and began to pace back and forth before the fire. "Look, I'll tell you what I do know. I wasn't there. I took a fistful of grapeshot in my thigh at Saratoga, and I wasn't with them, I was in the company hospital at Point Clarence. All I know is, it was bad. Artie was clean out of his head, after, much worse than lately. Dolly's brother, your cousin Eben, was dead. Dan's fingers was chopped off and he had a musket ball in his back. But you know that." Josh looked away.

"And Will? He was there, wasn't he?"

"He was. It was Will brought the others back. Him and that little fellow, Dodger. Where *he* come from I never knew, but he stuck to Will afterwards, and he's sticking yet. Flighty as a bird. Will would do most anything for Dodger, and the other way round."

"But surely there were rumors? Stories about what happened?"

"Some said ambush. Tories waiting, wanting revenge after Burgoyne surrendered. Some said massacre. Men wild with the fighting. It takes some men that way. There was stories. People lined up and shot. Women. Young ones. Some said worse than shot."

"By British troops, you mean? For revenge?"

Josh stopped his pacing. "No, my love. Our troops. Artemas. Daniel. William. Eben." He looked up at her. "And me, if I'd been there."

"But you weren't, my old dear," said Dolly, and went to him and took his hands.

"Thank God," he told her softly. "But don't glory in it. For if I'd been with them, I would have done no better than the rest."

Before she left Lamb's Inn, there was one more question Hannah had to ask, and she asked it as she pulled on her Uncle Henry's old boots by the kitchen fire.

"Dolly, when you stayed the night at Mrs. Emory's, did you notice a pocket? Fine grey linen with a worked design of briar roses and oak leaves?"

Her cousin looked up from the huge earthenware bowl of gingerbread batter to which she was adding a drop more rose water. "Pocket? Why, to be sure, she wore a pocket. Most of us wears them round the house." She glanced down at her own red-and-white-check pocket; it peeped out of the slit in the seam of her gown left for the purpose, and was now liberally dusted with flour like the rest of her. "But a fine worked piece? Wouldn't wear that, except maybe for Sundays. And she didn't go to Meeting." Dolly shook her head and pushed her straying hair under her cap with a molasses-colored finger, then stuck the finger in her mouth. "No, my dear. I never saw it. Now, are you sure you won't tarry to supper and have a slice of this gingerbread to take home to Jennet?"

THIRTY-ONE

PIECING THE LARGER BLOCKS

Hannah declined the chance of a meal with her favorite cousin. Josh saddled Flash for her, and she went home to Two Mills by the road she and Daniel had taken the previous night, the road that led to the Falls. Below her she could see lights moving on the High Road, men with torches, on foot and on horseback. They were no longer a mob, only a half dozen knots of men talking, shouting, keeping themselves worked up.

They could feel a power in themselves they were otherwise denied. Against taxes, against money, against the rises and falls of political theories and the rights of men to property, against their own despair—against all these things they were nothing. But against one man they were strong, omnipotent, and they did not care for his innocence or his lack of it. They wanted something to hate and to punish, and they meant to punish Daniel.

But they would have to find him first. He knew the woods better than most of them, the lumbering roads and the old Indian trails and the isolated cabins in cleared patches where he had sold settlers' lands for the Bristol Company. And he had friends there, too, trappers and loggers wintered into snug cabins, and even Indians, who had their winter earth lodges here and there. Wherever Daniel was, he would be safe enough tonight. Hannah could think no farther.

When she entered the workroom through the back door, she found there the last person she wanted to see—Jonathan Markham. By this hour—it was past seven o'clock—they usually abandoned the work on loom and quilting frame and carried small jobs, like carding or spinning on the linen wheel, into the kitchen to save fuel and candles. But tonight Aunt Julia had kept the fire going and there were several thick tallow candles sending their smoke and their scent of burning fat and bayberries toward the heavy ceiling beams.

Two Mills was the warmest house in Rufford because Henry Markham had built it solid, with an insulating wall of unfired bricks between the outer frame and the whitewashed wooden panels that lined the rooms themselves. When a fire burned at Two Mills, no ice formed in the fire bucket in the corner as it did at Phinney Rugg's.

Still, it was an indulgence to keep a fire in two sitting rooms at once. Hannah concluded that Aunt Julia, who had a way of getting wind of things before anybody else in town, had heard about the mob and about Daniel's flight. The fire was meant to be a comfort to her favorite niece. ·

But Jonathan's presence threatened to spoil it all.

"You're late home," he said gruffly. "I was concerned."

"Indeed? I stayed by your sister Dolly's fire while she made me decent."

She took off her cloak, and he could not help smiling at the oversized sack of a gown. But then his sharp, handsome features gathered into a frown again. "I'm sorry for what happened to you," he said. But even his apology was resentful. "I never meant it to go so far. But what I said was true."

"That I am Daniel's whore?" Now it was she who smiled. "I wonder when you think I should have time for it? And where would I be likely to invite my lord and master to bed me, sir? Here? In my aunt's back chamber? Or perhaps you think I tumble with him in the snow?"

"I never said you were a whore! Only—"

"You thought it. Others said it. And would have acted on the conviction, but for William Quaid."

"I stopped them. It was *me* fired that first shot, not Will."

"You wish to be thanked? Thank you."

"Why do you hate me?" He walked quickly across the room to where she stood, a little out of the circle of light thrown by the candles. Behind them, the quilt called Hearts and Bones, still in its frame, made a puzzle of squares and triangles, its interlocking pattern dissolved in shadow.

"Oh, Johnnie. I don't hate you," she told him softly. "When you were only a little older than Jennet, I used to take you skating. I taught you to play bowls, and sing 'My Love Comes Riding,' and make wreaths out of wild grapevines, and when Eben went to the war and you were wailing, it was me who made you stop. You remember?"

"I do, indeed. You got me down in the pumpkin field and tickled the mortal life out of me. After that, I had a fearful crush on you, Cousin."

He flashed her a twelve-year-old's grin.

But it didn't last long. Beyond, in the kitchen, the others were laughing and among the voices was the shrill giggle of Sally, Jonathan's new wife, and the babbling of little Peter, now five months old.

"When she isn't laughing, she's wailing over something," he grumbled.

"Sally will find the center of herself and gain her balance if she doesn't have to try so hard to make you love her." Hannah laughed. "She may even stop treating Peter like the Prince of Wales." She took a step closer to Jonathan. "At least be kind to her, Johnnie. To most people, that is all love is."

"But not to you." The boy let his fingertips drift across her battered temple. She barely felt the touch. "And not to Josselyn, neither. I guess that's why he steams me so. He's like you, and no matter how I try, I'm not."

"But you don't really believe he's killed two people. Do you?"

He kicked, boylike, at the carefully scrubbed and sanded floor. "No. I suppose not."

"And you'll speak for him to the others? You saw what they came near doing to me this afternoon. If they go after him into the Outward and find him there alone, they'll kill him. And I will not live to watch that."

He stared at her in silence for a time. "You mean that?"

"Yes."

"Then I'll do what I can to stop it," he said at last. "On my word, I will."

"Thank you. Johnnie, did you know Nan Emory at all?"

"Her? The bitch was mad as an owl, Hannah. No, I didn't know her, and I didn't want to. And I was home with Sally the night she was murdered, if that's what you're going to say next. Go in the kitchen and ask her if you don't believe me."

"I do believe you."

"But I know one thing." Jonathan walked a pace or two, then turned to face her. "I know Dunny Emory's no more dead than I am."

"How? What do you mean?"

"I used to drink with him and Jem Siwall sometimes. The three of us spent a night or two, rounding."

Hannah laughed again. "Sharing Molly Bacon between you?"

Jonathan glanced at her and grinned. "You are the damnedest woman, Hannah. But you're right. We took her to that old shack up past Seabrook's once or twice. She takes some pleasure in it and she keeps her mouth shut, for a shilling or two. Anyway. Dunny gets drunk as a lord one night last summer, says he's going off for good before the snow flies."

"Not just on a surveying trip?"

"No. Says he's got it worked out. Siwall will pay him for a job, pay in advance if he keeps his mouth shut, that's what he told us."

"What job? Did he describe it?"

Jonathan nodded. "Too drunk not to. There's this section of high timber, big section, west of here, he says. Three thousand acres. Worth a fortune in the shipping trade, good boards are in short supply in Europe. But Josselyn won't sell it for lots, won't cut it over. I don't know why, but he won't. Father says Siwall would cut every tree in Maine by next week if he could, and leave a desert behind him, he's that greedy."

"Because Siwall needs money. His housekeeper couldn't even pay me fifteen pence for some bread I sold her."

"So anyway, he hires old Dunny to survey that section and mark it for cutting behind Josselyn's back. Keep two sets of survey maps."

"And give Daniel one that shows that section still uncut."

"And the other to the cutting crew. By the time Josselyn finds out they're cutting his precious section, it's too late. Trees are down. Siwall's sold the logging rights and took the money. Sold a few homesteads in the cut-over lands. He's got all the money himself, and none of it gone to his partner nor the Bristol Company, either. It's easy enough to keep a second set of books, and put the money in one of the Boston banks, or even in London or Paris. And when Dan gets wind of it, Siwall just blames Dunny, says he sold it himself and cut out quick. By that time, of course, Dunny's long gone."

"No wonder he was willing to pay for Emory's silence in advance."

"Oh, he's a sharper, is Siwall. But not sharp enough. Because Dunny got the cash bribe, all in good silver, no scrip. Then he pretended to mount up a survey trip. You know he hired four fellows from Boston?"

"Yes."

"Well, there wasn't no fellows. He told Siwall and Josselyn he was meeting his party on the post road up from Salcombe, at Beale's Coach Inn. Well, he never had nobody to meet. Said he couldn't bear it with Nan anymore. Said she was crazy. Burned herself with candles. Tore out her hair. Cut herself."

Hannah sat down heavily on the settle. Memory washed over her, crushing her like a great wave, taking breath and vision for a moment.

"You all right, Hannah? What's the matter with you?"

"Nothing. Nothing, Johnnie. Go on."

"Well, that's about all, I guess. Except he took the money and lit out, and no survey made. Siwall was a fool to trust him. I wouldn't be surprised if Dunny's in Boston by this time, living like the King of France."

"The swindler swindled, then."

It explained why the Siwalls were so short of cash this season. And Daniel had had nothing at all to do with the disappearance of Dunstan Emory. It was Jennet's three thousand acres that were to have bought his escape from a tormented wife.

"So you think Dunny never went into the Outward at all?" said Hannah.

"Would you? He used to talk all the time about Boston. Philadelphia. New York City. He'd had enough of Maine, and more than enough of Anthea. It was her that wanted to come up here, not Dunny. Said he only came to keep her quiet, she's that mad. Was that mad, I mean."

"Why here, I wonder? Did he ever tell you whereabouts he'd met her? They came from somewhere in New York, didn't they?"

Jonathan nodded. "Oh, aye. Wide place in the road between Saratoga and Fort Edward. Think he called it Webb's Ford."

Sally and Jonathan stayed the night in the house, and Hannah was grateful enough for their presence, as it kept Julia busy until she was weary enough to fall into her own bed. Hannah went off to the chamber she shared with Jennet, changed Dolly's borrowed field tent of a dress for a plain skirt and bodice of her own, and waited in the dark until the others were settled and the only sound she could hear was her daughter's steady breathing from beyond the drawn curtains of the bed.

She pulled them back and climbed the two steps of the bed-stool up to the high feather mattress. Arthur the cat lay curled against Jennet's back, and Hannah picked him up all in a tail-to-nose package and put him in his basket on the floor. He grumbled softly in the language of cats, and tucked himself tighter against the chill.

But the minute his warmth was gone from her, Jennet was wide awake, peering out from between the bed-curtains.

"All right, come out, then," said Hannah to the two wide eyes gleaming in the darkness. She lit a candle, then another and another, until the room was a cone of brightness at its center, and dancing with shadows in every corner.

Still Jennet hung back. Hannah went close, and the child put her arms about her mother's neck and locked her small legs round Hannah's waist. She never used the steps to climb down. When Hannah was not there to lift her out of bed, she jumped down with a soft thud, light-footed as Arthur.

Hannah swung Jennet lightly to the floor, put on her the soft sheepskin slippers Uncle Henry had made for a Christmas gift, and wrapped her in a knitted rug. Then she went to the small linen chest under the slanted ceiling, opened it and took out the painted basswood box that contained her copy of *King Lear*; the pages of her journal, carefully tied together with some of the bolt of blue ribbon she'd bought for Jennet's hair; a bottle of reddish-brown ink she had made from barberries; and her turkey-feather quills.

She pulled her maple rocker—the only thing she had kept from her years with James Trevor—close to the table where the candles burned, and took Jennet on her lap. The small arms went instantly around Hannah's neck again, the soft, fine, reddish hair brushing against her cheek.

"Jenny, my love," Hannah said softly. "Can you hear me? Can you?"

Jennet's breathing quickened, and she lifted her head from Hannah's shoulder and wriggled closer to the table.

"I want you to know your name," Hannah said.

Jennet gave no indication that she could hear. She picked up one of the quills and almost knocked over the inkwell with it.

"Here." Hannah tore off a blank page from the end of the journal, took another of the quills, and dipped it in the ink. "Jennet," she said, and printed out the name on the page. "Jennet," she said again, and pointed to the word, then to the little girl.

She dipped the pen again, printed the name again, pointed again.

Jennet only stared.

Hopeless.

Hannah drew a deep breath of regret, tore off another page, and began to write, her own close, somewhat nervous handwriting. When she had finished, she stopped to blot what she had written, and it was only then that she saw Jennet.

The child had dipped a quill into the inkwell and was trying to write with it, tracing with grim determination over the letter *J* at the beginning of her name on the page. She held the quill so tight in her fist that she had broken its spine, and the ink had blotted and left the quill too dry to make any further mark. But Jennet continued her work, tracing over and over the letters one at a time.

Hannah could hardly breathe. She took another sheet of paper, and Jennet dipped the pen again. This time, Hannah showed her how to tap the excess ink from it. The line was still wobbly and Jennet pushed so hard she nearly tore the paper. But there it was at last. An almost recognizable letter *J*.

She looked up at Hannah, her head on one side, the telltale lock of reddish hair falling across her eyes. She put down the pen, closed her fists tight, and, wrists crossed just as Daniel had shown her, Jennet made the Indian sign that meant "friend."

Her hands were shaking so badly she could hardly manage to make fists of them. But Hannah made the sign in return.

"Friend," she said softly.

Better than mother. Friend.

When Jennet was back in bed and asleep at last, Hannah looked around for a hiding place, somewhere to leave the letter she had written for her aunt and uncle. She folded the closely-written sheet and put it into her volume of Shakespeare, then put book and writing box back in the linen chest where they belonged. It was, she supposed, a sort of will and testament, though she had nothing to leave but the knowledge of herself.

For a moment she stood beside the bed-curtains, listening to Jennet's sweet breathing, steady and slow. Arthur the cat, seeing no reason to sleep in exile, unrolled himself from the basket, leaped lightly up onto the bed between the curtains, and settled comfortably into his usual position against the small of the little girl's back.

Hannah reached in and stroked him softly, waiting until she could feel his rumbling purr. Then, feeling less alone, she took up the single candle she had left burning, went on tiptoe back down to the workroom and stirred up the fire. It was too dark to make fine stitches, but it was the rational pattern of the slowly forming quilt that had brought her there, the need to square the pieces of Anthea Emory's puzzle, to shuffle their colors on a clean surface and pick out the pattern if she could.

Triangle. Dunny, Anthea, Anthea's lover—or whoever it was that had left his child in her belly.

Triangle. Daniel, Hamilton Siwall, Dunny Emory.

Square. The place called Webb's Ford.

A triangle within the square. Daniel, Artemas Siwall, Will Quaid.

A circle set upon the triangle. Anthea. Anthea, who came from Webb's Ford.

And Dodger. What part of the pattern was Cornelius Dodger, who had appeared after Webb's Ford and never gone away?

More questions stitched themselves upon the shapes:

Why did Artemas Siwall die barely an hour after he spoke to Hannah about Webb's Ford?

If Daniel didn't kill him, how did the killer come by Daniel's sword?

Where did Anthea get the embroidered pocket that must have been the work of Charlotte Josselyn, the pocket that tied her to Daniel?

Why did Anthea take her children to Mrs. Dowell days before her letter said she feared she might be killed?

Why did she punish her own body as though she were guilty of some crime?

Why did she choose to come to Rufford, though her husband disliked it and she had no family living here?

Why did the man who killed her wring the neck of the bird and leave the dog to howl on the doorstep?

And there were two remaining questions, though Hannah Trevor did not put them into words as she had done the rest.

Why does no amount of reasonable thought explain Anthea Emory?

Why do I know nothing substantial, nothing reasonable about her, and yet seem to know her as well as I know myself?

Hannah banked the workroom fire again and lit a lantern from her candle. She carried it into the spring room that adjoined the back of the house, and carefully packed a loaf of bread, a quarter of one of Julia's remaining cheeses, some butter, sugar, and tea, and a flitch of bacon into a heavy leather sack. Next, she went into the kitchen and took two leather-and-horn bottles of Jamaica rum from the shelf, adding them to the sack, along with a wooden cup and a kitchen knife. Then she put on two extra pairs of thick stockings and a pair of her uncle's breeches that were just nicely dried on the rack over the workroom hearth, and pulled her petticoats and skirts down over them.

When she was ready, she padded in stockinged feet along the cold floors and up the stair again, candle in hand, to the room where Jennet was sleeping. Hannah parted the heavy bed-curtains and let the apogee of the circle of light fall onto the pillows. The child slept as before, on her side with the cat against her, her small knees tucked up and one hand tangled in her hair.

Hannah pulled the feather-comfort closer around Jennet, shut the curtains again, and padded downstairs, taking with her two woollen quilts from the linen chest in the hall.

Out in the mudroom, she rolled the quilts and tied them firmly into a saddle-roll, then dragged her feet into Henry's old boots, put on her cloak and a heavy knitted hood and mittens, and stepped out into the cold darkness, laden with her bundles. The snow had still not begun, but the clouds were very heavy.

"Flash, my old dear," she whispered to the sleepy little mare as she scooped oats into a nosebag. The stable was warm with the breaths of the oxen and the milk cow, and Flash herself had settled for the night against a heap of straw, a tangled collection of barn cats sound asleep around her. "I'm sorry, old Flash," said

Hannah, and the horse got to her feet with no more than a soft nicker—already waiting, by long habit, for the saddle and bridle. "We're going for a long, cold ride, my honey-love."

Hannah did not see the pair of eyes that watched her, nor the slight, shivering figure that slipped out of the house and stood watching until she disappeared along the narrow track into the black wilderness of trees that was the Outward.

Jennet, who was thought to be dumb.

THIRTY-TWO

WEAPONS

Daniel Josselyn had only one reason for riding into the Outward, and that was to find Dunstan Emory.

He had been reluctant to leave Charlotte with no more protection than the servants and good blustering John English, who would surely come in an emergency. But there was, it seemed to him, only one person who might have some idea who had really killed Anthea Emory, and that was her missing husband. And so far as he knew—for Jonathan Markham would have split and sewn himself up again with rawhide before he told Daniel what Hannah now knew—Dunny had disappeared into the wilderness and not come out.

They might have had some word of him, Daniel hoped, at the winter logging camp upriver. They called it Fort Holland, and fur trappers and far-ranging peddlers who traded with the tribes and with isolated settlers stopped there often and brought news. Besides, there was a small encampment of Indians at the Fort, and they made it their business to be aware of anyone who came or went within the territories that, in their minds, were still their own.

Daniel rose before dawn to make his preparations. He burdened himself with few provisions, taking only some smoked venison and cheese and two cannikins of brandy, with care that Mrs. Twig did not catch him in the larder. There was no need for much else, and he was ready for his journey long before the household woke.

In the matter of weapons, he was more particular. In addition to the French-made carbine he now used only for hunting, he provided himself with a pistol, silver-mounted and made by Hawkins of London—a gift from his father when he received his commission in the Dragoons. With his light officer's sword, and a wilderness knife and ax for firewood, it was all he needed— aside from ammunition and a flint and steel.

For the most part, he shunned even the sight of weapons. He kept them in a locked chest in the tack room of the stable unless he had to go into the Outward to supervise the cutting or to see one of the farmers whose notes were held by the Bristol Company.

It was only his grandfather's hunting sword he kept in plain sight, hanging over the library mantel, crossed upon its worked-leather scabbard. Even Charlotte found the antique weapon beautiful, and Daniel kept the blade polished and the swan's-head pommel shining. It was no good for real fighting, even a boy knew that. It could stab, but only at things that couldn't stab back.

But for Daniel, it was more than a blade. It was memory and ceremony and a life he would never know again.

Sometimes, he regretted it. Foolish as the county balls and fox hunts and presentations at court had always seemed to him, loutish squires and red-faced peers and potbellied princes were not all that England had to offer. At its best it had an elegance and a quiet that calmed the soul, a subtlety that challenged the mind, and a sense, not merely of power but of inherited responsibility—to learning, to courage, to whatever the future might become. The blade could cut, but you must keep it clean.

That responsibility, Daniel had brought with him—perhaps too much of it. But he missed the elegance and the subtlety in spite of himself. And he missed his grandfather.

Old Lord Bensbridge had been a quiet, bookish man who never

hunted at all, so far as anyone knew. Had he not inherited a title, he might have been a poor scholar or a country parson.

But he wore the sword whenever Parliament met, and it was, to him, a symbol of duty and pride and the defense of what is just. To a more jaded generation, the words sounded like an old man's babbling; abstractions were all very well, but you could neither spend them like sterling nor mount them like a horse or a woman. Daniel's father and his brother Geoffrey exchanged patronizing looks and yawned when the old gentleman began one of his elaborate proofs of the Nature of Justice or the Existence of God.

But it did not change what old Lord Robert believed, nor alter his behavior. Even after he retired to his books and resigned his lands and title to his son, the sword still hung above his library mantel.

When the letter from America reached him, telling him of Daniel's espousal of the Patriot cause, Lord Robert lay dying of a cough that grew suddenly worse after years of pesky hacking. The last thing he did was to send Daniel his sword.

"I rejoice," he wrote, "that you, at least, have learned the nature of Truth. You will pay its price, and it will be a dear one. I send you a good blade, with my advice. If you have enemies, use it to strike them. If it breaks, use the two ends, one in either hand. If you have too little money and must live, then sell it. It will bring a good price. And if you have too much of the life it buys you, and must die before it breaks you, then fall on the blade like a Roman. But be proud of the fall. It is all any of us has, in the end."

When his horse was ready-packed and he himself was dressed for the journey in his long, heavy riding coat, Daniel went into the library and took down the sword from over the mantel. It was very sharp. He ran his index finger along the blade and it cut him so cleanly that he was not even aware of it until he saw the tiny hairline of blood on his fingertip.

He slipped the sword back into its scabbard and laid it across his desk. If there were no truth? If he did not find Dunstan Emory, if Marcus Tapp trumped up such a case against him that they locked him away for the rest of his life, like old mad Dickie Bunch, or if they put a rope around his neck?

And what if they did not? If Will managed to find out who had killed the girl?

Even then, life would only go on as it had been. Would get no better and would grow daily—not worse, no. But more blank. Each day draining away an inch of possibility. Until colors were no longer different from each other. Until the wind made no sound in the trees and the mill turned without hearing and the face in the window glass was not your own nor anyone's you could remember. Until, if you lived, you moved through a wilderness deeper than any forest. The blank indifference of loss.

What were Daniel's choices? He could let them hang him, of course. He could disappear into the woods, perhaps find a life of some kind there, as the trappers and woodsmen did, leaving their civilized wives behind them and taking dark-eyed Indian brides who gave them a gaggle of squalling babies.

Or he might take his grandfather's way out. The third choice. *Be proud of the fall. It is all any of us has.*

Daniel glanced out the window at Two Mills across the river. There was no sign of Hannah, nor of his daughter, Jennet. He should have liked to see her again before he went away.

He hesitated for a moment, and once again he looked down at his hands as though they were separate from him and moved with a will of their own.

They hovered for an instant over the grip of the sword. Then they clenched themselves into fists and left it, lying in plain sight upon the desk.

When Daniel went upstairs to say good-bye to Charlotte, he found her already dressed, sitting in her chair as though she were waiting for him. Her embroidery work lay ignored upon the bed, and Abby, the maid, was nowhere to be seen.

"You're up very early," he told her, and bent to kiss the top of her head.

"I find it hard to sleep after daylight," she replied. She touched the wool of his coat. "Where are you going, sir?" she said.

"Oh, not far. Only riding a ways into the woods, as far as the Fort," he said, smoothing her sleeve with his hand. Charlotte complained of the cold, but she always wore silk. He took his hand away. "I don't intend a long stay, only a day or two, perhaps, while the weather holds. The logs at Markham's mill are badly jammed, and if there's a thaw, we'll have the Devil to pay. I'll get a few of the men from the winter camp to ride down and help shift them."

Charlotte did not contradict him and did not say that she knew anything of the accusation. "Should you go now, my dear?" she said. "The clouds look like more snow, Twig tells me." She paused. "I would not have you lost."

Of course she knows they will hunt me, he thought. He felt suddenly proud of her. Perhaps he had never loved her, but just then he might still have learned.

He sat down on the low footstool in front of her, his own face looking slightly up to meet her eyes. "Charlotte," he said quietly. "I'm sorry."

"I am sure you need not be, Daniel," she replied.

Charlotte laid her hands on his shoulders. So light, they were. So light.

His eyes closed. "We're a ruin, Mouse," he said. "I never meant it so."

"Let us go home, Daniel," she cried suddenly. "Please! I would be better at home, I know it!"

"Back to England?"

"Yes! Not London, oh, I don't mean London. But perhaps Salisbury or Portsmouth, or somewhere in Cornwall, even, some small place where—"

"Where nobody knows I'm a traitor and a rebel?"

"All right, then! Yes!"

He could not tell her no. If she believed the old life would heal her, then who could tell, perhaps she was right. But she had begged him before, and he had had physicians up from Boston to see her. They said the long voyage would kill her. Even to travel by coach to Salcombe or Wybrow was more than she could safely risk. Besides, there was a military warrant in England for his arrest. But he could not tell her no and leave her with nothing, with no escape to dream of at all.

"Perhaps, Mouse," he said. "When this is over."

"Now!" she said. "You can go by the post road to Boston now, and sail ahead of me and find a place, and in the spring, when John can find a crew for the *Lark*, then I shall follow you."

So that was it. She wanted him to bolt and run, and not look back.

"Charlotte," he told her. "I won't go alone."

She stood up and walked a few steps. He did not go to her, though he could see that standing on her own was difficult.

"Then take Mrs. Trevor," she said.

Daniel did not answer, only stepped to her and kissed her cheek, then turned and left the room. He went straight to the stables and did not stop again in the house, not even in his library.

If he had, he would have found that his grandfather's hunting sword had already gone.

THIRTY-THREE

On the Trace

It was the sort of day that is most beautiful in the woods in winter, the light pure and sunless, the frozen ribbon of the river the color of unpolished pewter, the sounds of birds and small creatures magnified, magical, and every bare twig and dead frond of fern bearded with frost from two days of fog now ended by the advancing cold. It would fall below zero before it ended, thought Daniel. But first, it would snow.

The road into the woods soon narrowed to an old Indian trail they called the Trace. It was barely wide enough for a horse to pass between the ice-laden spruce boughs that wove together overhead. The track ran parallel to the Manitac River, no longer navigable here, and at random intervals paths had been hacked through the trees, narrowing as they branched away from the main trail. These led to settlers' cabins, and from some of them, where the trees had been felled and small fields cleared for the plow, thin columns of smoke could be seen.

Some of the settlers, finding the going too hard or the poverty too grinding or the taxes impossible to meet, had pulled out or been thrown out, and in the farther cabins, otherwise abandoned, small bands of wild men lived, robbing trappers of their winter caches, smuggling rum and whisky down from Canada, sometimes preying on the settlers or even the villages themselves, dressed and painted like Indians or with sacks pulled over their heads and eyeholes cut in them.

It was possible that Dunstan Emory had been killed by these bandits. It was equally possible that he had become one of them himself.

But in either case, they would have heard of him at Fort Holland.

It lay a good day's journey upriver from the town. There was no stockade, only a large snug cabin of upright logs faced with milled boards and with a double chimney that served both of its rooms, one a kitchen and the other lined with beds for the wintering crew. Men who had wives and families mostly chose to spend the winter in the towns and pick up work there as they could. But many woodsmen were loners, and if they had wives, they were Manitawan or Mohawk or Iroquois girls and were less than welcome in the towns.

Such men spent their winters hereabouts, trapping mink and fox and beaver for Daniel and selling their skins on shares in spring. Some ranged up into Canada to trap where the pickings were free, and came back when their supplies ran low or they wished to visit their Indian wives in the half dozen mud-and-wattle lodges that squatted in the cabin yard or dug themselves partway into the hillside.

Daniel Josselyn reached Fort Holland at dusk, about the time Hannah was sitting with her Cousin Dolly and Joshua Lamb in the bar-parlor of Lamb's Inn. He knew nothing of Artemas Siwall's death, nor of the weapon that had killed him.

A handful of black-haired, blue-eyed half-breed children, dogs yapping madly at their heels, came to crowd around his horse as he dismounted, laughing and chattering and begging. They spoke too many tongues for any man to learn, but the sign language he had tried to teach Jennet, sometimes mixed with a French-Canadian patois, communicated well enough with most of them.

Daniel turned a half-grown boy to face him, and smiled. "Where is Uncle?" he said with his hands. "Oncle Pierre?"

The boy's face reminded him of Jonathan Markham's; perhaps the young are all resentful, whatever their race.

The half-breed boy said nothing, with his hands or without them. He only turned and led the way inside the cabin, and Daniel followed him.

A big fellow of past fifty sat by the kitchen hearth smoking a clay pipe and reading a Bible of prodigious size, the sort most often used in the pulpit. Pieter Soutendieck—known variously as Piet, Uncle Peter, and Oncle Pierre—was head of the Bristol Company's lumbering crew, part commanding general, part woodsman, part indulgent Father Confessor. He could cook and sew as well as most women, or cure a deer skin and brain-tan it till it was as soft as fine satin. Besides English and his native Dutch, he spoke a half-dozen Indian tongues and read French and even Latin, though where he had learned it and why, he could never be induced to say.

Piet was barrel-chested and bandy-legged, dressed in a fringed white hunter's shirt that reached below the knees of his leather breeches. The shirt was belted with a soft buckskin strip worked in the fine embroidery done by the Indian women, with dyed quills and colored beads in a pattern not unlike the crewelwork Charlotte fancied.

"So, Dah-niel!" roared the Dutchman, and stood up, spilling his tame raccoon from his lap. There was always some small animal with Uncle Peter, riding his broad shoulder or clinging with needle claws to his jerkin or hidden in his commodious pockets. "Come to the fire, my friend, and thaw your arse. Good you come before night. Tonight, it snows, you watch! Or maybe tomorrow. Susan! Louisa! Bring His Lordship some food and fatten him up, he's thin like a stick!"

There were three or four Indian women moving about the room, and one of them went to a huge pot, spooned a thick stew into a shallow wooden bowl and handed it to Daniel. He smiled at her, dipped his fingers into the food and put them in his mouth, then smiled again.

She waited until this gesture was completed, then returned to her friends with no sign of acknowledgement. Her face betrayed no emotion. It was not a thing you gave away to strangers, especially to white men. Daniel wondered whether this was so because she was an Indian, but he suspected it was because she was a woman. Would Hannah or even Charlotte in such a place have been much different?

Daniel knew the Indian woman vaguely. She was one of Piet's four wives.

The big Dutchman lighted a pipe for Daniel, scooped up the fidgeting raccoon, and settled down again. Uncle Piet was round-faced and balding, with a fringe of corn-yellow hair brushed smooth, then cut off blunt at his shoulders and worn loose. His eyes were bright blue and the upper lids drooped slightly, so that he seemed always to be considering the world and finding it absurd and mildly amusing. He had a bulbous nose, thick lips, and a chin scraped religiously clean each morning. Piet Soutendieck had been in the woods, it was said, longer than the trees had. Nothing came in or out of them that he did not know about.

"I brought you some brandy," said Daniel, working at the bowl of stew. Part of the meat was venison, but Piet didn't mind what else he threw in—muskrat, badger, now and then wolf. He drew the line at skunk, at least he said so.

"*Ja,*" he said, "brandy's good. Only I rather have beer." Piet studied his employer. "I hear Dah-niel is in the lion's den. They going to stretch your neck, my friend?"

Josselyn set down the bowl. "How did you know?"

"One of Uncle Peter's nephews went to town yesterday. Jean Le Petit was in Hobart's store to buy tobacco, he hears the talk. How that rich bastard Dan Josselyn puts his high-and-mighty pecker into poor little crazy girlies and then breaks their necks." He looked out from under the sleepy eyelids. "Either you didn't do it or they couldn't prove you did. I see they got no chains on you yet."

Josselyn set down the bowl. "Not yet. Soon, maybe."

"They got to catch you first. In these woods, in the winter? After the snow, even your tracks will be gone." He laughed and picked the raccoon off the back of his neck.

"I didn't kill the girl. I won't run, Piet."

The Dutchman put the little animal on his lap and began to stroke it with his thick fingers. "Maybe you're a dumb-ass, then, my friend. If they hang a dumb-ass, it's just as well. The world don't need no more of us."

"Since you know everything, you probably know what I came to ask you."

"Probably. Jean says the girlie's man came in the woods and never came out."

"Last November. Late in the month."

"Goddamn fool."

"He was a surveyor for us. I tried to talk him out of it, but he wouldn't be stopped. I sent Georges and Francis Dumaines to look for him in December and again in that thaw we had after the New Year. They said there was no sign of him or the others who went with him."

"There's been no surveying party in the woods this winter, I can tell you that. But there was something."

Piet lighted a lantern, then wrapped himself in a long striped blanket coat and led the way out into the compound, parting the children and dogs in front of him like the Red Sea. At the edge of the yard, near the palisade of sharpened saplings, there was a tightly-built shed where furs were stored until they were taken downriver to be sold to buyers who came up on Munday's sloop each spring.

There was a heavy lock on the door. Piet dug under his shirt, pulled out a bunch of keys, fumbled for the right one, and finally swung the door wide.

"Over here," he said, and threaded his way past stacks of cured

mink, fox and marten pelts to the back of the shed. "There." He
held up the lantern so Daniel could see.

It was a plain wood coffin, roughly made from what boards
were handy. Though the shed was well-chinked because of the
valuable furs, and was proof against mice and small animals, they
had weighted the lid of the coffin with rocks, as if what lay inside
might come out and do them harm.

But the man inside was past harming anyone. Piet lifted away
the rocks and pried up the lid to let Daniel see.

There was not much left of Dunstan Emory, but more than
you would have supposed. The deep cold had come soon enough
to freeze his body and even now some of the flesh remained on
his bones. His face was nearly gone; animals recognize no distinc-
tion between one kind of food and another, and—the ultimate
rationalists—they eat whatever is good for them.

They begin with the eyes, the lips, the meat of the cheeks,
because it is tender. But they often leave the ears and nose, the
cartilaginous parts, until nothing else is left.

It was the ears that made Daniel certain. No two ears are ever
quite alike, and even on the same head they seldom match exactly. In Dunny Emory's case, this was certainly true. Not only
was one of his ears observably larger than the other, with a longer
lobe, but the right ear was set perhaps an inch higher on the
head than the left, so that he looked as though his face sloped
downhill toward his left shoulder.

It was impossible not to notice. Daniel remembered, and knew
him at once.

"Black Ezra found him, no more than a week ago. Not far in,
by some rocks near where that fool Dysart and his woman lived."
(The Dysart family had been evicted during the late summer, the
land bought by the Siwalls, like most of the rest.) Piet frowned.
"You think it's him? Your surveyor, the husband?"

"I'm sure of it." Daniel explained his reasons.

The Dutchman nodded and sucked at his pipe. "We will bury
him decent when the ground thaws. You see how he died, Your
Lordship? The neck broke."

"I see."

"And the arm. It was the same with the girlie?"

"Yes." Daniel put down the lid of the coffin and slammed it tight with his fist. "I don't understand it, Piet. You said he was found in rocky ground. Was there anything with him? His survey- ing equipment? There would have been a tripod, a lens—"

"Is the stuff worth money?"

"Only to another surveyor."

"Then I doubt Black Ezra kept it for himself. He'd steal your teeth if you sleep with your mouth open, but he's no fool. Maybe when the snow melts, we find it, though."

"If he was going in to survey, what the devil was he doing up near Dysart's, anyway? He should've been headed north and west, not south. I don't understand."

"They will say you killed him, too," said Piet quietly. "You know that, don't you, Lordship? Your constable and your sheriff and your fine friends. They will say you killed him so you could fuck his little wife."

The Dutchman used the word as a simple Anglo-Saxon verb, neither impolite nor profane. It meant something very specific, and he had no delusion that he had originated the procedure it defined. It suited the case, that was all.

"Even if you prove it to them, they will hang you anyway, because they have to hang somebody. And if it's you, it ain't them."

Daniel didn't answer, just walked out into the compound, tak- ing deep breaths of the cold air. Inside the shed, he could see the Dutchman kneeling beside Dunstan Emory's makeshift coffin, and hear the booming voice at prayer.

He stayed the night at Piet's fire, but he was already packed and mounted when the Dutchman came sailing out to say his good-byes next morning. The sleepy blue eyes looked up at Dan- iel sadly.

"So. You are going back anyway, Lordship?"

"Yes."

"Why? Your honor? Or your sick wife?"

"Both."

"Stay here. I get you another wife. Two wives, not sick. I got four wives here and another in Amsterdam. I'm an old sinner. But I'm alive." He laughed softly. " 'O Dah-niel, servant of the living God, is thy God able to deliver thee from lions?' "

Josselyn did not answer, only nudged his horse's sides and rode out of the compound, back the way he had come.

THIRTY-FOUR

Snow

It began as a few dry flakes that seemed nothing to worry about. In less than a quarter hour it was falling fast.

After that, the wind came. It lashed the icy branches on either side of the Trace, snapping some, turning all of them into weapons that could knock you off your horse in no time and leave you floundering and blind, buckling against the stinging wall that was snow.

After the wind, the drifts.

After the drifts, the dark.

Above all, under all, in the heart and bone of the snow, the loneness. That you were no longer where the eye of God could reach you. That the universe consumed itself and the daylight would not come back.

That no matter if you walked or did not walk, breathed or did not breathe, thought or could not think, the snow had eaten you like grief and you were already dead.

He saw her as something blocking the path and thought she was a tree blown across the Trace or some animal, a deer perhaps, or a moose, stumbled into a drift and floundering.

Then he heard the horse screaming above the wind. He

shouted, but the wind ate his words and he could not even hear himself, thought he had imagined shouting.

It was a risk to dismount, but he did it, up to his hips in snow, his long coat trailing after him, dragging the wild-eyed sorrel by the halter. If you stopped, if you let the horse stop, if you got stuck in a drift and lay there, if a branch struck you unconscious, then you would be dead. Even if you kept moving, your nose and your fingers and toes could freeze.

He had lost the pistol fighting his way out of a drift, and the carbine, too, was gone, slipped away and eaten by the snow. He had only his sword, now, and the knife and ax, but how could you cut the snow and the wind?

There was snow in his eyes and his mouth. He was drowning in snow. He was sailing, and he had gone overboard, and there was no water, only an ocean that was snow.

Then he heard the other horse scream again. He kept walking, swimming, dragging the reins. Why he did so, Daniel did not know. Surely it was not courage. He did not hope to rescue anything, even himself.

Only he wanted to touch something that was still living.

At last he tripped over her. She hit out, connected with his chest. He could not let go of the reins. He would have to mount again before long or his feet would freeze. He tied the reins to his arm and pulled at her body with the other. The big sorrel bucked, screaming, scenting the other horse nearby, dragging at the reins until Daniel thought it would dislocate his arm.

He had no idea who she was, it was too dark to see faces. She was heavily wrapped, her eyes barely showing, her clothes so thickly crusted with snow that he could hardly feel her body under them, could not be sure if her shape was man or woman. But it did not matter. She was a thing still living, like himself.

He couldn't lift her, couldn't even try to catch her horse and free it from the drift. Somehow he got her onto her feet and she gave a cry, wild, not of pain or even fear, but of a kind of furious anger, as though she would like to kill him for touching her. It was the snow she was fighting. He let her go free.

She could stand alone, but at the first drift, she fell again. There was a break in the trees and he thought he knew where they might be. It was a trail to one of the abandoned settlers' houses, a dugout built into a hillside.

He couldn't get her up again. She couldn't walk anymore. She put both her hands around his wrist and let him drag her as he dragged the sorrel, Yeoman, and he seemed to feel his own body separating between them, being split apart and torn, deep, deep inside himself.

He thought he might die now, suddenly, in the snow, with the horse on one side of him and the woman on the other. He thought his heart might stop beating and find some kind of rest, and his mind might stop thinking and lie quietly, while the animals feasted on his eyes as they had on Dunstan Emory's. He did not grudge them. Let them use him as they could.

He did not see the front wall of the dugout; he crashed into it, and knew he was not yet dead, because he felt pain.

The back of the place was dug into the hill, the front built of rough logs. There was a door, still tight, and a window, the glass not yet broken. And there was a stone chimney.

He kicked at the wall in front of him and the ice that had frozen the door shut gave way. Daniel dragged the woman—still only a shape that seemed to grow out of his wrist—as far into the house as he could and tried to drop her, but her hands were locked tight and would not let him go. He pried them away, the horse still tied to his other arm, then went back into the snow and looked around for shelter for his sorrel. There was no stable, but there was a lean-to next to the dugout, open on one side but roofed with saplings and sound enough.

He led Yeoman inside and tethered him, and by the time he had taken off the saddle and provisions, another dark shape loomed up beside the lean-to. The woman's horse had kicked free of the drifts and followed the path they had left, more afraid of being alone than of the snow and wind. He murmured to the little mare and leaned against her, calming her, calming himself. He was unaccountably glad to see her. Even crusted with snow as she was, he seemed to know her, and she him. He led her into the shelter and put his face against her nose, his arms around her neck. Perhaps he lost consciousness, but only for a few moments. When he returned to life, he was sobbing, the mare's breath warm on his cheek. He took his arms from her neck and unpacked her, fed her, fed Yeoman.

The storm had not lessened. Daniel was not sure when his toes and his face had stopped aching, or when his hands had become blunt clubs. He slung the saddle sacks from both horses over his shoulder and began to feel his way along the wall of the lean-to, then the house wall, until at last he found the door. The woman had not shut it, and snow had blown in and almost covered her with the drift of it. He fell inside, clawing it away from her, his mouth and eyes full of snow, his body partly tangled with her own.

He could not move at first, could not even kick the door shut. He felt her breathing, like the mare, and it seemed strange to him that they two were warm when everything else was cold. Her body moved under him, trying to free itself.

"I'm hurting you," he said, but neither of them could possibly have understood what language he was speaking. It was no language anyone had ever heard, for it was the snow that spoke.

His body was like a puppet with cut strings. The intention to move, to lift his arms and legs, resulted in nothing, as though his brain had no more connection to him. It lived somewhere in the cold dark room that smelled of earth. Perhaps he had fallen into his grave.

The woman moved under him and at last he fell away from her onto the floor. It seemed a long fall. He lay on his back, and it was then that he realized his toes and fingers had begun to ache again, and his face was throbbing. Daniel sat up and dragged the baggage off his shoulder, then kicked the door shut with his foot.

The woman lay still beside him. He brushed the last of the drifted snow from her and fumbled for her hands, then pulled off her heavy wool mittens, which were frozen stiff. The fingers were not frozen and he began to chafe them as hard as he could, rolling them between his palms, breathing on them. He found her head and pulled off her knitted hood, but he could not see her. He let his own fingers move across her face. She was very cold; he could not tell how cold, whether there was frostbite or not.

He dragged himself to his knees and felt in the pocket of his greatcoat for the small box with his flint and steel. You kept the things you could not survive without in your coat pockets, in case your horse was lost. In the other pocket was a silver flask with some of the brandy, and he opened it, took a sip, then lifted the woman's head and found her mouth and made her drink.

Some settler's wife, he thought, caught out alone, gone to help a sick neighbor or barter for meal or sugar. This late in winter, supplies were always short.

Her hair was soaked and it stuck to her head. It was short, fitting her head like a cap. Perhaps he was wrong, perhaps it was a boy, not a woman after all. Daniel let his hand drift down her body until he felt the swelling of her breasts under the wet cloak and the gown.

Short hair. Only one woman he knew cut her hair so short.

"Hannah," he said. But that, too, was another language.

A Night in the Grave

He was lucky. The fire caught quickly, after only twenty minutes' laborious fumbling with the flint and steel. He had crawled to the wall where he knew the fireplace must be. There was no dry wood. He had felt the leg of a trestle table in his crawl; he found his ax and hacked at the table. He splintered the braces for kindling. The top was made of two huge split logs and would last, with luck, until the storm let up and he could find more fuel outside and dry it.

Once there was fire, there was light. It was faint and strange and never stopped moving, and it made the darkness—which was most of the room and most of the world—seem liquid, like the bottom of the sea.

Hannah made a few small, indistinguishable sounds when he carried her to the fire and took off her cloak and her boots. He could almost have laughed when he encountered Uncle Henry's breeches underneath, but there was no time to waste on laughter.

He took the breeches off her, and her stockings, too, and the sodden petticoats and skirt, touching her as little as he could while he worked. Her shift was dry enough, and he left her that. The quilts in her saddle roll had had the leather bag of provisions on top of them, and were still fairly dry. He lifted her and wrapped her in one of them, then put the second over her.

The worst edge of cold was gone from the room now. There were no candles, but the firelight was enough. Daniel sat down on a small bench and pulled his own boots off, and the wet stockings. There was a bedplace against one wall, a platform strung with ropes and laid with a cornhusk mattress that crackled when he lay down on it. Someone had left an old rag coverlet behind, thick-woven but faded and worn, and he pulled it over him gratefully, and slept.

It was still dark when he woke, and he did not know if he had slept hours or only minutes. Hannah was sitting on the low bench by the fire, still wrapped in the quilts, her body rocking back and forth so that the bench tipped off the floor, then went back down with a tapping sound, as though the wind were banging a door.

That was what had wakened him, but she had not meant to do so. Daniel got up from the bed and went to her and sat cross-legged on the floor in front of her. "Shall I make you some tea? I think there's a kettle, and I can get some snow and melt it. You have tea in your bag."

"No."

"You ought to eat something."

"No."

"Let me feel your toes," he said, and slipped his hand inside the quilt. "Can you feel that?"

"Yes."

"And your face? Your nose and ears?"

"I know what frostbite is. Let me alone."

His hand still lay on her foot and he could feel her body shaking. He remembered it. It was the way she cried, with no sound nor any tears, but shaking like earthquake or the end of the world.

"Why are you angry at me?" he said softly.

"Because," she said. "You touched me. When I was so cold, and I was helpless. You touched me."

"I had to, you know I did. I took no advantage. If I hadn't—"

"Because you touched me and I couldn't even feel it and it went all to waste!" She made a soft moaning sound, her breath catching in her throat.

He said nothing, only bent so low over her feet that his body was almost doubled. She saw him lift the corner of the quilt to his face, saw him hide himself in it, as he had hidden against the neck of the mare.

She slipped down from the bench, then, and held him as she might have held Jennet, rocking him back and forth, letting him rock her.

Daniel wondered afterwards whether they would have come together even if they had never known one another until that hour, if they had been strangers who had survived some other kind of death in one another's company, and were slightly mad. After a battle, he had known men stumble together that way and stroke each other's bodies, make love to each other, not knowing even so much as names, scarcely caring for faces or whether their limbs were still whole or whether they bled from wounds.

If Hannah had wounds, they were invisible in the firelight. She led him carefully, as though he were a boy, an innocent, and he let her. Waited quietly while she undressed him. Lay watching the shape of her as she moved, pale in the liquid darkness. She seemed to drift down onto him like a leaf on water, her thin shift moved by the draft, and he felt his sex rise to meet her. She knelt above him and took both his hands in her own and leaned over him, her breasts brushing his face for a moment.

Then he felt her body arch backward suddenly, as though she would break, and the same cry came from her that he had heard in the woods, half-angry, wild. As he watched her, Daniel felt alone, as though she had left him again, or had never been there. Whatever enemy she was fighting, it had no more to do with him than the snow had, or the wind and dark.

Then she relaxed onto him and pulled the quilts over them. She was with him now, and gentle. He had imagined the rest.

"Put your arms around me," he told her. "Hold on to me. I need to feel your arms."

"Yes," she said.

They lay locked together for a long time before he spoke. "Why did you come?" he said. "You had no business. Why the hell did you come?"

"After we talked at the Falls, I found I couldn't do without you anymore."

"You could have found another man."

"It was not the man I couldn't spare. It was you. The thing in you that is myself. The thing I threw away." She lay quiet. "I thought I might find a way to die in this place."

"Hannah—"

"Why didn't you let me?" Her voice was clear and calm and as much without expression as the face of Piet's Indian wife. "I wanted to die in the snow, where it was clean."

"No, Hannah, you don't want to—"

"I do. I want to die and lie still and not think anymore."

"Why?"

"I can't ever have you. I can't ever keep you. I'd lose myself and I *won't* lose myself, not even for you. There's nothing between but desert. I want to die." She got up and padded to where her cloak was drying, wrapped it around her and came back to sit on the bed. "Tell me," she said after a long while. "In the spirit of scientific observation. How do I compare with your other whore? The one in Boston?"

Daniel closed his eyes. "She's not so bold as you, and has not so much imagination. But that is because she does not love me and need not keep proving it to herself. She can spare me some tenderness, since she risks nothing. She need not defeat me every time."

"And I *do* love you?"

He got up, holding the quilt around him. "Yes."

"Need is not love. You're very sure of me."

"Oh yes. I know you better than you know yourself."

"You presume a great deal, sir, after eight years."

"I presume nothing. Have I gotten drunk in Edes's tavern and told lewd stories about you?"

"No."

"Have I taken liberties with you? Have I caught you in your uncle's barn and rolled you in the straw?"

"No, sir, but—"

"Have I made any claims upon you or upon our daughter?"

"*My* daughter!"

"And mine! That is my crime, isn't it, Hannah? I've made the terrible mistake of existing. I'm a fact you can't get around. I'm not James Trevor, no matter how much you punish me as if I were."

He found a stool and sat opposite. He could see her battered eye in the firelight, and the way her mouth was split and swollen. It was more than the punishment she had taken in the storm. Someone had hit her, beaten her. He took her hands and held them, and she did as Jennet had done, let her fingers travel over the stumps of his two ruined ones, now gloveless and cold. She bent her head over his hand and kissed his palm and then his fingers.

"It was a lie that I never loved you," she said. "That I wanted nothing but the child from you and used you to get it. That was all a lie."

"I know."

"But I lied to myself, too, not only to you, my heart. Only I didn't want to love any man, ever again. I thought I could not bear it."

"I'm not James. I told you that."

"No. I knew it from the first. But I was still afraid." She looked at him. "I am afraid now."

"Tell me about James. What he did to you."

"I can't. I can't do that."

He stood up again, stirred the fire, laid on more of the wood. "Then I see no hope for us," he said at last.

"He wasted me!" she cried suddenly. It was a shrill sound, unlike her voice, and seemed to come from the fire that blazed up. "Twenty years of my life that will never come back! Now I'm old and my children are dead and I can't ever have them back and I can't ever have myself back! Those years that—"

Daniel sat beside her on the bench, but he knew he must not touch her now, or she would shatter like glass. "Tell me about your children," he said softly. "Tell me how they died."

He could feel her shaking. She clasped her hands together in her lap and he could see she was pulling hard, one hand pulling at the other, fighting herself.

"I married as silly girls marry. I was eighteen, bold and stubborn. He was handsome, full of dreams. Fine talk. What did it mean? I didn't understand that it would never be over, that even now that he's dead, I could never be myself again. Something is gone in me, Daniel. He took it away from me."

She drew a breath and it came out of her in short, cruel stabs. He put his arm behind her and she leaned on it as though it were a rock or a tree.

"Did you never love him?" he said.

"I think so, once. I can hardly remember."

"Did he hurt you? Beat you?"

"No. He wouldn't have been brave enough for that. He was only stupid. Selfish and stupid. When I realized it, he knew. He read my thoughts and began to hate me then, and punish me. In small ways at first, but . . ."

She leaned nearer to him. "I had three children in four years," she said. "Susanna. Martha. Benjamin."

The last name made Daniel close his eyes. Pressed for a name to carve on the tombstone, he had named the mangled parts of his own dead son Benjamin.

"We were living in Boston. It was a bad summer, hot. There was fever in the town. Diphtheria. Children were dying. My own were still healthy. I wanted to bring them here, to my aunt, to stay the summer with them in Maine until the fever burnt itself out. He— James— He wouldn't let me go. I begged. On my knees. Me." Again she paused. Her voice was a low monotone. "He said he would not leave his business. He wanted his wife with him. Not me. Not Hannah. His wife. His cherrywood desk.

His snuffbox. His hunting dog. His wife. I must stay and the children must stay. I wasn't to go to my aunt's alone."

"But you did go."

"What else could I do? My children—" She paused again. He wondered if she were crying, brushed his hand across her face. No tears. "I borrowed a cart," she said, "and hitched the horse to it. I took the children and their things. Clothes. Susanna's dolls. A wooden horse on wheels for Benjamin. My sewing. He— James sent— A constable after us. He said it was against the law for me to go without my husband's permission. That I was a runaway and James could bring charges against me. I told the constable why I was going. He said it didn't matter. That it was the law."

Daniel knew it was true. "Did James really take you to court?" he said softly.

"No. He killed my children."

"The fever?"

"Yes. He dragged us back. I tried three more times to get away from him, to take them away. Why didn't I kill him? I let them die. I killed my children."

"Hannah! You're not responsible!"

"I have saved other women's children. They are alive because of me! Me! But my own— They died burning up with fever and choking. I couldn't help them. I want to die, Daniel. Please let me die."

She began to sob at last, and the tears that came from her were torn away like splinters of her bones. He didn't try to hold her until she sat hunched and spent beside him. Then he put both arms around her.

"What a cruel bastard God must be," she said softly, letting Daniel brush her hair with his fingertips. "To let me save other women's children, and none of my own. Or yours." She pulled him to her and held him and they sat very still.

"It was James who brought them back to Boston, my love," he said at last. "It wasn't God. Tell me the rest, now. How you came here to Maine."

Her voice was low and he strained to hear it. "When the War

came, James was afraid. They began to break into the houses of Loyalists in Boston. Sometimes they kidnapped the men and boys and they disappeared. We didn't know where. They never came back. There were terrible stories about what they did with them. James was afraid. One day he came to me. 'We'll go to your aunt now,' he said. 'It will be safe for me in Maine, at least for a while.'"

Hannah broke away from him and got up, moving into a corner of the dugout where the firelight could not find her. Daniel did not follow her where she had gone.

"He wouldn't save my children, but now he would save himself. I picked up an ax from the firebox. 'If you try to make me go with you,' I said, 'I will split your head apart.' He knew it was true. So he went by himself."

"He left you alone there in Boston, with a war starting?"

"He hated me, I told you so. I didn't want him. I didn't want anybody." A silence. "I had no neighbors. They were afraid to be kind to a Tory's wife. It was dark in the house. If you lighted candles, they saw them and punished you for having light. I had some food in the house, but James took most of it. When it was gone, no one would sell me more. Once or twice I stole bread. I went into a shop once. No one would look at me. I went home and sat in the house and waited for dark. I don't know how long. Days, weeks. Once I got a knife and cut off my hair. It was long, then, down to my waist. I chopped at it with the knife and some of it I pulled out with my hands. When it was dark again, I cut myself. Across my wrists."

Her body slid down the rough wall until she sat in the corner. Daniel went to her, lifted her, carried her back to the fire. He had known, of course, about the cutting. He had seen the scars. But he had made up some story for himself—that she had been hurt in some accident, tangled in wires, caught in brambles.

Had he wanted to believe that the wars of women are not so bitter as the wars of men?

"But you did not die," he said.

"No. Even at that, I was clumsy. I didn't die. I don't know how long I waited. My uncle had grown worried when I did not follow James. He and Jonathan came for me, and Eben. The rest you know."

"That you came here and lived with James again until he ran away north. You had no choice. I understand that now."

"Only one choice. I would have no more children for him to waste." She turned to face him. "Daniel, you do not know me, how cruel I am. I found myself with child by him twice after we came here. Each time, as soon as I was certain, I killed it in my body."

Another delusion, he thought. He knew such things were common enough, but he would not have believed her capable. Why not? he wondered. Of what was Hannah Trevor not capable?

"You say you killed it, but the child was not born, it was barely conceived. It had no life. No real being." He wanted to make her innocent. But she would not have it.

"It was alive. I felt it there. I killed it. There are plants. Certain funguses that are almost always effective. It was a better death than my three children had. Better than your own son's." She studied his face. "There," she said. "Now I have ended it. Now you cannot love me. I see it in your face. You can go back to Charlotte now, and visit your mistress in Boston twice a year and be happy. I'm a monster. I kill unborn children. I wonder, do you think I wanted your son to die, and rejoiced when Clinch mangled him?"

He took her by the shoulders. "I have killed. Am I a monster?"

"That was war."

"And yours with James was not? You fought for the life of my boy. I watched you do it. You kept my wife alive, you were kind to her. You had no reason, but you were."

"I had Jennet. She was my reason."

Daniel looked at her steadily. "I have found nothing in the world to love but you," he said. "It changes nothing. It creates no obligations. It gives me nothing but pain. No hope of happiness. We are no fairy tale. It's there, that's all. Without it, I might as well live without skin."

"Even if you were free, and there were no Charlotte," said

Hannah suddenly, "I would not marry you, Daniel. Though I love you dearly, I want no more marriages."

"Oh, I have had enough of marriage, too." He smiled. "That surprises you, doesn't it? You should see the look on your face." He reached out a hand to her. "Come to bed now."

"And if I find myself with another child of yours? There is no James to blame it on this time."

"Then you will do what you have always done," he said softly. "You'll do what seems best to Hannah Trevor. Come to bed."

They lay for a long time without touching, side by side on the crackling old mattress, the quilts and the rug and their own wraps heaped on top of them. The wind had gone down outside, but the snow was still falling and it was as though it fell upon their grave, as though they came to each other in their single grave, the smell of the cold, dank earth heavy around them in the little dugout room.

There was no battle this time. No cry of despair or of triumph. When he touched her, she scarcely felt his fingertips stroke her, and when he entered her it was so slowly, with such delicate deliberation that she seemed to reach up and find him and grow her body around him.

At his climax he was still as the snow outside and he made her so, both of them motionless, waiting. With a soft moan her belly arched under him, and she felt his seed pulse softly into her. It came with the exquisite release of breathing in sweet sleep, of rising to the surface and breaking through into the air and filling the lungs, and afterward, she felt clean, unused. Free.

"We could go away somewhere," he said, slipping away and lying beside her, his hand tangled in her short curls. "There is always the West."

People who wanted to leave their outworn lives took the wilderness roads, or followed the rivers into the wilds of Pennsylvania, Ohio, Tennessee.

"We couldn't," she said.

"I suppose not. Only I want to do something for you. Please. Something."

"You just *did* something. And I did as much for you. Say thank you."

"Thank you. Very much."

"That pays all debts. Still. There *is* something else you can do for me," she told him.

"I suppose Madam wants her cup of tea now?"

"No," said Hannah. "I want you to tell me about the massacre at Webb's Ford and how you came to know Anthea Emory."

PIECING THE EVIDENCE:

Records of the Courts-Martial of the Continental Army Concerning the Incident at Webb's Ford, Proceeding of the Prosecutor-General Against: Artemas Charles Siwall, Captain; Daniel Edmund Josselyn, Lieutenant; William Ephraim Quaid, Sergeant; Thomas Jakes, Frederick Patterson, Richard Rawlings, Privates

Testimony of Lieutenant Josselyn
Major Edward Lambrick, Prosecutor

PROSECUTION: State your name and rank.

JOSSELYN: Sir! Daniel Edmund Josselyn, Lieutenant, Upper Massachusetts Militia, sir!

P: Am I correct in informing this court, Lieutenant, that you were formerly an officer in the British Army, serving under General Burgoyne?

J: That is correct, sir.

P: With what rank, sir?

J: Sir! The rank of captain, sir.

P: You may be at ease, Lieutenant.

J: Sir.

P: What brought about your decision to desert from the British Army?

J: Sir. I did not desert, sir. I resigned.

P: Very well. You left your post. Under what circumstances?

J: After the invasion of Canada and the siege of Montreal, I was— I had reached the end of my agreed tour of duty. I chose to resign my commission.

P: You were a career officer. Why did you do so?

J: Because I chose to.

P: That is not a sufficient answer. You may have left a letter of resignation behind you, but you rode out of Burgoyne's camp during the night and presented yourself a week later at the camp of the Upper Massachusetts Militia, as a volunteer, later requesting assignment to the company in which you are now a Lieutenant. Is that not correct?

J: Yes, sir. Substantially so.

P: The company of some twenty or more men who had come from the vicinity of Rufford, Upper Massachusetts, sometimes known as Maine. Why did you seek out those particular men?

J: I did not seek the men especially. It was a place I had seen when I went to join my regiment in Canada. It seemed . . . worth fighting for.

P: No other reason?

J: That is all, sir.

P: I submit to you that you had advance information of General Burgoyne's movements. That after his army left Canada, he sent you into the American camp as a spy.

J: No, sir.

P: I say you are a spy, sir.

J: Major Lambrick, sir. I was detailed to the transport of Loyalist prisoners and their wives. They could, I believe, be expected to be privy to very little useful knowledge of the military plans of their captors.

P: Well. Hem. Very well, then. Let that pass. We shall proceed. Did you fight with the Rufford company at the battle of Saratoga?

J: Yes, sir. I did.

P: In the first line of horse deployed against Burgoyne's right flank, I believe?

J: Yes, sir.

P: You received a commendation for that action, did you not?

J: I did. So did several of the others. Lieutenant Markham. Sergeant Quaid.

P: Captain Siwall was to have been promoted Major, I believe, on the strength of his command against Burgoyne?

J: Yes, sir, that is what we were told. Before Webb's Ford.

P: Ah. Were you deployed there? Were you sent as a wood-gathering party, for instance? Or on a foraging mission?

J: When we—the regular troops, I mean, sir—were told of Burgoyne's surrender, we were issued double ration of rum and the camp went wild. Some—I may say many—became separated from their regiments. In general, our only order was to pursue the rear guard of the British troops and capture as many as we could. Many had deserted Burgoyne before the actual surrender, hoping to find other regiments and attach themselves elsewhere.

P: Capture or kill? That is what you were told?

J: That is correct, sir. When the British units began to desert in numbers, Lieutenant Markham was seconded to a scouting party. He was a skillful woodsman, and they needed trackers. He left camp early in the morning, some two days before Burgoyne's surrender was announced.

P: Tell us what you yourself did on that night, Lieutenant Josselyn, after the surrender of Burgoyne.

J: I . . . drank.

P: To excess?

J: Fairly heavily. I had just heard by letter of the death of my father. I believe I read aloud the Service for the Burial of the Dead in my prayer book.

P: The Church of England Prayer Book?

J: It is called the Book of Common Prayer, sir. Yes.

P: And you drank as you prayed?

J: Yes. Somebody had found a barrel of rum and a cartload of ripe apples from some farmer's orchard, and a barrel of cider. It was October, fine weather. Some girls had come into camp from one of the villages. Willing girls. There was dancing. We roasted the apples. The men were laughing. It was a long time since they had been able to forget where they were, what they had . . . become.

P: And you, Lieutenant? Did you forget?

J: As I have said, Major Lambrick. I drank. It was only in part effective.

P: And in the morning?

J: It was still dark when I woke. Cold. Most of the others were asleep—from the rum, you see. A sentry rode in, along with one of the scouts from Lieutenant Markham's party. On their way back to our camp, they had discovered a company of Burgoyne's foot soldiers hiding in a wood two hours' ride away from us. The British had dispersed when they were pursued, and some had been killed and captured, but the remnant were thought to be hiding in the farms and villages in that area.

P: And what were your orders that morning following Burgoyne's surrender? October—what was the date?

J: October the eighteenth, sir. Major Patrick Ballard, who was then in command, ordered Captain Artemas Siwall to search out the enemy and destroy him. To burn the barns and haystacks in which he might hide. To be certain insufficient provisions remained in the small farms and villages to succour him. To punish any who gave him shelter willingly and provide an example to those who might do so in future.

P: And did you find these orders distasteful?

J: I found them—harsh. Perhaps necessary. Certainly impractical.

P: Impractical, sir?

J: Our officers had encouraged a night of drink and revelry, and we were all the worse for it, Major Lambrick. Many of the men were still drinking, having found a nearby farmer whose wife had just finished her ale-brewing. They had consumed not only the barrels of rum and cider, but three hogsheads of new ale. And they had had women for the first time in some months.

P: So they had lost all sense of discipline.

J: They had remembered another life than war, sir. Captain Siwall did his best to remind them of orders. So did Sergeant Quaid and I. Had Lieutenant Markham been with us, we might have had better success. He was much respected among the men.

P: Would you say he was beloved?

J: If leaders are ever loved, yes, sir. I would say so.

P: But he was not with you.

J: No. As I said, he had been sent on ahead and was with the scouting party. We formed our men up into something like a column, and rode out in the direction of a village to the north of the wood where the British regiment had been discovered.

P: The village of Webb's Ford?

J: That is correct, sir.

P: Go on, Lieutenant.

J: The wood where the British had been hiding was two hours' ride but we took four to reach it. The men were surly and quarrels broke out among them. Some at the rear of the column dozed off in their saddles, the horses wandered. We reached the wood just after noon, but we did not stop for food. Captain Siwall thought—and rightly—that if we let the men stop, we would never get them onto their horses again.

There were three small villages and half a dozen outlying farmsteads in the low hills on either side of the wood, which had a wide stream called North Brook running alongside it. We watered our horses, and traveled along the stream on the near bank, waiting for a proper ford to cross, as it was fairly deep and fast-running, and badly obstructed with rocks in many places.

We came to the spot called Webb's Ford at near three o'clock that afternoon, and crossed the brook to the village. There were but five buildings. Two large dwelling-houses, well-kept. A great barn and storehouse built between the dwellings. And a small cottage, aside from the rest. At the back, an orchard. We rode over the fallen apples as we came up from the ford, I remember their scent rising from the grass. A large garden plot. Late cabbages. Corn, drying in the husk. Ripe pumpkins. An arbor of black grapes. Chickens, geese. Maple trees in the yard, red with the first frosts, and a few late flowers still blooming.

P: And where were the inhabitants?

J: At first, there seemed to be none.

P: Go on. Lieutenant? Please go on.

J: Until— Until we saw the flies.

P: Flies, sir?

J: There was an object in the yard. It was black with the crawling bodies of flies. When I heard them, I thought at first it was wind, or cicadas. But it was too late in the year for cicadas. And there was no wind. It was the flies, buzzing.

P: And what did the object prove to be?

J: It was the corpse of a man, sir.

P: A soldier?

J: Yes.

P: British or American?

J: What remained of his uniform was blue.

P: American?

J: Yes.

P: He had been shot from ambush?

J: Shot, yes. I do not know the circumstances. His weapons were nowhere in sight, and his horse was gone. I do not know, but—

P: Go on.

J: He had been mutilated. Hacked to pieces. Even that, I think, would not have been too much for us. We had seen such things before. But for the flies. They covered his face and what was left of his hands. His belly, where it was cut open. The hole where his private parts had been. The humming sound, very loud. We heard it before we saw him. The black, glistening bodies. I took off my tunic and beat at them to get them away from him. But they were implacable, you see. They left us nothing. No more hope. There was the sun and the smell of the apples and that sound of buzzing, terrible buzzing. Eating at the heart of the world. And then I saw the men. Their faces.

P: Take some brandy, Lieutenant, before you proceed. You are not well.

J: I looked down, where they were all staring. His feet. He was wearing Lieutenant Eben Markham's boots.

P: But surely boots are not so distinctive as to—

J: I have said. Eben. Lieutenant Markham. He was a woodsman. He did not wear boots, precisely. They were Indian leggings. Cree, I think. Brain-tanned deerskin, painted in a pattern of green and blue. Very soft and long-lasting, laced up to the knee with rawhide thongs.

P: Unique, then.

J: I never saw a pair like them.

P: So the men saw those leggings and assumed—

J: Not assumed. Knew. It was Eben lying there with the flies black on him.

P: But surely the Indian boots might have been stolen or bartered or—

J: No! Don't you understand? We— I. Battered the flies away from
him. What was left of his face was—Eben. Lieutenant Eben
Ma— Markham.

P: Take this brandy, sir.

J: No! There was a musket ball through his belly. He had died
slowly, and they had left him there in the yard to do it, and
then come out when he was dead and hacked him up. There
was an ax in the chopping block nearby. A mowing scythe
leaning on the barn. There was blood on the scythe.

P: And they left him unburied, for the flies.

J: Yes.

P: Who had left him? Tories? The people in the house were
Tories?

J: No. They were not known Loyalists.

P: Very well. Not known. What happened next?

J: A woman appeared at the door. A young woman with a baby
at her breast.

P: And?

J: Captain Siwall started for the door to speak to her. His pistol
was drawn. The last of our men were still straggling in from
the orchard. Sergeant Quaid and I were trying to get them to
fall in, but they wouldn't come away from Eben's body. I saw
a movement in the window of the small cottage at the edge of
the compound. A glimpse of a face.

P: Man? Woman?

J: I cannot say. A whitish blur.

P: A wig, perhaps? Such as the British officers wear?

J: There were old men at the place. They wore wigs. Their own
hair was white. There were no young men at Webb's Ford. I
saw only women, children, old men. No British soldiers.

P: You saw none. That does not mean they had not been there and killed Markham, perhaps waited in ambush, using his corpse as a bait.

J: No, sir. There were no British! I—

P: What happened next, Lieutenant?

J: There was a musket shot. I saw Captain Siwall dive for cover, but he was not hit. I looked at the young woman in the open door. There was blood on her breast and on the child she carried. It was dead. The ball had passed through the baby and into her lung. I think she did not live long after. She collapsed at the door, on top of Siwall. I saw him sitting on the doorstep holding the dead baby. Then I turned and saw a musket in the hands of Private Fenly. It was still smoking.

P: Private Fenly has deserted his company. He cannot corroborate nor dispute this accusation, sir.

J: Yes. I am aware of that. It was not an accusation, merely a fact.

P: Go on.

J: I cannot.

P: Some brandy now? I believe there is a physician in the court.

J: No, sir. Only I remember nothing else plainly. I made to wrest the gun from Fenly, and a minute later I took a musket ball in my back, near the left shoulder.

P: Who fired it?

J: One of my men, sir. Private Dunbar.

P: Why? One of your own men? Why would he shoot you?

J: I am of English birth, sir. You yourself accused me of being a spy. At that moment, I was the enemy. The color of my coat mattered no more to Private Dunbar than the color of Eben Markham's did to the old men and women and children of Webb's Ford.

P: Please spare us your theories, Lieutenant! Continue.

J: Will Quaid—Sergeant Quaid—shoved me aside, or I might

have taken the shot through my heart. I fell near the root of one of the trees in the yard and lay there on my side. I remember thinking that I had to keep the flies off me or I would surely die. I remember the men, their feet running past me, toward the house. Wild, like mad things, screaming. I saw Quaid go after them, shouting orders, firing his pistol in the air. Nobody listened. He disappeared into the house nearest the orchard. I remember hearing screams, women's screams. Children's. Shouting. Guns firing. Smoke. Then I fainted. That is all, until—

P: Until what?

J: When I woke, it was almost dark. I was lying on my back then. There was a young woman sitting cross-legged near my left side, keening. She had a little girl with her, eleven or twelve years old. The woman had a knife on her lap, and she was holding something that looked like uncooked meat, and something else that shone in the darkness by the light of her lantern. I had no notion of it then, and I fainted again a moment later. She must have thought me already dead. But—

P: What was it that she held?

J: Two of my fingers, sir. The thing that shone was my wedding ring on one of them.

P: And you remember nothing else?

J: I remember Artemas Siwall, screaming, screaming.

P: What else?

J: Nothing. I awoke next on a wounded cart, sir. Sergeant Quaid and Private Jakes were with me, and Captain Siwall, who was bound and gagged to stop his screams. They told me Lieutenant Markham had been decently buried.

P: He was murdered by these Loyalist madwomen, then. And according to orders, your men punished them for their treacherous—

J: No, sir! We had orders to punish British sympathizers, not to murder old men and rape women and children! You must let me finish—

P: You yourself have said you saw a movement at the cottage window. No doubt the remnant of Burgoyne's defeated army—

J: You wish a simple answer, and there is none! The people of Webb's Ford were helpless, peaceful. The war had taken too much from them. From all of us. When you teach plain men and decent women to kill and kill, and show them they can be snuffed out in an instant at any fool's order, then sometimes they break, sir. Suddenly, in a minute, over a little thing. Red coats, blue coats. What did it matter? They didn't shoot Eben Markham for politics. They didn't even shoot an American soldier. They shot a uniform, because a uniform was the War, and the War would kill them. For days they had listened to the guns from Saratoga. Their sons, their young husbands, were all taken from them. Those women in the house, the woman who took my fingers. The ones who left Eben to the flies. My own men. Myself. We wanted to punish the world for what it is, and we ran mad, sir. If that is madness. I tried to stop them and they shot me, but if they had not, I might've done as bad as they. My men killed the girl and the baby and then they went into the dwelling-houses and found the others. An old man and woman. Two little boys. A young woman and the little girl I saw.

JUDGE-ADVOCATE: That will do, sir! It was an action against Loyalist traitors!

J: They used the women and girls! They killed children!

JUDGE-ADVOCATE: That is hearsay, Lieutenant. You are speaking of American troops, Patriot troops. Besides, you saw nothing of this yourself, for you were at the time unconscious. You have admitted as much. You may stand down.

J: No! I will be heard! We must accept the guilt of it! Captain Siwall witnessed what they did. Our own men!

P: Siwall is distracted, sir. You yourself are not yet of sound and healthy mind. You are dismissed, I say. Stand down, sir!

J: I will be heard, sir. I wish to be punished with my men!

JUDGE-ADVOCATE: This Court will hear no more slander against American heroes! Bailiff! Help him from the room!

PIECING THE EVIDENCE:

The Decision of the Courts-Martial
Concerning the Incident at Webb's Ford, New York,
18 October 1777

It is the judgement of this Military Court that the defendants Siwall, Josselyn, Quaid, Jakes, Patterson and Rawlings be found guilty of the charge of being drunk on their duty watch on the afternoon of October 18, 1777. They shall be given each one hundred lashes before their company, and rationed on bread and water for one week. Confine them to barracks.

On the charges of Rape, Murder and Mutilation of Civilian Sympathizers with the British cause at Webb's Ford, this Court finds the defendants Not Guilty.

It is, further, the opinion of this Court that Lieutenant Ebenezer Markham died of wounds inflicted upon him by fleeing Soldiers of the British Crown, abetted by the suspected Loyalist sympathizers living at the place known as Webb's Ford.

Addendum: In the case of Captain Artemas Siwall, sentence is commuted as the defendant is distracted in his wits and would not benefit from correction. In the case of Lieutenant Daniel Josselyn, sentence is commuted on advice of Army physicians, his wounds and state of health being such as correction would put in grave danger of death.

Nota: Sentence was carried out upon Sergeant William Quaid and Privates Jakes, Patterson, and Rawlings at six o'clock on the morning of December 20, 1777, before their Company assembled.

As Witness: Cornelius Dodger, Civilian Clerk to Major Edward Lambrick

$\mathscr{M}$ORNING

"Mr. Dodger was an old schoolmaster, so they said, out to pasture at his age and taking no more pupils, and they'd made him the court clerk in those parts. When they convened the court-martial, there was nobody else about who could write so well." Daniel had left Hannah's bed and gone to stand alone by the banked fire, wrapped in one of the quilts she had brought. "Major Lambrick commandeered him, more or less, along with the meeting house where we were tried. Dodger was no fighting man in his best days, and years too old, and so he had been left behind. He did have a wound, though, for his head was bandaged, and he said he had been slashed with a saber in battle." Daniel shrugged. "Saratoga, I supposed."

"So that's where he and William met?"

"Yes. Poor Will. I thought he would die of that flogging."

"A hundred lashes for nothing." Hannah shuddered. "For I'm sure he had no part in the terrible work that was done at Webb's Ford. Not Will."

It was unthinkable.

"And Mr. Dodger perhaps thought the same," Hannah went on, "that William had been unjustly sentenced. And so he befriended him."

"Well, certainly old Dodger was there on the day of the floggings. Four days before Christmas Eve. He was the Court's witness, he had to write the whole thing down."

"And where were you, my heart?"

"When I was well enough, I did what I could to stop it. They
did not confine me to barracks like the others, since my sentence
had been commuted. Josh Lamb was out of hospital by then, and
he put in a word for Will with the court. It did no good. We
sat up with Will the night before, playing dominoes. In the morning, they came for him. Marched him to the yard. Tied him to
the sentry post."

"Like Artie Siwall."

"Yes. Like Artie. Except Will's back was to the barracks. All
the men turned out to watch. They stripped off his shirt and for
a minute there wasn't a sound. He'd been beaten before, you
know, when he was a lad, by the British. The scars were—"

"I know. Hetty told me of it. But never that there were *two*
floggings."

"I doubt she's ever heard about it. Afterward, we made a promise. Josh and I, one or two of the others. To say nothing about
Webb's Ford, ever, nor about how Eben died. Not only to spare
ourselves. There was your aunt and uncle and yourself to think
of, and the Siwalls. Some of the others still have families here,
too. Of all people, Will wouldn't tell Hetty."

"No," said Hannah, softly. "No, I see that."

It was the way of human things to trust those least whom
they should trust most entirely. She herself had surely
proven that.

"When it was done, Josh and I carried him back to barracks.
The company surgeon gave him a half bottle of rum, but Will
took a fever. Old Dodger sat with him for days after."

Hannah lay still on the bed, her knees tucked up under
her, watching the ice-frosted windowpane grow brighter. It
would be a morning of blinding sun on hard, wind-crusted
snow. Mentally, she began to calculate how many hours until

the Rufford mob might thrash its way through the drifted
Trace and find them.

That was the worst thing in the woods. There were too many
trees an innocent man might be hanged from.

She shook off the panic. They might still have days together
here before the Trace was passable.

"I don't understand," she said. "Why Dodger? What did he want
with William?"

Daniel shook his head. "How it came about, I don't know. But
the old man wouldn't stir from Will's bedside till the fever was
burnt out. The shame that came afterward, none of us could do
much about that."

He came padding over, soft-footed as always, and sat on the
edge of the bed beside her, let his hand slip inside the quilt to
lie upon the cage of her ribs.

"For days, we couldn't get a word out of him. Then, one night,
it was, when he was alone with old Dodger, and we were across
in the duty room, having a pipe, we heard him. William's
voice, singing."

"Singing? After a flogging and a fever?"

He nodded. "You know that old ballad, 'Katy Cruel'?"

> " 'I know who I love,
> And I know who does love me,
> I know where I'll go,
> And I know who'll go with me.' "

Having no voice for singing, Hannah spoke the words, but the
next verse, Daniel sang to her, a sweet, clear, unselfconscious
tenor.

> "O that I were what I would be,
> Then would I be what I am not,
> But I am what I must be,
> What I would be I cannot . . ."

"He sang," said Daniel, when the verse had ended, "all that long night. It was almost the New Year, then. And he sang the year in. 'Old Hundred.' 'Sir Patrick Spens.' 'Barbara Allen.' 'Butternut Hill.' 'Springfield Mountain.' Until finally he slept, with Dodger still beside him. Next morning, when he woke, you would have thought there had been no fever, and no flogging, either, and no Webb's Ford at all. In less than a week, we were on our way to Rufford."

"And he said nothing of it?"

"Never a word, to this day. What his part in it was, what happened inside that house—he said nothing. Well, at least not to me. Will's term of service was up after the New Year, and the company surgeon said I was unfit for duty till I healed better, and somebody had to bring poor Artie Siwall back home. So we three came away here together, and Dodger with us. And I found you, my heart and bones. The rest, you know."

"Did you never inquire of Mr. Dodger why he devoted himself to William so entirely? A civilian and a stranger—it's hard to credit," said Hannah.

"I asked him once, yes," replied Daniel. "When Will still lay fevered, and we took turns watching over him. 'You are a good friend to him, sir,' he told me, 'and so you are a good fellow to me.'

" 'Is he some relative of yours, Dodger?' I said. 'Or how come you to care for him so?'

" 'I, sir?' he said, quite agitated, and jumped up from the joint-stool where he sat and began to pace. 'Why, I am no man's friend, sir! Not worthy, oh no! *Nullius addictus iurare in verba magistri.* Horace, sir.'

" '*Not bound to swear allegiance to any master,*' I said, for I knew the verse well.

"He nodded. 'I watch and listen, sir,' he said. 'Sometimes I venture to pray a space. I write down facts when required, for my eyes are too sharp and my ears, also. Too sharp, too sharp.'

"I scarcely realized that he had begun to weep until he took off his little black cap and wiped his eyes with the tassel. Then he put it on again.

"'I prevent what I can and defend what I may,' he said. 'I attend the world as a fearful midwife, sir, and hope it gives birth to no more monsters. No more monsters.'

"Then he darted over to where I sat by the hearth and knelt down in front of me, a tiny little man like a child's wooden toy to be pulled on a string.

"'Only I beg you, sir, of all things,' he said, the tears rolling down his face again, 'God save us, do not tax me with being his friend.'"

When Daniel fell silent again, Hannah thought for a moment, trying to piece together the ragged scraps of his terrible story, to make a single pattern of it. The women and children and old men, maddened by fear, who had seen a uniform and known that death lived in it, no matter whether it were red or blue. Who had shot down poor Eben and then hacked at him, not knowing his name and not caring.

Women who like herself had quilted and woven and stitched and sewn. Women with axes and scythes, at war and killing a thing they could not see, killing death itself in a human shape, until Eben lay mutilated and barely recognizable except by those jaunty Indian leggings he had always sported and laughed about.

Women at the walls of ancient cities under siege had done no less and been called heroes, and had poets singing over them for a thousand years. And men came and found them, too, and punished them, as Anthea Emory had been punished to death.

I attend the world as a fearful midwife, and hope it gives birth to no more monsters.

But one monster had killed Nan Emory and Artie Siwall, and from what Daniel had told her as they lay together, the same monster had followed hapless Dunny Emory into the heart of the winter forest and killed him, too.

Who, then? Which of the men Hannah knew and in some

part valued might have done such a thing and put the blame on Daniel?

"Mr. Dodger came from the neighborhood of Webb's Ford, then. Did he know Anthea Emory?" she asked him. The hand that lay now on her breast under the quilt was his left. She could feel the strangeness of it, the two fingers and thumb that stroked her clumsily.

"I've no notion," he replied. "But certainly he's not strong enough ever to strangle her or her husband. Nor to drive a sword through Artie Siwall, neither. And how could he ride into these woods alone and kill young Emory?"

"Daniel?" Hannah hesitated before she asked the next question. "Did you know where Nan came from, did her husband tell you when you hired him?"

"John English hired him, not me. I only spoke to him as a matter of course when his contract was let, and again to dissuade him from going so late into the woods." Daniel spoke sharply, then stood up and went to poke the fire again. "I had no idea where Mrs. Emory came from, Hannah. Not until a moment ago, when you told me Jonathan's story. I beg you to believe that."

"I do, my heart. If you tell me, I believe it."

"Thank you. But if she was at Webb's Ford on the day of the killings, she must have been very young."

"It's more than eight years. She was barely twenty. You said there were two little boys and a young girl—"

"Of eleven or twelve. Yes. The girl I saw when they took my fingers."

It made Hannah's bones ache to hear him speak of it so calmly. "You're not wearing your glove!" she said, suddenly realizing.

"No." A brief smile played round the corners of his mouth. "I do not make a habit of wearing it to bed." Then he grew sober again. "Though if you prefer— I hadn't realized. After all these years, you must find it most distasteful. I should have—"

"Don't be a fool, Daniel! I was only thinking— You don't take it off around many people, do you?"

"Not many, no."

"Artie Siwall? When you visited him, was it your custom to remove it?"

"Oh, I never took it off with Artie, no. It troubled him, made him wild to see damage of any sort. I always wore the glove, and even kept my hand in my greatcoat pocket for the most part. We met almost always in the open, you know."

"The execution post. The chain."

"Yes. The chain." He sat down on the low joint-stool, the quilt still wrapped round him like a blanket on an Indian wise man. "But I see what you're getting at. If I lost that glove and someone found it and put it on poor Artie to lay his dying at my door also, then it must be somebody I'd be willing to show this mangled mess of a hand to in all its glory."

"John English?"

"Yes, certainly. When we're at work. In my own house. But never in his." He looked over at her. "He has young daughters, you know. And a pious wife. Pious women have little stomach for other people's imperfections, I find."

"Magistrate Siwall?"

"Never." He smiled. "Wouldn't give him the satisfaction of demonstrating a flaw."

"But he might have come by it easily enough. He had access to your study, for the company papers are kept there, are they not?"

"Why, yes. And old Twig is always keen to oblige Siwall." Daniel grew more excited. "She'd have let him in if he asked it, whether I were at home or not."

"And if he feared you might learn of his treachery over the survey maps and his bargain with Dunny Emory—"

"He might be anxious to get me out of the way for good and take over my shares at a bargain."

"His wife says Siwall was with her when Nan Emory was killed," said Hannah reluctantly. "But wives have been known to lie for husbands."

"She's a cold woman," said Daniel. "To tell truth, I've wondered myself if Siwall might have a mistress somewhere in the town. But one so young as Mrs. Emory?"

"Ham Siwall grows old, Daniel. Perhaps he felt young again in her company, or perhaps—"

But Daniel shook his head. "We go too far, Hannah. There is no proof of anything, not even Siwall's bargain over the maps. We have only your cousin's word for it, and a court would require a good deal more. We must not paint Siwall guilty so easily of three deaths, and one of them his own brother."

"Very well. Who else might have laid hands on your glove, then, when you were not wearing it?"

He shook his head. "Not many. Josh Lamb—Dolly has a strong constitution, it doesn't shock her to see my hand. Will and Hetty."

"And Dodger. If you lost the glove at Will's place, Dodger might have found it."

"But Hannah, I told you, he hasn't the strength to strangle anybody! To break the woman's neck? It would take a giant, a man who barely knew how strong he was."

"Who could snap an arm like a twig by accident, without realizing? As he held his victim down, pinned the arm to the ground?"

"Or the bed." Daniel had begun to pace again. "Not Dodger."

"No. Is John English strong enough for that?"

"Might be. The woman was slight, and Dunny was a string bean."

"English has access to your study, has he not? And he works for Siwall as well as for you, you are partners."

"So we are back at Siwall's door again, are we? You mean, did Ham Siwall pay John to get both Dunny and me out of the way? And perhaps share the profits from his fraud?" He paused, a little stunned by the thought.

But again Daniel shook his head. "It doesn't wash, my dear girl. I grant you, John's not a rich man, but he's comfortable off, and his wife's a clever one at saving a shilling, though she *be* too pious for my tastes. Still, he might've been tempted into it, or tricked somehow and trapped, for Siwall's clever, I'll give him that. Only one thing. Kill Dunny Emory to shut him up. Kill Nan Emory, too, maybe because she knew what her husband was up to and they didn't want her telling. Make me look guilty of her death to get me hanged and let Siwall get the timber rights cheap when the county seizes my lands from Charlotte as a felon. But Artie? Why should they need to kill Artie? He knew nothing of our business dealings, his brother's and mine. Even at Webb's Ford, he was guilty of nothing. He ran mad from too kind a heart, and was too gentle for his memories."

Now it was Hannah's turn to consider. Certainly Hamilton Siwall had given no sign of anything but mourning over his brother's death. But there was one last candidate. She approached him slowly, dodging his shadow because she herself could hardly bear the thought of it.

"Daniel?"

"Yes, my love?"

"Could it be William?"

Daniel stared into the fire. "No," he said stubbornly. "Never."

"He went to the Grange looking for you the morning you left for the Outward. He might've seen your grandfather's sword on the desk and taken it then. While you were upstairs with Charlotte or—"

"Will Quaid? Kill a girl as that girl was killed? Never!"

"She was there, at Webb's Ford. She was the little girl who watched while her mother or her aunt or her sister cut your fingers off. When she came here, Daniel, Anthea Emory was no girl, you may believe me! And she knew something, and Will knew it, too. And what Will knows, Dodger knows."

"You're mad! Will's your friend, for the love of God."

Hannah got up and marched over to the fire. She spoke quietly and steadily. "What did Dodger tell you? 'Do not tax me with being his friend.' I am your friend and more than your friend, but if I knew for a surety that you had done what was done to Nan Emory and to Artie Siwall, I would kill you myself."

"And you think I must do as much to William?"

"If he be guilty."

"That is the point, my dear. There's nothing at all to tie him to Mrs. Emory except the fact that he was at Webb's Ford."

"The dog," she said suddenly.

"What dog?"

"Nan's dog, Toby. He growled at me and would have bitten, but he took food from Will. And he stopped barking when Will spoke to him."

"A dog? He makes friends with every dog and stray cat in the village, you know that!"

Hannah shook herself, relieved. "You are right." She held out a hand to him. "I was wrong to suggest it."

"No," he said. "I told you just now of other decent men who did mad things. It made you doubt the surface of the world and the masks it wears. So you had to face it out. But these are other times. And our Will is not a murderer, no more than I am."

"No," Hannah agreed. But she had one last question, the one that had been bothering her ever since her visit to Charlotte Josselyn's bedchamber that foggy night.

"Daniel, my love. When Will and I went into Nan Emory's house that day, there was a pocket hanging on the chair in her chamber, folded with her clothes. It was embroidery work, and I notice such things," she told him. "That same night, your wife called me to come and see her."

"Charlotte? Sent for you?"

"She had heard of Mrs. Emory's letter and wished to ask my help in clearing your name."

"She asked *your* help?"

"Your lady-wife is stronger than you think, my love. And clever with a needle. In her chamber, I saw more embroidery work, a design of briar roses of her own drawing. It was the same design as the wool work on Mrs. Emory's pocket, Daniel. She could only have come by it from Charlotte, and yet according to Abby, your wife's maid, Nan Emory never worked at the Grange. But she did work at Burnt Hill, when the Siwalls butchered. Perhaps a few other times. I meant to go to Mrs. Emory's house and take the pocket myself and ask Charlotte what she knew of it. But I had no time before I came away."

Daniel turned suddenly and began to rummage in the pockets of his greatcoat. At length he pulled something out and handed it to Hannah. She took it and smoothed it on her knee: Mrs. Emory's pocket, in the crewel design of briar roses.

"I took it from the dead girl's chamber," he said, "because I knew it would be traced to Charlotte. I could not have her plagued with questions. If she were summoned to Magistrate's Court, or had to testify at my trial at Wybrow, the strain would kill her."

Hannah looked up at him. "And besides, you know how Mrs. Emory came to have it. Don't you? Did Ham Siwall take it when he was in your house?"

Daniel met her gaze, then glanced away. "My wife sometimes gives such things as small gifts to women of the town, when any of them comes. They do not come often. But I recognized the work, just as you did."

"Could she have given it to Mistress Siwall?"

"No." His tone had grown formal, as if the night between them—the firelight, the warm nest of the bed—had never happened. "Not Mistress Siwall."

"Tell me, damn you!" Hannah cried suddenly. "Do you wish to be hanged?"

He fixed his eyes on the shape of her, but he seemed to see her at a distance, as though she were very small.

"I gave the pocket to Hetty Quaid," he said.

THIRTY-NINE

The Miller's Son and the Midwife's Daughter

The drifters and idlers and hotheads of Rufford, who had almost been a mob on the night of Hannah's departure, had been shut up in scruffy cottages while the storm raged, with babies bawling and sour-faced wives scolding. When the morning dawned bright and clear, they were ready for rum and rabblery, and as soon as the Red Bush opened its doors at eleven o'clock, they began to drift in, stamp the snow off worn boots, and pick up where they had left off.

"I've a craw full of the bastards, and no mistake," growled Tom Whitechurch, wiping the last of a pint of ale off his lip.

"I hear Will Quaid took Edward Fairbrother off to Debtor's Jail last week."

"Only 'cause he couldn't lay hands on you, Phinney!" Joseph Cool, a fisherman who had little to do but drink and jest when the cod weren't running, jabbed Phineas Rugg in the ribs and helped himself to another mug of spiced cider from the huge pewter punch bowl that sat steaming on Bill Edes's bar.

"I ask you, though!" insisted Nathan Berge. "There's no more decenter fellow than old Ned Fairbrother in all of Rufford and Wybrow, yes and even so far as Salcombe, too, I'll venture to say."

"When he hasn't taken a drop too much of Edes's flip, that is," joked Cool.

But they ignored him. It wasn't a day for jests. Nor did they notice Jonathan Markham enter the inn parlor and take a quiet seat at the back, far from the fire.

"And what if Ned *should* owe Master Siwall seven pound, because he had bartered a dozen of Siwall's hens for the milking of his own red cow for a year?" said Phinney. "Is it Fairbrother's fault the cow run dry before Christmas? And Siwall might've had the hens back again, too, only except he wouldn't take 'em."

" 'Tis Edward's land he wants. Says he has no more use for the hens. Says he wants the milk or the money. And he up and signs a complaint for debt against the old boy." Tom Whitechurch slammed his meaty fist against the bar counter, making the apple slices afloat in the punch bowl dance. "Ned Fairbrother's seventy-four, and his wife Liddy's no younger, and while he sits in Salcombe jail for debt, who shall cut her firewood and see she's food in the larder?"

"Not Ham Siwall, that's certain!"

"And how can you buy another cow and make good the bargain, when you're locked up like a clam in a shell? If Siwall wants his milk—"

"Milk, my arse!" cried Whitechurch. "Siwall wants the land at auction now, when he can get it cheap while there's a debt against it. Attach the land and he has only to pay the seven pound to get it."

"That's fine land, it's worth a hundred!"

"Seven pounds for the use of a cow!"

"Who'll be next, that's what I want to know? You, Tom? Or me?" Nathan drained another mug. "If old Phinney's place was worth a shilling, he'd even want *that*, I'm bound! He's made of greed, is Siwall, and hard as iron."

"And his lordship-partner no better!"

"*And* they own Will Quaid, lock, stock, and barrel."

"Aye, Quaid does nothing without Ham Siwall's say-so, or Josselyn's!"

"Otherwise, why has he not gone into the Outward and brought back that murdering bastard Josselyn, snow or no snow? I ask you, why?"

"We know why!" shouted Tom Whitechurch. The other voices had merged into a chorus now, and to be properly heard and taken note of, Whitechurch leapt onto the bar. His voice was thick with drink and his eyes were glazed in the firelight. "We know bloody well! Because the life of a poor man's wife means nothing to these rich bastards, no more than it did before the War! Dunny Emory's likely dead in the woods, too, with another of His Lordship's fancy swords stuck through him like Artie Siwall, but that don't spell nothing to the Siwalls. Artie was gone mad, and that's one less useless mouth to feed, and another shilling in his brother's purse!"

"Aye, that's the truth of it!" Even Joseph Cool had lost his sense of humor now. "Us and our wives and our troubles is nothing to them lot! They'd as soon turn us all to fodder, so's they could sell our bones."

"That Emory lass, spoilt and murdered! 'Tisn't right. It's not what I dragged through them years of war for."

"If we leave things to Quaid and his masters, we'll all be murdered in our beds, and our wives, too. And worse than murdered!"

"When I went for a soldier, we knew what to do with traitors, all right," cried Whitechurch. He held one hand above his head and, giving a jerk to an invisible rope, let his tongue loll out and his eyes roll.

"Tom's right! What are they else but traitors, the lot of them?"

"I got a new hank of hemp in my barn," cried someone.

"And there's trees a-plenty in the Outward!" shouted someone else.

"Let's give the bastards justice!"

From the back of the room, Jonathan spoke quietly, but his voice was clear and strong. "And how will you track Josselyn? There's a foot of new snow over his trail."

"No need to track him." Whitechurch was determined not to be cheated of his moment of glory. "Just follow the Trace. He's gone to Fort Holland and that old Dutch devil, Uncle Piet, where he can hide out warm in some squaw's blankets till spring. They're all pirates and blackguards in there."

Jonathan stood up and sauntered to the center of the group to lean against the fireplace. "Snow drifts into the Trace deeper than Edes's roof beams, Thomas. After yesterday's wind, you won't get through unless your horse has wings, not till the weather warms a bit."

"You've gone and changed your spots since a day ago, Johnnie," snapped Nathan. "I thought you was all for giving Josselyn a new hemp neckcloth yourself."

"Well, now. Perhaps he's been and had a heart-talk with his cousin," said Tom Whitechurch. "Mistress Hannah Slut."

Jonathan moved so quickly that Whitechurch had no time to defend himself. He dived for the big man's ankles where he stood posturing on the bar, grabbed them, and felled his opponent like a tree.

In another minute, the inn parlor was chaos. Bill Edes came out from behind the bar swinging his trusty pike handle, Jonathan's friend Martin Wilks began to pommel Phinney Rugg, and most of the others fell in a flailing mass upon the two prime battlers.

Jonathan was strong and young and supple, but most of his strength was in his brain, not his arms. Tom Whitechurch's gifts, on the other hand, were mainly brawn and endurance, and it was not long before Johnnie lay at the bully's feet, eye blackened, nose streaming blood, cheek already swollen to twice its size, ribs badly bruised, and breath coming sharp and painful. Martin Wilks lay unconscious till Edes threw half a mug of ale in his face. He woke, sputtering, but he had had enough. Forgetting his battered comrade, he scrambled to his feet and made for the door.

Whitechurch stood swaying above Jonathan. "Well, then," he said, and spat blood and a broken tooth onto the scrubbed-pine floor. "Leave the little boys at home behind the midwife's skirts, if it pleasures them. We've got men's work to do yet. Anybody got a high sledge with runners that'll cut through them drifts in the Trace?"

"Oh, aye," said somebody.

"And a good team of Dorset plowhorses. Near nineteen hands, and bellies that'll clear any amount of drift. I use 'em for sugaring, and we been caught out in worse weather than this, too. They won't mind this little bit of snow, I guess."

"Then I got but one word more to say boys!" Whitechurch glanced down at Jonathan, who had begun to stir. "Justice!" he cried. "And death to Tyranny and them that serves it!"

"Justice!" shouted the others. Somebody liberated a keg of Edes's cider, somebody else a dozen bottles of rum, and they were gone.

"Where is the girl?" cried Aunt Julia Markham. Skirts caught up, cap askew, cloak flapping, she came wading precariously down the deeply drifted path to her husband's mill, trailed by Jennet and the one-eared cat, Arthur. "Husband, where is Hannah?"

"What?" Henry, imperturbable as usual, could not hear her above the rasping of his saw against a length of pine from which he was building a draw-chest for young Jennet.

Julia pursed her lips and seized the saw from him. "I said, where is my niece? Where is Hannah? You know she was gone at breakfast. I supposed she had been called during the night to attend Mrs. Burton's delivery, for we knew her child would come soon and had promised to go to her. When I saw that Hannah's cloak and boots were gone, I thought she had not liked to rouse me and had gone alone."

"Oh, aye?"

"Oh, aye, indeed! Now, not twenty minutes ago, comes young Penthea Burton to say her mother is unwell and would Mistress Midwife Trevor come as quick as can be." Julia stamped her foot, fuming. "Booby! Do you not understand me? She never went to Burtons. I sent Parthenia and Kitty to look for her, and she's vanished. Hannah is nowhere to be found!"

"Not quilting, is she?"

You could almost have seen smoke coming from Julia's ears. "No, sir, nor milking nor churning nor hiding under the bed with a pint of rum! Do you not suppose I have looked for her? She's gone, you old fool! She's taken food with her, a loaf and some of the bacon, and two of her quilts. And Flash is gone! The horse, booby! Flash, my mare, is gone from the stall!"

"Oh, aye?" The old man straightened his back. "Then perhaps Hannah's gone some distance."

"Well, saddle a horse, confound you, and go after her! If the storm caught her without shelter—"

"Well, now. There's inns a-plenty on the road to Boston, my dear."

"Boston?" Julia peered at him. "And what, pray, would she be doing in Boston?"

"Now, then, haven't you been nagging after her to marry that Reverend, what's-his-name?"

"Bosh! You know as well as I do she would never do that, nag or don't nag. Not so long as Dan Josselyn's still breathing."

Henry nodded. "Aye. He's away, too, is Daniel."

Julia considered. "Ah. So you think she's gone to—" She paused, thinking. "You may very well be right," she said at last. "The girl is fool enough to run off with him. We might, I suppose, send Jonathan on horseback along the post road as far as the first inn, to see if they've been heard of?"

"We might, at that."

During this plausible but entirely misguided discussion, they had all but forgotten the silent presence of little Jennet, who had not gone inside with Julia, nor even stopped in the mill yard. With the cat trailing after her, she had kept on along the path that led to the Grange ford, where the frozen Manitac lay smooth with trackless snow.

When Julia caught sight of her from the open half-door of the mill, Jennet was already standing on Daniel Josselyn's dock, over on the opposite bank.

"Jennet!" cried the old lady. "Come back here this instant!"

"No use shouting," said Henry. "Child can't hear you, no more'n she can hear the sun nor the cold."

"Well, go and fetch her back, then!"

With a sigh, her husband trudged out the door of the mill and headed for the frozen river ford. The child had already taken the road that led past the front garden of Mapleton Grange—the road into the Outward, where the trees stood black and heavy-laden with snow.

Jennet stumbled and fell, picked herself up and waded on again, up to her armpits in deep snow, the cat now riding precariously on her shoulder.

Suddenly Julia's breath caught in her throat. "Husband!" she cried. "Where is the child going?"

Henry turned back. "From the look of it, my dear," he called to her, "I'd say Jennet knows better than we do where Hannah's gone, and 'tisn't Boston, neither. Looks to me as though the lass is bound into the Outward to fetch her Mam." He took a deep breath. "And that's where we'll find your Hannah. If ever we do, indeed."

"Where's Hannah?" said Hetty Quaid.

Jonathan Markham sat in her kitchen at the Forge, allowing Will's wife to minister to his black eye and his bloody nose. The ribs would have to wait until he went home and Sally could bind them up. She had grown good at it, he thought ruefully, all the tavern brawls he'd had since they wed.

"Hannah?" he said, surprised.

"Yes, she'd promised to go up to Nell Burton's when her babe was come. Well, Nell's eldest, Penny? She was in here a while ago, and she told me she'd been to Two Mills to fetch Mistress Trevor, and not hide nor hair did she find, nor did anybody else, neither. Your Mam's fair beside herself, Penny says. Where's Hannah gone off to, do you think?"

Hetty swabbed at the last of the blood on Johnnie's lip, and the boy winced. "How should I know?" he said, frowning. For a while he was silent, but then he pushed aside the basin of water and stood up.

"Hold still there, I'm not finished yet!" she cried, clucking her tongue.

"There's no time to fuss, Hetty. I must find William," he said. "And quickly."

"I told you. He's gone to see if the road to Salcombe's open, in case Sheriff Tapp got caught in the storm. They'll go after Daniel together, when the Trace is clear enough. But Will won't be back till past dark, I expect."

"Hetty, there's a bunch of fools and hotheads stirred up to go into the woods after Daniel. If they find him, they'll stretch him. And if Hannah's up and gone in to find him, if she's there when that bunch catches up to them—"

"Dodger!" cried Hetty, wasting no more time. "Mr. Dodger! You're wanted, Dodge!"

In another moment the old fellow trotted in, his black nightcap askew upon the carefully powdered wig. A bunch of keys jingled at his waist—the keys to William's jail—and he carried a wooden trencher with the remnants of a meal of stew and bread and Hetty's corn pudding. He had been taking the noon meal to old Dickie Bunch, the permanent resident of Rufford Jail.

"Mr. Bunch sends his compliments, Ma'am," he said. "And commends the meal most highly. He is a philosopher, is Mr. Bunch. And he plays a fine game of draughts."

"To the Devil with Dickie Bunch! You must find William, Dodge, and quickly!" cried Hetty. "Johnnie says there's a mob of idiots gone into the woods after Daniel and Mistress Trevor. William must put them in their places before they do harm, or get lost in the drifts, drunk as they are!"

"But William is in the Forge, is he not?" The old man blinked. "Surely he's making a bolt and a hinge for Mrs. Emory's door, where the old one was broken?"

"No, no! Will rode out this morning, bless you!" Hetty was fairly dancing. "He's halfway to Salcombe by now. After Sheriff Tapp. And you must bring him back!"

Cornelius Dodger stared. For a moment he stood motionless, as if lightning had struck him. "Away!" he whispered. "Away without Dodger! Away and alone!"

Then suddenly he turned and trotted off through a door and down a narrow, cold hallway. Jonathan followed him into Will and Hetty's small bright bedroom with its quilted bed and red-and-white-check tester. At one side of the room was a tall draw-chest with brass pulls and locks on all the drawers. Mr. Dodger fumbled with the bunch of keys, found a small one, and unlocked the top drawer.

Again he froze, arrested in a space that seemed to terrify him. When he turned to look at Jonathan, his small bright eyes brimmed with tears and his mouth hung slack.

"Gone, sir!" he said.

"What's gone, Dodger?" said Jonathan gently.

"The pistol, sir," the old man replied. "The pistol from Webb's Ford. He has taken it and gone. He has not gone to fetch the sheriff. He's off into the woods to kill them both, or die. Or both together." He looked up at Jonathan sadly. "That's all a pistol's good for, you know, sir. Kill or die."

Above the bed, a framed motto in bright-colored cross-stitch on thread-counted grey homespun was caught in a spill of cold sunlight:

We thank Thee for our Peaceful Sleep, that Wakeful Thoughts from Sin doth Keep.

FORTY

The Pursued and the Pursuers

It was not that day that he found them. It was clear and bright, and William wore the snowshoes Eben Markham had once made for him from bent willow woven with rawhide and seasoned till they were tough as any steel. But he had the horse with him, and the big bay gelding sank into the deep drifts of the Trace, flailing and screaming until it fought free. Once or twice, he had to dig the horse out, poor thing, scooping great handfuls of hard-packed snow with his blackened hands.

As he worked, he sang, his deep voice booming.

> On Springfield Mountain there did dwell
> A likely youth that I knew well;
> His father's only son was he,
> Who died by the foot of a black oak tree.

There were birds in the woods, struggling to find some food that the snow had not hidden, for a bird must eat many times its weight of food in a day to keep alive. High in the spruces that rose up, leaning their heavily laden boughs over the trail, chicka-dees and siskins and red-birds gleaned the seeds from whatever cones were clear of snow. Now and then a pair of squirrels chased

271

each other madly up a nearby trunk, shaking a burden of snow off some limb to fall with a thump into the drifts beneath.

> *On Friday morning he did go*
> *Down to the meadow for to mow;*
> *He mowed and mowed around the field*
> *Till a poisonous serpent bit his heel.*

A family of young foxes crossed his path, trotting lightly on top of the snow. Through the darkness of the thicker trees beyond the trail, he glimpsed a wolf, circling the carcass of a frozen elk the storm had done for, sniffing the wind for competition as he tugged and tore at his meal.

> *Madam I will give to you*
> *The Keys of Canterbury,*
> *And all the bells of London Town*
> *Shall ring to make you merry!*

It was a good enough world, he thought, if you could have been alone in it. Here in the woods, he could almost forget that he had killed Anthea. She had wished it, begged him for it, and in the end, he had done what she asked for, and more. He knew how the wish for dying felt, like a heavy weight that dragged and dragged upon the heart and filled the bones with ice. It had been a mercy to her, she had said as much herself. There were times these last nine years when he had begged the same mercy from God, though he had never had it.

No, surely he felt no guilt for her death, only surprise that it had been so easy. Her life had broken with as little strain as the snap of her thin arm when he leant on it, once she was dead.

He was glad she had not felt the pain of it, for he had never wished to cause her pain. It was she who fed upon self-damage. The marks she bore—the torn hair, the battering, the mystical burns from the candle flame—she had given herself. He had always known she was madder than Artie Siwall on his madman's

chain. For madness is seldom a thing you can find and set a lock
to, and keep on a chain. And the mad can be tender, as she was
at times.

After Webb's Ford, remembering the things she had seen there,
Anthea had carried on her slender back the guilt of the universe.
The guilt of her sisters and her mother and father was her own,
and of her brothers, little more than boys themselves, who had
shot Eben Markham from ambush and ridden away to be bayoneted in their turn by the frightened, fleeing British, and the guilt
of those same British, and of the Rufford men, too, himself among
them, who had run mad at the sight of their mutilated friend and
stormed into the house and killed the old man and raped and
ruined the women—their guilt, too, was hers, because she had
been raped like the others and was a child and a girl and could
not stop it. And the guilt of her sister, who had stumbled, shocked
and half-naked into the yard and taken Dan Josselyn's fingers like
a child gathering blossoms—that guilt had been Anthea Emory's, too.

It was the guilt of breaking, and crashing in pieces against the
hard face of the world.

Until they were all punished, the whole universe of them, she
alone was still to blame, and so she tortured herself. She was
guilty of the great pit that had opened before them all that day,
and she wanted more than anything else to die for it.

But she would not die alone. She would see them all in Hell.

So he had got old Dodge to write the letter, as she told him.
To point the finger at Siwall and Josh Lamb and Daniel, that was
her plan. She had not found the others, those who were guilty
of the worst of it. But she would settle for what she had.

She trusted Will because of Mr. Dodger, who would have done
anything for him, so it seemed. It had taken all her growing years
to learn the identities of the Rufford men, a mere list of names
and ranks that had no faces till she talked her husband into coming here to settle. She had only married Dunny Emory, she had
told William, because a woman could not travel alone nor live
alone without prying noses plaguing her.

She knew Josh Lamb's name, but she did not remember his face when she saw him. In truth, he had never seen Webb's Ford, never been there. But it did not matter. He was guilty in Anthea's eyes.

She went out to work at Siwall's and saw the madman on his chain and remembered him, and though he had taken no part in the raping and killing and cutting, she believed as Artemas himself did, that he was guilty, too, and deserved execution.

She saw Josselyn when her husband went to work for him, and saw the fingers missing from his hand, and remembered how she helped her sister take them. If they had not thought he was already dead, they would have driven the knife into his heart and called it justice.

How could she know that Daniel had tried to stop the others, not join them?

If she had known, it would not have mattered. The guilt of it lay in the fact of living, that they were alive, and that part of her dark heart had been dead inside her rattling box of ribs since Webb's Ford.

William Quaid she did not remember, or if she did, she pretended otherwise. William Quaid who had put a pistol to her father's skull and pulled the trigger. William Quaid who had tried to rape her sister and failed, as he failed with all women, flinched at the last moment and slunk aside. He had only watched while some of the others raped the little girl they called Nan, three of them, grown men, otherwise decent enough, their sex engorged now with the power they suddenly had over her, over the world. They had passed her small body from one to another as you might pass a cup you drank from, or a pipe of cheap tobacco.

And when he could watch no longer, William Quaid had fired his pistol again and put a bullet through the left eye of Private Abel Hutchings, and another through the belly of Private Jabez Wilks, and yet another through the groin of Private Lucas Breedlove.

Not because he could not bear what he was watching. Because he could do nothing *more* than watch.

It was the same thing he had felt as a boy, when his father had put the noose round his neck and hanged him.

But it was the first flogging, the one he had had as a lad from the British officers, that had withered his manhood inside him, or so he had always thought.

Perhaps the second, after the court-martial, had awakened it dimly, with old Dodger's kind care to heal him. But if so, it made no difference in Hetty's neat and comfortable bed. There, William was helpless, though he loved her with all his heart.

No, it was Anthea who had at last taught him the skill of it. In her bed, with her battered body beneath him, her thin hands clutching at the scars on his back, Will Quaid came alive with a great wild cry that tore his throat and made it ache. At the last, in the long winter darkness, he had wanted nothing but her, had come to her again and again, each night when he finished riding the town boundaries and before he went home to Hetty's cozy supper table at the Forge.

There was no one to tell Hetty. Nobody knew. Only Dodger, who owed him everything, or thought he did.

And then, that last early, dark, cold morning, Nan had taught him what he really was, what he had always been. She had made him rape her, just as the others had done that terrible day at Webb's Ford. If she had not, he might not have been able to kill her.

> Madam I will give to you
> The Keys of Canterbury,
> And all the bells of London Town
> Shall ring to make you merry!

He fought the drifts most of that day, making little headway, but he could not let the darkness catch him in the open. The wolves were prowling thick, now, gathering the corpses the storm had left to feed them. William found a clearing among the trees, cut branches and built a lean-to, made a big fire of a fallen hemlock tree that lay rotting nearby, and waited out the night.

He did not sleep. When there were wolves about, you could not risk it. He crouched in his brush shelter, watching, and beyond the fire the eyes of the wolves came and went in silence, glowing red-gold in the dark. When William could no longer bear the sight of them, he fired his pistol at them, the same pistol he had had at Webb's Ford.

He had saved that gun to kill himself with. In the first years after the War, he had planned it again and again, reenacting the death of the old man and the others in the farmhouse, executing himself like Artie Siwall at the end of his madman's chain. It was a common enough thing, he had been told, among soldiers. The long unspoken guilt. The aching envy of the peaceful dead.

But now he had no intention of dying. That was the terrible thing Anthea Emory had done to him. For now, whatever he had done, whatever the guilt of it, William Quaid was awake and wanted nothing so much as to live.

In the morning he would set out on the Trace again and try to find some word of Daniel. For if Will Quaid was to live, then Dan Josselyn had to die, and so did Hannah Trevor.

Daniel and Hannah did not try to leave their warm bunker in the hillside that first day, nor the second neither, not until the sun had been out long enough to sink the worst of the drifts and harden them under the horses' hooves. It was past midday when they set out, on foot and leading their horses.

"I know of a place we can stay the night," he told her. "If the Trace is passable that far by now, we should get to the Farrow place before fall of night."

Hannah knew the homestead, a tiny patch barely hacked out of the trees—Moses Farrow and his scrawny wife and four little boys. With Will as an escort, she had ridden out to deliver the latest of the boys in autumn, just before the Manitac froze.

"Are we really so close to Rufford, then?" she asked him. The Farrow homestead had taken no more than two hours' easy ride into the woods when she went there with Will.

"On a clear trail," he said, "we might have been home yesterday with ease. But in these drifts, with the horses, it may take us yet another day to get back home."

Hannah studied her lover's placid features, as unreadable as Jennet's. When she asked, he said little more about the embroidered pocket. He had taken it to Hetty as a small gift after one of Charlotte's illnesses in the autumn, when Will's good wife had been especially kind.

"When you saw it among Mrs. Emory's things, why did you not ask Will plainly how it came there?" Hannah asked him suddenly, as she packed the rest of their supplies into the leather scrip.

"I told you. The pocket was Charlotte's work. I didn't wish to involve her."

"Besides, it made you suspect William, and you did not wish to suspect him."

"I will not! And neither should you! You are hasty, as you always are. Hetty is a good soul and kind to everyone. Nan Emory was long alone, and her life was poor. Charlotte's work was handsome."

"It would be like Hetty to give it away again to someone who needed a bit of gentling," agreed Hannah.

"Of course. But you are right. I should have spoken to Will. It was foolish of me to take the thing and keep silent." He picked up the heavy bag and studied Hannah's face. "Does it make you doubt me?"

She spoke without hesitating, but she felt her breath catch as she did so. "Not you, no."

"What, then?"

"I . . . cannot tell. Myself. The clearness of things." She paused for a moment. "Daniel," she said quietly, "when you get home, they will take you to prison. With chains on you, like Artie Siwall. It's too much to bear. Could you not stay here until William finds whoever is guilty?"

"A man doesn't die of shame, my heart," he said as he helped her fasten her cloak. "I must go back, chains or no chains. What they do to me, that they must do, and you and I the same."

FORTY-ONE

THE BREAKING OF HEARTS AND BONES

As for the mob from Rufford, they were not sure *what* they must do. In Nathan Berge's sledge, pulled by the two great Dorset drayhorses he kept, they had reached Moses Farrow's homestead near dusk of the previous day and had sheltered in his narrow barn that night, eleven men sharing two narrow stalls with a bad-tempered black cow and an ox that liked to kick.

Next morning they were of divided will. By early afternoon, the last of the liquor was gone, and they were still arguing.

"I say head home and to the Devil with Josselyn," muttered Phinney Rugg, who had slept nearest the business end of the ox. "And the Devil with Justice, too, blast her."

But Tom Whitechurch, reluctant to surrender his power over them, insisted. "We come here to do a job, brothers!" he cried. "There's a killer loosed on us and Power and Greed protect him! We have a rope and good stout trees. We can't shirk the business for a little snowfall!"

"Shirk or don't shirk," said someone. "I've a shop to keep and harness to mend, and I can't mend it here."

"Aye, either we go on or we go back, Tom Whitechurch, for I've no mind to spend another night in that stall!"

"The Trace will be better open farther up, where the trees grow thicker and will stop the drifts. I say keep on."

"I've a job waiting at Silvanus Whitney's. If I'd known we was coming to the woods to sleep with a she-devil of a cow—"

"Look there!" cried a voice.

It was Will Quaid they saw plodding through the snow on the back of his bay gelding. With yesterday's sun and last night's cold, the crust of the sunken drifts would hold the combined weight of horse and man fairly steadily now, the hooves only breaking through when the horse shied at something in the path or changed its gait upon command.

Seeing the aimless mob of them gathered in Farrow's farmyard, Will turned his horse's head toward them, and the animal lunged and screamed as it broke the crust. Will urged it a bit with his heels and the gelding fought free. They rode at a deliberate walk into the farmyard, Will singing one of his famous songs.

" 'Gallants attend, and hear a friend, Trill forth harmonious ditty,' " he roared. The men watched him in silence, wide-eyed.

Will Quaid's lank dark hair hung loose over his shoulders, the small black ribbon with which he tied it long lost and forgotten, the hair covered with frost. There was hoar-frost clinging to his unshaven upper lip, too, and dripping in icy runlets down the corners of his mouth. He had a pistol laid across his saddlebow and a musket in the crook of his arm, and the leather sleeve of his jacket, too, carried a thin coating of frost.

But for the frost, all this was familiar enough. It was the chains that frightened them.

They were long and thick and had heavy locks hanging from them, and iron cuffs to clamp round the wrists and ankles of prisoners, and because they were long and heavy and might strike the horse and frighten it, he had wrapped the chains around his own body, around his waist and chest and around his neck, and the great iron cuffs and the locks hung downward, clanking with every pace of the horse like the forging of coffin nails. And the chains, too, were white with frost.

" 'Strange things I'll tell, which late befell,' " he sang, " 'in Philadelphia city!' "

William pulled up the horse with a clatter of chains and looked at them all and laughed, and though they had thought nothing could frighten them more than the terrible chains, they were wrong. For the laugh was worse, and the way his lips remained parted afterward, with the cold breath coming out of them like steam when he plunged a red-hot iron into a bucket of icy water in the Forge. It was the way you hardened iron, and the steam of his breath, too, made the men afraid. For the first time they could see that Will Quaid had a deep core of iron, red-hot and still being forged.

None of them spoke this knowledge. Perhaps they did not clearly think it. But they knew.

"I'm damned if you lot don't look a sight," he said. "Phinney, what you been up to this night? Tumbling some poor lass in the mire, were you? Look like you been kicked by an ox! And Tom Whitechurch, your face is paler than that snowbank. What you need is a glass of Edes's brandy, now." He turned to Nathan Berge. "Nate, what you got your sledge out for? Won't be sugaring time for a good two months yet. Best go home to the missus, she's bound to be needing firewood hauled in by now."

"We come out to find Josselyn, William," said Whitechurch. "Seeing as you didn't give much promise of it yourself."

He was as frightened of the apparition before them as the rest, but he could not surrender control so easily, and when it was challenged, he grew surly and belligerent, as he had with Jonathan.

"Now, Tom," said William mildly. The voice itself seemed distant, as though it were muffled by frost. "You was ever a half-cocked marksman. What else do you think I'm doing out here in the snow, but going after him myself? Go home, now, and let them see to the business whose business it be."

"We'll go with you, Will," said someone. "Lend a hand."

"Aye, he's got friends in these woods," somebody else cried.

"Lumbermen, trappers. Some of them Indian runners of Uncle Piet's at the Fort."

"He's right, William. You can use our help," said Phineas Rugg.

Will grinned, his eyes bright under the heavy dark brows. "You, Phinney? What kind of help you think you'll be? Why, I could knock the lot of you down with one of these here chains."

Suddenly the huge chain was in his hand and he swing a wide arc with it. Phinney Rugg took it in the chest and fell, swearing.

"Bloody bastard!" cried Whitechurch. "Siwall's sent him!"

A handful of them rushed at the horse, and again the chain cut through the cold air. It felled Whitechurch only momentarily, but it struck Andrew Pierce hard on the temple and he collapsed, bleeding onto the trampled snow.

"Who's next, boys?" cried William, the broad grin never fading from his face. "Come ahead, then!"

Nobody moved.

William collected the chain and wrapped it again around his chest and shoulder, leaving a long and dangerous length swinging loose in his hand. The men stepped hurriedly back, dragging their felled comrades out of range.

But he did not swing the chain again.

"Nate, better hitch up them fine greys and make for town while the trail's open. Thomas, you and Phinney give him a hand," said Will, "and you'll be toasting your heels at the Red Bush before—"

"Why, there's Josselyn coming for his rope!" cried Tom Whitechurch in triumph. "There! Him, and that slut Hannah Trevor with him!"

There was a flash of cardinal red through the trees where Daniel walked, leading little Flash and his own great sorrel, with Hannah in her red cloak on Yeoman's broad back.

"Take him!" shouted one of the others, and William's chain was forgotten as they ran through the snow toward their quarry.

William spurred the gelding and charged it past them, and was level with Daniel before Whitechurch and the others had time to make it across the muddy yard.

"I got a fine length of hemp rope here!" cried Nathan.

"Get him on a horse!" shouted Whitechurch.

"Stay back!" said Will, and felled two more of them with the chain.

But this time they had sighted their quarry, and Will Quaid was not proof against their greed for power, for it made them strong, and braver than most of them would ever be again. Tom Whitechurch, the biggest and strongest of them, dodged the flying chain and, reaching the heaving side of Will's gelding, pulled the constable off into the snow, where he lay as if unconscious. Before Daniel could draw sword or knife, half a dozen of the others seized him, while the rest dragged Hannah off the sorrel.

"The chains!" cried Nathan Berge. "Put the chains on him, lads! Ropes break, but chains will see him to eternity, the murdering bastard!"

And so they did not use the length of good hemp rope. They unwound the chains from William Quaid's chest and looped them tight around Josselyn's neck, and four of them lifted him onto the horse's back and walked it under the overhanging limb of a huge oak at the edge of Moses Farrow's small pasture. They got the other end of the heavy chain over the limb and then they were ready.

"Say some words," said Nathan Berge, who was a notorious Christian.

"Death to Tyrants!" cried Whitechurch.

"Say hello to King George when you meet him in Hell!" shouted somebody else.

"We commend this sinner to the mercy of Almighty God," intoned Berge.

Daniel sat perfectly still on the horse, the great chains so tight around his throat that he could hardly speak. The horse jittered, and Phineas Rugg made ready to smack its rump and end things.

"William," whispered Hannah hoarsely. "Please, God, wake up. Will!"

The constable lay facedown in the snow, unconscious or dead. Hannah herself had fallen very near him, and Will's pistol lay close to his knee, dropped from the saddlebow when they dragged him off his horse. Hannah tried to inch her way to it, crawling on her belly in the snow, fingers creeping slowly toward it until her cheek brushed William's boot.

Suddenly a huge hand clamped down over her own. It was William's, alive indeed, and playing possum.

"Thank God, Will," she said, no louder than breath. Daniel had been right. To doubt Will Quaid was to doubt that trees had roots. "What shall we do, Will? They'll kill him by accident, the damn fools!"

"Hush," he whispered. "Give no sign. Just you leave this to me, my dear," he said.

In another instant, the pistol had slipped into his hand, and William was on his feet.

"That'll be all now, lads," he said gently. "Though by rights I ought to thank you. You've chained him up proper, and saved me the trouble. Best take that other end from the bough, there, Phinney, and put the irons on him. He'll be tried fair and square. Only I'll bring him back on my own, if you please."

"William, no! Not chained! You must know he's done nothing!" Hannah caught at Quaid's arm.

"Law's law. He was under bond and he broke it. We shall see what we know at the inquest, Hannah-girl," he replied. The pistol moved an inch nearer to Daniel's head. "But he's been a friend to me, and the trip back will give me leisure to make my peace with him. One of you help Mrs. Trevor to her mount, now, and ride out, and Daniel and me will follow. There's still a few points I'd put to him, and I can do it best alone."

"Points, my arse! You want him alone so you can let him go, off into the woods and nobody the wiser!"

"Nate's right!"

"Aye, by God! The hell with inquests, and trials, too. He's taken two lives at least, Will Quaid, and if him and Siwall's bought and sold you, then they haven't me! Go on and shoot me if you want! For if you fire that pistol, Josselyn's a dead man anyway!"

Tom Whitechurch was right. Daniel's horse was wild-eyed now, ready to bolt at any minute. No matter what it was aimed at, if the gun were fired, the chains would strangle him and snap his neck.

All through this wrangling, Daniel had said nothing. Now at last he spoke.

"William," he said hoarsely. "Look at me."

"What?" Nathan Berge squinted and frowned. "What did he say?"

"Look at me, William!"

Quaid's breathing was heavy and harsh as he looked up. His dark blue eyes were black in the sunshine. "What's amiss?" he said.

"Daniel has done nothing," Hannah told the men again. "Ham Siwall wants him out of the way of his profits, that's all. He paid Dunny Emory to draw false maps and then killed him so he wouldn't talk. Go to the Fort. Ask the Dutchman to show you Emory's bones. If you must hang somebody, go and hang Siwall!"

"What's she blubbering about?" Even the sullen Whitechurch was growing uncertain.

But William did not take his eyes from Daniel's face.

"It's no crime to have loved her, William," said Josselyn gently.

"Loved?" Will murmured.

"I saw you. You know I sleep badly, and often I ride late along the Falls road. I have seen you leave Mrs. Emory's house three times, near to morning. I told nobody. It was your affair, but—"

"I? With Nan Emory?"

Daniel continued, the half-smothered voice forced out of the trapped throat painfully, as though he had swallowed glass. "I saw the pocket, Will, at Mrs. Emory's. Hetty's pocket. I took it and said nothing, and I wouldn't have told them. For I don't believe it was any more than loneliness between you, and I know what that is, surely. I wanted to keep you clear of it, and Hetty, too. But now . . ." He could move nothing but his eyes, and they were terrible, sunk deep in the cavern of his skull.

William's pistol turned to point at him. The huge blackened forefinger moved slightly, almost unconsciously, farther onto the trigger. "I don't know what you're saying, Daniel. Be easy, now. Be still."

"I knew you went sometimes to other women. Hetty knew it, too. Mary Seaforth. Even Molly Bacon. So when I saw the pocket in the bedchamber at Anthea Emory's house—"

"Women like that Molly, they were no good to me, not a one of them," muttered William. The pistol moved an inch closer to Daniel's skull.

"Here is the pocket Daniel speaks of," cried Hannah to the others, unwrapping it from her saddle sack. "I found it draped on the chair beside Nan Emory's bed where she lay dead. An embroidered pocket, Lady Josselyn's own design and her work. And given by her as a present to Hetty Quaid."

Daniel looked away. "It was so," he whispered. "My wife was ill again last Christmas. Hetty sat up with her. Charlotte sent the pocket as thanks, and I stopped at the Forge and left it there with William."

"And he gave it to Anthea Emory. Who was his lover." Hannah held up the pocket. "I examined it closely the day I found Mrs. Emory, I saw the mark on it. See there? Soot does not wear off, nor wash out easily. And William's hands are never anything but black, no matter how he scrubs them. I said nothing until I might have a second look at it. But you knew at once, and because Will is your friend, you took it and kept it for him, Daniel. Because you were sure, as I am now, that William has done no wrong but the need of loving. That's why the dog knew him, Mrs. Emory's dog Toby, who saw him come and go so many other nights, and knew the scent of him well. Did you always bring some scrap from Hetty's table to quiet him, William? As you did the day we found her dead? How cruel it must have been for you, to find her lying so."

She came to stand beside Will, very close indeed, her voice soft and kind. "You had no children with Hetty, did you, my dear? Love her though you might, it was no use. And to have Anthea die so cruelly when she was carrying your child—"

He turned to stare at her, blank-eyed, the gun wild in his hand. "Child?" he whispered. "She was with child? My Nan?"

"Of course. It was in the report. The results of Dr. Kent's dissection. Didn't Dodger read them to you?"

"She told me nothing of any child! It's lies! You want to trap me with lies!"

Hannah stared. "Why no, Will. Why should I lie? It's true, I promise you."

"What good are women's promises?" he shouted. "You're mad, the lot of you. She was mad. What but a mad thing would wring the neck of a songbird in a cage? 'I think you love it better than me,' she said, and then she wrung its neck. So I put the dog out in the cold, then, or she'd have killed him, too."

Hannah's voice shook when she spoke next and the roots of the great trees themselves seemed shaken. "William. She killed the cage-bird herself?"

"Aye. But there was no child. She was never with child."

"The letter she left said the killer wrung the bird's neck. The man whose hands she feared so."

"Letter! Why, she'd wrote that letter a month before ever she—"

"Before she killed the bird. And she showed the letter to you, she read it to you, didn't she? Oh, she pretended to Mrs. Kemp at Burnt Hill that she couldn't read, but she told Dorcas Holroyd she read sermons at home instead of going to Meeting. Her father was an educated man himself, and her uncle was a schoolmaster. He had taught her to read and write, hadn't he, William?"

"No! I don't know! It's lies, I—"

"You heard all her plans. Knew all her anger. But not quite. You didn't know she was carrying your child."

"I tell you, it's not so! She loved her children dearly, she'd never have—"

"She made you kill your own child, Will. The child you wanted so much. It was there inside her when you killed her."

"I killed nobody! I—"

"She wanted you to betray your friends, just as you killed your own child. As she betrayed you, my dear."

Daniel could bear it no longer. "Hannah, you go too far. This is nonsense, and cruel. I cannot believe that—"

A strange sound came from Will Quaid's throat and he seemed
to sway where he stood, the pistol raking the group of men, then
returning to aim itself at Hannah.

"My own child," he groaned. "Ah, Christ."

Daniel was shaken, but he was not convinced. "What about
the others? What about Artemas and young Emory?"

"They had to kill Artemas Siwall to be sure he would say nothing. For he knew, didn't he, William, that Mrs. Emory had persuaded you to follow her husband into the woods last autumn
and kill him, too?

"Artie was in the yard as always, was he not, the day you and
Nan Emory made your plans? Was it in the autumn, when she
helped Mrs. Kemp with the butchering before Thanksgiving? Just
about the time young Dunny left for the woods, or so we all
thought. You, at the magistrate's house on some legal business,
and Nan in the yard at her work. And Artie's nephew, Jem Siwall.
I have wanted myself to believe his father was guilty, but Jem
was the only one who knew that Dunny Emory meant to go to
Boston to spend his bribe, that he was deserting his wife and
never coming back, and not going into the woods to survey at
all. But Jem couldn't kill anyone, he hadn't the nerve. So he and
Nan persuaded you that day. She wanted to be free of Dunny,
and you wanted anything she desired, did you not? And Jem
needed the money Emory was carrying, his father's bribe, to pay
his own gambling debts."

Hannah's voice was low and quiet, but there was no other
sound in the farmyard, the men shamefaced and afraid, and even
the wind no longer moving the snow-laden branches. Her breath
came sharp and painful. She was not in Moses Farrow's yard now,
she was locked in a house in Boston, lying in the cold darkness
on her own quilt-covered bed, and raising a newly-sharpened
blade to draw it gently across her wrists.

That was it, of course. The reason she had felt so deeply the
death of Anthea Emory, the reason she seemed to know the woman's mind. They had both been bitterly used, their lives squan-
dered and thrown away as if they had no value in themselves.

Hannah hated only James, who had done it. But Anthea had hated all men, all human beings who had not been so hurt as she. It included the men of Rufford, guilty or innocent, who had been at Webb's Ford. And it included her husband, Dunstan Emory.

There is a line you cross, Daniel had told her. Anthea Emory had crossed it. And so had William Quaid. You had only to look at him now, to know it.

"You didn't kill Dunny out on the Boston road, of course," Hannah went on. "How could you? You had to be sure the body would not be found, so it would seem he had disappeared in the Outward. So you tricked him into the woods or forced him there. Or did you arrest him and make up some story? And then you strangled him, just as you did Anthea. Tell me, Will, was Jem her lover, too? I'm told he'll bed most anything. Maybe it was his babe in her belly when she died, after all."

"Shut up, you bitch!" he cried. "Shut up your mouth!"

His great hand swung in an arc like the chain, and when it struck Hannah's face, she did not fall, would not give him the pleasure of it. But she could feel her bones grate. The tooth that had been plaguing her for days broke loose in a gush of blood and she looked up at the man who had so long been her friend.

Whoever he had been, he was not Will Quaid now. He was alien. He had no songs, no name, no friends, no wife, no hope of life.

Still, he *wanted* to live. She could see it in his eyes. He wanted to live, if it meant killing every human thing in sight.

Hannah spat the blood and the broken tooth onto the ground at his feet.

"Christ," whispered Will Quaid. "Forgive me that. You mustn't— I was provoked, Hannah. Jesus forgive me."

Daniel sat his horse now like a statue wrapped in the chains, the end of them still looped dangerously across the branch above his head. He was overburdened, fighting for breath in order to speak, and his eyes were on Hannah's bleeding face.

"William," he said softly, and the pistol turned slowly in his direction once more.

"Yes, my dear?" William replied. His voice, too, was a hoarse whisper and the gun shook wildly in his hand.

Tom Whitechurch nudged Phinney in the ribs and he began to shin up the tree and ease his way along the branch to the chain, to drop it to the ground where it would do no harm if the horse bolted. He was a pigheaded fool, was Whitechurch, but he would not kill without what he thought was justice on his side.

Daniel had to keep Will's attention off the movements in the tree, or he might shoot. "Why did you have to kill Artie, William? He loved you."

"He was a madman. Madmen have loose tongues, you know. He'd heard us, as Hannah says. Heard us talking of killing Dunny, maybe. And his eyes—"

"He knew what you did at Webb's Ford, didn't he? Did he drag himself in from the yard, wounded, and try again to stop the men? Did he remember Anthea when he saw her at Burnt Hill?"

William did not answer, only began to laugh softly, a sound no louder than the wind that blew the snow in sheer veils from the branches.

But Daniel did not let up. "And you put my glove on Artie to make it look as if I had been there. Just as you wore it the night you killed Mrs. Emory. Was that her idea? Or yours?"

"You left it at the Forge, didn't you? Careless. 'Twas a fine bit of leather."

"And I left my grandfather's sword on my desk at the Grange."

"I come up to ask you that morning. Old Mistress Twig showed me in the room and went waddling out and left me alone there. The idea come to me, clear. Nan always wanted you blamed, you see, you and Josh and the Siwalls. 'Twas her idea I should double my fingers into that sewed-down glove of yours when I killed her, to leave the marks on her you'd have made."

"Why, William?" asked Hannah. "Why Josh and Daniel?"

"Her whole family died at Webb's Ford. She didn't care who

done what. She wanted them all punished at last, that's all. Natural enough. She were but a lass, and they took her and had her. More than once, her and her sister. I watched 'em. Her Pa dead. I done that myself, though she didn't see it. All her own people killed."

"Except for old Mr. Dodger," she said. "He lived in the cottage, didn't he? The small cottage beside the barn as you came from the ford. Who is he? Nan Emory's grandfather? Uncle? But there's one thing I don't understand, Will. Why didn't Anthea accuse you along with the others? You were there. You say yourself you'd killed her father. If she hated all the others, how could she have forgiven you?" Hannah paused. "But then she didn't, did she? She'd found another way of destroying you. The child you gave her. She must have hated you more than the rest."

"No!" he cried. "She did love me, and was gentle, for I shot the men who hurt her, when I come to myself, and I cared for her, after, and Dodger, too, when they sliced open his head with a sword! She did love me, Nan did! If she died with my child in her, then she was too mad to think of it anymore!"

Phinney Rugg had crawled far enough along the branch now to reach the end of the chain, but he slipped on some ice and when he grabbed for purchase on the limb, a load of snow plopped down at Will Quaid's feet.

Startled, scarcely knowing what he did, William turned the pistol's mouth upward and before anyone could stop him, he fired.

When Hannah tried to remember them afterwards, the next few moments broke into mad spinning fragments, like the legs and arms and severed heads the preachers said would be joined together at the Last Day.

There was Phinney Rugg's scrawny shape falling, falling from the limb and landing sprawled over the rump of Daniel's horse.

There was the great horse, Yeoman, wild-eyed and rearing, the men trying to hold him still.

There was Will Quaid, rolling in the blood-flecked snow with Tom Whitechurch as they struggled for possession of the pistol.

There was the limb with the chain upon it, cracking and breaking and crashing down on them where they fought.

There was Daniel, still weighted with chains, thrown off the horse and dragged through the snow by his neck, his hands torn and bleeding and clinging to the chain to keep himself from being strangled as the horse reared and bolted. Later, when they pulled off the chains, there were strange marks on his throat like a hundred cruel fingers that had no hands attached to them.

And there was Jonathan Markham, who came riding full-tilt into the Farrows' yard with tiny Mr. Dodger, in double cape and plumed tricorn, perched precariously behind him, just as the gun went off.

And there was Hannah, blood still oozing from her mouth, with Will Quaid's musket useless in her hands.

Jonathan spurred his horse and grabbed Yeoman's halter. He leaped down, caught the chain and held it hard, letting himself be dragged a few feet to take the tension of Daniel's weight from it. When the horse stopped at last, with three men holding his foam-flecked head, Johnnie let go the chain and bent over Daniel, whom Hannah and old Dodger were already laboring to untangle from the stranglehold of the chains.

At first she thought he was no longer breathing and she felt, for a split-second, the crushing weight that is dying fall down on her own body.

Johnnie grasped her arm and jerked it, hard. "You've saved other men from drowning, Hannah. Worse men. Do it now for him. Now!"

The weight of it still lay heavy on her. "Turn him, some of you," she cried, still at a distance from herself. "Flat on his back." She put her two fingers inside Daniel's mouth and made sure he was not biting down on his tongue, that the throat was clear and could receive breath and send it to his lungs.

Then, herself again, Hannah Trevor did as she had done with countless babies unwilling to draw their own first breaths in this inhospitable world. She put her mouth to Daniel Josselyn's and forced him back to life.

Under the fallen limb, William Quaid and Thomas Whitechurch had ceased to struggle and lay still, the both of them.

"Pull the bough off 'em!" cried someone.

"He's done for, old Tom," said somebody else.

There was a whimpering sound from a snowbank, and Phinney Rugg emerged, his mouth full of dirty snow. "I'm shot!" he whined. "Shot to death."

Some of the others hurried to him. "Ain't nobody ever been sent to St. Peter from a bullet in the arse, Phinney," hooted one of them.

"No more than a cat scratch, at that!" said somebody else.

Daniel was waking now, struggling to sit up. In another minute, they had helped him to his feet.

Alive, thought Hannah, as the death-weight lifted from her mind.

And then the great fallen limb seemed to heave itself off the two men beneath it and Will Quaid, huge and crusted with the load of snow and ice whose weight, once Phinney's was added to it, had broken the branch, rose up like one of those dragons the old sailors once believed lived in the deep waters between England and America.

Death had not left Hannah, nor any of the others in the yard. Will Quaid was Death, and the pistol was still in his hand, and Tom Whitechurch lay dead beside him in the snow, his head lolling at a mad angle, his neck broken like Anthea's, like Dunny Emory's.

"Now, then," said William quietly. "Where's Josselyn?"

"I'm here, Will." Daniel's voice was hoarse and uncertain, and he swayed slightly in the cold wind. The chains lay at his feet.

Shaking loose of Hannah, he moved to face his friend, and the others stepped back. Jonathan and old Dodger, however, inched closer, the old man jittering like a colt.

"I done terrible things at Webb's Ford, Dan," said Quaid softly. "I didn't know what was in me till I came there. But she knew."

"Nan?"

"Aye. She was a mad thing, mad with pain. And she made me mad, too. She made me do plain murder, not killing, like it was back there in the War."

"If you did horrors, it was because you had horrors in you," said Hannah. "At Webb's Ford, and here."

"No, my heart," said Daniel softly. "We did not altogether choose what we were that day, nor what we did, any more than you chose to bring your children back to Boston when there was fever raging there. Great batterings are sometimes leveled at the heart. We all break, as you did when you cut yourself and prayed to die. Only with some, the broken ends turn outward and do others harm, far worse than we do ourselves."

William nodded. "It's true. I would not have done such terrors for the wide world, if I had known what I did. But a wild thing come on me there, and maybe it was madness and maybe 'twas something else. For it lasted but a moment, and I scarcely remembered what I'd done, after. I seen the young girl there, and old Dodge, half-scalped by a saber, and I took 'em up and tended 'em, for I was myself again, you see. 'Twas only when she came here, to Rufford, and I saw her again. Then I remembered, and grew mad again. I wished to love her. I expect that's madness enough."

For a split second it seemed that he would drop the pistol in the snow. But he did not. His voice went on, dead calm.

"I bid her ask anything of me and I would do it, whatever she asked. She laughed and kissed my mouth. And then she asked me to kill her, for she wanted the worst of all to die, and be at peace." Will was very close to Daniel, the pistol held against Josselyn's temple. "Only she's not at peace, and won't be, not till you're dead, Dan. And me, as well." The black index finger brushed the trigger. "So I shall kill us both. I owe her that. What do I not owe her?"

"You can't kill us all, Will," said Nathan Berge. "Some of us will take you back and see you hanged."

William Quaid smiled. "Well, now, I don't mind that, Nate. For haven't I been as good as dead all these nine years, ever since they did lay the stripes on me in the barracks yard?"

Perhaps he was right, Hannah thought afterwards. She had watched many men and women and children die, and there is a moment when death comes, a still moment like the sudden dropping of a wind that has blown for days, or like coursing water that falls into a deep pool and can go no further. In most people, it is something like peace, or it seems so to those who only watch.

But if it came so to Will Quaid, it must have come long ago—perhaps, as he said, at the flogging he took after Webb's Ford, or perhaps in Nan Emory's bed. Or perhaps it had come during that long, cold night he spent with the wolves, their pale eyes on him in the darkness.

He shoved the pistol hard against Daniel's ear and braced himself to fire, and it was not until then that little Mr. Dodger spoke.

"Put down the gun, sir, oh, put down the gun and bury it!" he cried. The great pile of tangled chains lay at his feet. "Bury the chains and the locks and the keys. On another such day, you saved my life and the life of that wretched girl, who was my brother's child. The others would have shot her, when they had finished with her, for it is the way of guilt to put the stain on the innocent. But you shot them, all three, and saved her, and you found me hurt and kept me living, and when they put the whip to you, I tended you in return. For there is seldom anyone to tend the damned and the guilty, though the innocent have kind folk enough. And when I knew you were mad, and when I knew you were broken, I followed after you. For a debt—good or bad—must be paid. You know that. She knew that. She was wise, like all the mad. So I watched and listened. I kept you always in sight." He kicked at the chains. "You wore no other chains, sir. And I was always there when wanted. Always there, though I do not interfere. God does not interfere. He sets us to work and watches. He lets us do evil and have evil done unto us and does not interfere till the Day of Judgement. It is come now, sir. It is come now." He removed his hat and looked up, small bright eyes brimming.

"I knew she would die for it," he said. "But the choice was hers. The dead must be buried, sir. Chains must be broken and debts must be paid. Must they not? Oh, must they not?"

"Go home, Dodge," whispered William.

He turned back again, jammed the pistol to Daniel's ear, and again braced for the recoil. Josselyn fixed his eyes on Hannah, then closed them, wishing her to be the last thing he would see, and when she heard the powder blast an instant later, Hannah did not look at the snow where she knew he must be lying dead. Instead, she stared down at William's useless musket, which she had picked up again. Though it was still unprimed and unloaded, she almost believed she had fired it herself.

"I owed her a debt, Dan," said the constable's soft voice. "How could I live till it was paid?"

Hannah looked up, stunned, and let the musket fall.

For a moment, Will Quaid stood very still, blood soaking through his heavy coat and spattering the snow at his feet, and his pistol still aimed at Daniel's head.

Daniel, unharmed, had turned to face him, and suddenly the constable's huge body swayed and the eyes closed and opened again and one blackened hand reached out and seemed to grip the air, the fingers opening and closing on some invisible barricade.

Josselyn put his arms out. "Ah, Christ, Will."

"Oh, my dear," said William, and stepped into the embrace.

They fell together onto the trampled, bloody snow, and Daniel sat there with his friend in his arms, his mangled fingers smoothing the frost from the dark, shaggy hair.

Behind him, Johnnie Markham, his musket still smelling of hot powder, stepped near and slipped his arm through Hannah's.

"There, now. I've saved him for you twice," he said gently, and pulled her close. Hannah could feel his body shaking and hear the faint whine of breath that fought its way from him.

"I'm grateful, Johnnie," she said, leaning against him.

"I only hope," he replied, "that he was worth the price."

Dodger, too, was now kneeling on the ground beside Will Quaid's body.

"Bury the chains with him," he cried suddenly, his shrill voice echoing across the small farmyard where the silent Rufford men still lingered, watching the end of the world. "He was a good man and a kind man, with an evil man and a wild man inside him, kept in secret chains. I loved him and watched over him, though I am a fool and a sinner, and now I have paid him all my debt. I beg you to bury his chains!"

FORTY-TWO

The Journal of Hannah Trevor

22 February, the year 1786

I write this on General Washington's Birthday. A great celebration in all the towns from here to Wybrow Head.

The morning warm and bright. We heard in the night the cracking of ice upon the river Manitac, and my Uncle fears a flood from the great jam of logs beyond the mill. Major Josselyn and Mister John English have brought a crew of woodsmen to shift the jam with powder, which makes a great noise. Jonathan helps them, for though he is sobered and means to be a good husband, now, to that chit Sally, he is still half a boy, and anything to do with noise gives him joy.

God send they blow off no one's feet and do not deafen me before they finish.

My daughter Jennet studies the Indian finger-talk from Major Josselyn, to what purpose I know not. He has taught her to say Mother and God and cat and some other words else. The Words of Women bear Slender Stalks and are easily Trampled. Still, the thought is kind, and it does me good to see them side by side.

He does not come here, for Prudence speaks against it. Patsy, the daughter of John English, fetches the child to their house, where Jennet's own father waits for her.

I have not written that word of him before. It is a danger, for what is written in secret may too easily be spoken aloud.

I shall amend. Jennet goes to the house of John English, where Major Josselyn waits for her.

With Aunt and Uncle, attended yesterday the funeral of Will Quaid. The Elders would not bury him within the churchyard, for he was a confessed felon. I grieve for him and miss him sorely. May God pardon his secret Soul and Cleanse it of Wrong, his own and that which was done to him. For there are many rapes done in this world of tears, and not all to the bodies of women.

May his long pain end here.

I was called to bear witness at the inquest in the borough court at Wybrow. No evidence could be presented of Mr. Siwall's bribe of Dunstan Emory. Though he is no longer Daniel's partner, for they have had a Great Strife over it, and come to blows, Hamilton Siwall is still Magistrate and Moderator of the Congregation.

The Rape of War. The Rape of Greed. The Rape of Power. The Rape of Great Loss.

How deep I trusted Will Quaid. How little we know the minds of others. I think have almost forgiven James Trevor, for I shall not be made to carry his guilt as though it were my own, and kill or die for it like Mistress Emory. Who knows but James was broken, too, in secret.

Poor Hetty Quaid is gone to Boston with Mister Dodger. Perhaps she will marry the Reverend Rockwood, for my Aunt would surely have Somebody to marry him, and I shall not. Attended Mrs. Pomfrey's delivery. Six shillings and a bundle of flax, which my Uncle breaks for hetcheling. We are short of candles. Made three dozen in the small molds, to last us until the weather is good next month for dipping.

TO MOLD FINE CANDLES

Put the sharp end of your candle mold into a potato with the end cut off flat to rest on, and the tallow will not run out before it sets. Use good beef tallow, and the wicks of best new linen tow, stiffened with tallow beforehand, and hung out straight till they be set. Harden in the molds two days, away from the fire but out of the deep cold, lest they freeze and crack apart.

Visited Mrs. Burton, to whom my Aunt did deliver twin boys in my absence. Little George Burton hearty, though Jacob not so, for he has a twisted foot. I am sorry for it. I can do nothing.

The girls would not do the washing today but let it tarry until the morrow, for it was Washington's Birthday, they declared, and wrong to have wet wash strung about before the fire.

Aunt and I baked fine Shrewsbury cakes for the celebration. Daughter pounded the mace and cinnamon and broke up the cone of sugar and powdered it with the pestle. My Daughter Jennet comes on well with the skills of women. I am glad of her, though she is silent.

✑ MY AUNT'S RECEIPT FOR SHREWSBURY CAKE

One pound flour
One pound butter
Three quarters pound powder sugar
A little Mace, Cloves, and Cinnamon
Four Whites of Eggs mixed and beat till Light
A little Rosewater or Orange-Flower Water, and
A little Sack or Spanish Sherry, if it can be had

Break the Butter fine and work with the Flour and Sugar, beat up the whites of eggs and mix with the spice and rosewater sirup. Work up the dough with some warm cream, till it is thick and light.

Roll and cut into Small Rounds, like Biscuit. Bake in a Light Oven, not too brown.

TO MAKE ROSEWATER SIRUP

Take a quart of fine, clear water, and put into it half a pound of beaten rose petals from damask roses. Set them a-stewing on the embers. Strain off and put on fresh water twice each day till they be changed a dozen times, or fourteen. After this be done, put to every pint of rose liquor a pound of sugar, and boil it down to a good thick sirup. The thicker it is, the better it will keep all the year around.

I think often of Mrs. Josselyn now. Shall send Kitty with some of the Shrewsbury cakes, and a bottle of my decoction of Feverfew, Pennyroyal and Camomile. Perhaps it will give her ease.

I shall not have them say the cakes have come from me.

Jonathan Markham, my Uncle's son, is named Constable of Rufford, in the place of William Quaid, who is dead, and Peter Fellingham will be his clerk, though he cannot write so well as old Dodger. God grant Johnnie may be as true a man as Will, though calmer in his mind and clearer in conscience.

For all his wildness, Johnnie is just when error is proven upon him. He never killed a man but William, and he mourns for it. When he was a boy, Will Quaid and Eben taught him to shoot a musket and track rabbits, and took him first into the Outward.

William's dying was the end of Johnnie's youth, I think. He has an honorable calling now, and serves Justice, of which he has always spoken much.

As for me, I mourn for Hetty more than for Mrs. Emory. It is one thing to wish life away in hating, as I have done myself, and another to have it fall away beneath the feet of kindness, honor, and innocence. I resolve I shall waste no more time in hate, nor in the vain denial of loving, which is much the same.

Tomorrow I shall attend the dissection of old Absalom Blunt, whose body was found yesterday, cast through the ice of Blackthorne Creek. It is thought he was pushed by his daughter Melinda, and she is now under surety and cannot leave the Bounds. I do not credit it, though her father often beat and threatened her. It is said she will hang.

Dr. Cyrus Kent is ill with colic and Sam Clinch will dissect the body of Mr. Blunt.

God Help the Cause of Justice, and help Linda Blunt. And so shall I.

I have begun to read Mr. Shakespear's King Lear again. I have not read it since before my children died, though I did keep the volume fondly.

There is a verse of his: Men must endure their Going Hence, even as their Coming Hither. I think it is a thing only a man would needs have written down, for every woman knows it in her bones. I shall work it in a sampler and send it to Hetty Quaid, when she is settled.

Have finished the quilt called Hearts and Bones, of appliqué-work and piecing. I draw out the pattern here, to keep it in my memory for Daniel's sake.

For my heart does treasure the name.

The ice at Blackthorne Falls is melting. The fearful jam of logs is broken, and the river runs free. I thank God I am the same.

Writ by Hannah Trevor, in her own poor hand. 1786

AFTERWORD

There is a peculiar familiarity about Hannah Trevor's world. It strips away two hundred years of smug progress like a false beard. It is 1786, the edge of the Maine wilderness. The beginning of something. The end of something.

The government is chaotic and useless. There is no president and the country is like a riderless horse. The mails are hopeless. Foreign trade is a dead issue. There is no treasury, and America owes forty-two million dollars in war debts. There is paper money everywhere, but you can't buy anything with it, let alone pay your debts. The poor are drowning. The middle class is under siege. Suicides are more frequent, outcasts take to the woods and prey on travellers, violent crime is common and often sexually motivated. Money may not buy love, but it sustains it; some will always break as they are broken. Men battered by years of struggle find themselves deep in debt to a rising class of money-men who have no loyalty but to gain, and the spectres of foreclosure and debtors' prison quickly put paid to the dream that all men are created equal. It is still the rich who own the world. Perhaps it will always be.

But what of the woman? What are her dreams?

If she is married, she is subsumed in her husband. She has no existence under the law. She cannot sue or be sued, nor give evidence against him if he beats and brutalizes her. Her children are legally his, and if he dies, though she regains some rights, she must find another man—a grandfather, uncle, family friend— to be her guardian and her children's, unless she can prove her own ability to support and protect them. Even if she is single, she cannot legally own a business—though she may operate one if it belongs to a man—unless she petitions the state for special permission, which may or may not be granted, for the courts are capricious and they are run by men.

But certain women—women like Hannah Trevor—do not wait for permission. They have a unique skill which they barter with their neighbors for an independence that circumvents courts and lawbooks. They are the women healers, possessed of a traditional knowledge everyone needs and no man can lay claim to. They are midwives, nurses, herbalists, experts in the skills of childbirth and the ills of women, babies and young children. They battle the epidemics of cholera, yellow fever, smallpox, scarlet fever, and diphtheria. Their gardens grow the plants they need, and their stillrooms and kitchens make the ointments, syrups and decoctions that often prove more effective than the male physician's bleeding, blistering and purging. Doctors are still learning the human anatomy by dissecting the bodies of hanged criminals or the victims of violent death. And even there, the nurse-midwife is indispensable. By law, a woman is required to attend all autopsies, for male physicians have been known to drink and place bets on the condition of corpses, or to sell bodies to medical schools for study and bury empty coffins. When there is crime or unexplained death of any sort, the midwife sees it firsthand.

I think it is not so much that the past is dead, as that we are not alive enough to reach it.

Let me tell you about my Aunt Mag. She was in her eighties, and I was a child, but I think I knew even then that she had come from another century. She wore long skirts and tight-fitted bodices and a strange little cap she never removed except to wash and sleep. She lived at the edge of town in a tumbledown house with an overgrown garden and a thousand half-wild cats. She crowed with delight at the foibles of fools and said what she thought in language that withered the faint-hearted. She could make a perfect copy of any dress from a catalog drawing, no matter how intricate, and the stitches on her quilts were too tiny to count. She knew that a poultice of comfrey would heal a festering wound or a cracked rib, that if you drank catnip tea before bed you wouldn't catch cold, that yarrow would stop bleeding and a poultice of onions on the feet would draw out fever. She was stiff-necked and strong and had a mind like the point of a steel pin. I am proud to be named for her. Whatever lost world she came from, Hannah Trevor lives there too.

—Margaret Lawrence
January, 1996